THE AUTHOR

Nick Cann was born in London in 1959. Since 1981 he has worked as a freelance journalist and graphic designer.

In 1989 he moved to Northern Ireland where he works as a design consultant.

Nick Cann's debut novel *Jake's Eulogy* was listed as a number one bestseller in the *Belfast Telegraph*, 20 August 2005.

Father's Day is his fifth novel.

KHARA PRINGLE

It's long

GW00320181

Nick

15.12.20

FATHER'S DAY

BY NICK CANN

indiego

indiego.co.uk

FIRST PUBLISHED IN THE UK IN 2020 BY

indiego

HOLYWOOD, COUNTY DOWN

© **indiego 2020**

TEXT © NICK CANN

ALL RIGHTS RESERVED

Nick Cann is hereby identified as author of this work in accordance with
section 77 of the copyright, designs & patents act 1988

ISBN 978-0-9549066-4-1

WRITTEN BY NICK CANN

EDITED BY VICTORIA WOODSIDE

PRINTED BY GRANGE PRINTING

BOUND BY ROBINSON & MORNIN BOOKBINDERS

FOR DAWN CANN

WITH THANKS TO:
Sophie, Chloe, Jack and Poppy and Dave The Dog
Steffan, Wendy and Judy
Derek and Valerie Geddis

WITH SPECIAL THANKS TO:
The surgeons, doctors, wonderful nurses and staff
on Ward 16 at the Ulster Hospital
without whose expert care ...

ACKNOWLEDGEMENTS:
Chloe Cann, Sophie Cann, Al Cassels, Scott Beadle, Tim Lamb,
Jo Rice, Paul Hewitt, Ricky Alexander and Caterina Pini

1

Saturday, 20 March 1993

The Wellington House Hotel, Rye,
Sussex (South East England)

The man slumped across the couch opposite the ladies loos had been staring at his shoes for the last fifteen minutes. Deep in thought he'd become oblivious to the drum and bass thumping through the double doors at the end of the corridor.

"Oh, for some Motown," he had murmured when leading his girlfriend away from the wedding reception to guide her to the conveniences.

Numbed by red wine and deep in thought, Patrick McDade had stopped worrying about what his date may or may not be doing on the other side of the toilet door a few feet away. That she'd downed a bottle and a half of Asti Spumante and could be choking in a pool of her own vomit didn't occur to him now that he was lost in a daydream – a near narcoleptic state that had been his undoing at school and often led to a clout round the ear or bang on the head from an expertly thrown blackboard duster.

Marriage was the subject of Patrick McDade's musings today. Aged twenty-four, he had come to realise that he had an extreme abhorrence of both wedlock and weddings. He had always tried to be an eager participant in the nuptials, especially since his peer group had started to sign up to the institution of late, but now realised that weddings were anathema to him.

And even if he could conjure up a fiancée, marriage would be totally impractical since, unlike most of his school friends who were already making their way in the world of work, he was still stuck at college in Falmouth struggling through the final term of a master's degree in architecture.

It didn't help that he felt uncomfortable and awkward at nearly all social gatherings too. Just couldn't be doing with formal occasions that required good manners, small talk, a tie and any kind of behaviour that didn't come naturally to him. Weddings, therefore, came right at the top of the list of events he would rather not attend.

Today's nuptials typified all that he disliked most about them: the service, the vows, the vicar, the bride, the bridesmaids, feral children, fixed grins, speeches, stiletto heels, peach chiffon, the cake, the extravagance and the hypocrisy. That Natalie, his girlfriend of six months, had got overexcited, over-intoxicated and had fallen asleep during the meal and then flopped face first into her raspberry panna cotta in clear view of the groom – Patrick's cousin – Patrick's cousin's bride and Patrick's favourite aunt and uncle, all perched above them along the top table, made an already tense situation far worse.

Patrick suddenly became aware of an aggressive voice barking at him. One that he didn't recognise.

"Budge up! Come on! Budge up!"

"I'm sorry?"

"You heard. I said, 'budge up'!"

"How about 'please'."

"Just move over."

"It doesn't take much to say 'please'."

"Are you always this fucking arsey?"

"R-r-rarely," Patrick replied, in a barely audible murmur, but sliding across to the far end of the couch as requested. He buried his head in his hands.

"What?"

"I-I-I didn't say anything," Patrick muttered under his breath, while trying not to engage with the stranger and attempting to suppress his stammer.

"OK, but you want to, don't you? You look like you want to say something – something half-witted and arsey. You do, don't you? I can see it in your face. You're one of those pass-remarkable types, aren't you? Can't help yourself, can you?"

"Well, no. I don't think—"

"Then why do you look so fucking miserable and so fucking disapproving? I only wanted to sit down. Is your backside that fucking huge that it has to take up the whole fucking sofa?"

"No."

"What, then?"

"I-I-I didn't see you, OK? I-I-I was lost in thought."

"What's bugging you? Your face looks like a slapped arse."

"N-n-nothing."

Patrick McDade sneaked a peek at his adversary, then immediately averted his gaze back to his shoes. He could see madness in the young woman's eyes; a fierceness that knew no bounds – but there was beauty too: an impish grin, fine bone structure and fiery green eyes. She had a demeanour that he imagined once fired-up on cheap champagne would free her inner Boudicca. Angry and attractive – a combination that would terrify most men, Patrick McDade in particular. And for someone who used swear words with such liberal aplomb she had what he perceived to be a pretty cut-glass accent.

"Why are you hanging around the toilets like a stale fart?"

"I'm waiting for someone."

"What's your name?"

"Yo-yo-you don't want to know."

"Oh, go on. Be brave. Try me."

"P-Patrick. You?"

"Kat."

"Appropriate."

"Fuck off. It's Kat, as in Katrina, you idiot. Katrina Wyatt-Browne."

"Ah."

"I presume you're one of the Irish ones, then?" Katrina Wyatt-Browne asked after a short pause to allow for a change of mood. "I expect you're one of Sean's lot? Are you? Are you one of Sean's lot?"

"Yes. A cousin. I'm Sean's cousin. You?"

"I'm Katrina from Cornwall. St Ives. Sean used to work for Pa. He was our estate manager for a while."

"Fuck."

"What?"

"Nothing."

"Anyway, I thought you Irish were supposed to be good fun at parties – you know, great craic and all that? It's a fucking wedding. What's wrong with you?"

"Nothing. I'm perfectly happy, thank you very much."

"Well, you don't fucking look it. What are you doing here? Who are you waiting for – a man? I can't believe any woman would want to be seen dead with a miserable-looking cunt like you."

"I'm waiting for my girlfriend," Patrick replied, nodding towards the ladies.

"Likely fucking story."

"Are you always this rude?"

"Rude – you call this rude? I can be a lot worse, you know. A lot worse. Especially after a couple of gins. You should see me when I'm being really angry and abusive."

"Err ... no thanks."

"So where is she – or *he*?"

"I told you."

"No, you didn't."

"Where the hell do you think? Oh, hang on ..."

The door of the Ladies suddenly swung open to the backing track of a whirring hand dryer revealing a dishevelled auburn-haired woman frozen to the spot, her head drooping forward, arms outstretched and hands jammed against the door frame. A

4

pair of spindly legs were struggling to support her stick-like physique.

Patrick McDade was about to jump up and offer his girlfriend a hand when she lurched forward, eyes half-closed, striding like a mechanical doll, tottering towards the leather couch and – about to sit down – bent over double and spewed a shallow wave of pink vomit across the floor.

"Shit! My shoes! My fucking shoes!" Katrina Wyatt-Browne wailed as her legs were doused in a fine spray of the offending liquid.

"Oops!" Patrick said, smiling for the first time since he'd left his parents' house that morning. "See weddings? They're nuts!"

"Oh, fuck off, you Irish pillock!" Katrina Wyatt-Browne shouted, jumping up, pushing past Patrick's girlfriend and disappearing into the ladies.

"Who the fuck was that?" Natalie slurred as Patrick steered her towards the disabled toilet to take advantage of its generous floor space, calm ambience, privacy and sink.

*   *   *

The weddings that Patrick McDade was invited to were usually held in the most inaccessible parts of the country, entailing complex travel arrangements and an overnight stay in some godforsaken two-star hotel, Premier Inn, B&B or pub. The travelling could be endured on the outward journey but often proved tortuous on the return leg following an all-day drinking session – the after-effects of which invariably left him not only hungover but also wrestling with a dark and dismal mood.

Waking up on the morning after his cousin's wedding, Patrick McDade's mood descended to a new low when he found himself alone in bed and then lower still when he read the crumpled note that Natalie had left for him on the dressing table of the room they were sharing. Not that he could remember sharing it with her much as they'd hardly been in it

5

since dumping their bags and doing a quick wash and brush-up before the wedding service.

The note attempted to offer an explanation for her absence:

Patrick,

I'm sorry but I forgot to tell you that I bumped into a girl from the office at the reception last night. She offered me a lift back to London with her this morning.

I hope you don't mind but it turns out she has to leave right now. I mean, right now. It's early and she's in a hurry.

I tried to wake you but you weren't for moving and I've got masses to do today and, as you're heading straight back to Falmouth, I thought you wouldn't mind if I cadged a lift with her now.

It's nothing personal ... I'll call you later.
Nat xxx

Patrick wasn't sure whether he'd been dumped or not but it certainly felt like it. The phrase *'it's nothing personal'* hinted as much. Her choice of words struck Patrick as being rather coherent for someone on their last legs through drink. He suspected that she may have had a helping hand in the note's composition. That he'd spotted Natalie's ex-boyfriend, Hugo Henderson, during the wedding service and then observed him hanging around her late into the evening, regardless of her dodgy breath, left him feeling more than a little uneasy and now deeply suspicious. There had been no sign of her in their room when he went to bed or during the night as far as he could recall from his drunken stupor. Though he did remember hearing feet scampering about around daybreak.

Having rushed through breakfast with the last of the wedding party, checked out and said his goodbyes, Patrick headed off to Rye Station for the train journey back to London and his connecting train on to Falmouth.

He arrived at Paddington Station in good time for the onward journey. If anything, he was a little *too* early he realised when sitting alone on Platform 4, a good thirty minutes before the arrival of the 13.03 to Falmouth via Truro.

That it was sweltering hot, that he had a heavy bag to lug about, that it was still a five-hour journey on to Falmouth, that he was thirsty but couldn't be bothered to walk back down the platform to the station foyer and the overpriced shops just made his mood worse. But then his train arrived. And on time.

There was a large crowd waiting to board but he was right at the far end of the platform and could see that there were plenty of seats free in the leading carriage as it pulled up beside him. As soon as those arriving had disembarked he dashed on board and nabbed a single window seat with a table – the seat facing towards the front of the train, a small luxury. He dropped his copy of the previous day's *Guardian* on the table to mark his territory, put his feet up on the seat opposite, sighed, leaned his head back and tried to doze off. He smiled when the train pulled away with a slight jerk. Sleep came easily but was soon interrupted.

"Get up, please. Please, get up!"

"What?"

"Get up! I need to sit there!"

"Katrina?"

"Yes, Patrick, it's me. And, I need to sit there! There, right there, where you're sitting."

"What? I'm sorry? Why, for God's sake?"

"Look, I need to sit there NOW!"

"If there's nowhere else for you to sit, I'll move my feet and you can sit opposite me."

"No, not there. I can't travel backwards. Let me sit there! I need to sit right there where you're fucking sitting!"

"Are you kidding? Is this some kind of joke?"

"No. I'm deadly serious. I need to face the way I'm travelling or I'll be ill – really ill."

"For God's sake, Katrina! What the hell makes you think I'm going to move for you?"

"Because if you don't, I'll probably be violently sick all over you."

"Do you have a handicap or something? Are you with child? Are you old or infirm?"

"Vertigo. I suffer from fucking vertigo if you must know."

"Vertigo?"

"Yes, vertigo! And I need to sit down IMMEDIATELY! Right away. I can feel motion sickness coming on already."

"Vertigo? Isn't that a fear of heights? We're not halfway up Everest or Kilimanjaro, are we by any chance, Katrina? No, we're travelling on a bloody train!"

"Google it, you plonker! It's an inner ear thing. It affects your balance. Whatever! I need to sit down or there's a good chance I'll throw up all over that lovely Ralph Lauren shirt."

"Is there nowhere else?"

"No!"

"I don't bloody believe this! Here you go, then," Patrick said slowly getting to his feet. "But I warn you, you'd better not talk to me or wake me up again if you're going to sit there for the next four or five hours."

"Deal."

"You sure?"

"Yes!"

"Good!" Patrick McDade growled before allowing her to squeeze past him in the aisle. Glancing down he noticed how much smaller she was close up – tiny, elfin and blonde. Placing his hands on her shoulders so as not to overbalance he felt empowered by his superior height. He, an Irish wolfhound; she, a petite English poodle. When Katrina peeked up he noticed beauty in her large emerald eyes. They weren't glaring now. She looked vulnerable. But he still wasn't going to chat, preferring to snuggle down in his seat to snatch some sleep. He closed his eyes and tried to nod off.

"Can I read your paper, please, Patrick?"

"Ah, there you go! See? You're talking again!" he said sleepily.

"But I was being polite."

"Yes, but you were talking."

"Hardly."

"You were moving your lips up and down and uttering words. That's talking," Patrick pontificated without opening his eyes.

Silence prevailed. Patrick snoozed.

Ten minutes hadn't passed before he felt a tug on his sleeve.

"What!" Patrick shouted, sitting up abruptly and making enough noise to cause heads to turn. "What the hell's the matter now?"

"It's this!" Katrina Wyatt-Browne said, smiling and waving Patrick's copy of *The Guardian* in the air.

"What about it?"

"I see you've finished the crossword – well, all bar one clue, that is."

"I usually can." Patrick yawned, leaning forward and resting his elbows on the table feeling smug.

"You usually can what – finish the crossword? Shit, really?"

"Why? Are you interested? Do you do crosswords?" he asked employing a superior tone.

"Kind of."

"What does 'kind of' mean?"

"Sorry, no. I love crosswords – cryptic crosswords," she said smiling warmly.

"Touché!"

"But only the one in *The Guardian*," Katrina added.

"Yes, it's the only one I can be bothered with too. The cryptic one in the *Daily Telegraph* is good, but then I can't stand the *Daily Telegraph* if you know what I mean."

"So, Patrick, do you do *The Guardian* crossword every day?"

"Not *every* day, but most days."

"And do you finish it most days?"

"I can usually do at least half."

"Just half?"

"Yes, but then I always seem to finish it on Saturdays – well, mostly. More often than not, say. Strange, really."

"Why Saturdays?"

"I don't know. Perhaps it's easier on Saturdays. Maybe it's because I'm simpatico with the setter on that day or something. You know, like we have a great empathy – a natural connection. If it's a woman, who knows? Maybe we were born to be together. Maybe we were married in another life! Maybe she's my soulmate and we're destined to be partners!"

"Do you think?" Kat said smiling.

"Why? What's so funny? What's it to you?"

"Oh, nothing, nothing."

"Katrina, what did you mean when you said you 'kind of do crosswords'? What does 'kind of' mean?"

"Can't you guess?"

"No."

"It means I write them. I compose crossword puzzles, Patrick."

"Do you? Really?"

"Yes."

"Who for? Where would I see one?"

"In *The Guardian*. I've been doing it for two or three years."

"Really, Katrina?"

"Yes."

"Exclusively in *The Guardian*?"

"Yes, Patrick, exclusively in *The Guardian*."

"Oh, on what days? When would I see them?"

"It varies a little but mostly for the Saturday paper, I suppose. Yes, mostly on Saturdays."

"Just a minute! You're not Artikan, are you, by any chance?"

"Yes, that's my tag line. It's, it's—"

"An anagram – it's your bloody name! It's obvious! I should have guessed!"

"Yes, you should."

"Bloody hell! *You* are Artikan! Oh, my God!"

"And what's the clue you couldn't solve yesterday, Patrick?"

"Eight across. It's five letters."

"Let's have a look. Ah, yes, here it is. Eight across, I remember. *Strange the two of us on one road*?"

"Yes, that's the one! What's the answer?"

"What, you can't work it out?"

"Oh, please, just tell me."

"But it's easy. It's so so obvious."

"Please, Katrina, just tell me."

"Are you sure?"

"Yes. Please."

"It's weird, Patrick."

"I know, but what's the bloody answer?"

"Weird."

"Eh?"

"That's the answer – *Strange the two of us on one road*. See? It's *weird*. *We* then *i* then *rd*."

"Shit! Of course it is. But then so's this."

"What?"

"Meeting you, Katrina. It's weird. Too bloody weird."

2

The small dark figure scuttling along the pavement was hunched against the wind and rain, his teeth clenched with grim determination.

A blanket of cloud had cast a dull and dusk-like gloom over the North Dublin backstreet. At the top of the road lay his destination, a four-storey building that had the appearance of a factory. Forties or fifties in style, dour and unadorned, it dominated the skyline dwarfing the surrounding clutter of lock-ups, commercial premises and terraced housing.

The walls of the red-brick building ahead were pockmarked with square windows that added little or no character. The small figure imagined that the place would look Sunday-serious and sober even on a bright summer's day. Today in the wet it appeared grey and sinister. There were no signs of life.

As he struggled into the gale, the only movement he was aware of was the rain smacking off the cobbles and the streams of water gushing down the gutters; the only sound the distant rumble of thunder over the Wicklow Mountains, the occasional flash of lightning overhead and the gusting wind.

The street was deserted. Neither cat nor dog would venture out in this, he thought. The young man assumed the residents would either be at work or sheltering by the hearth. The smoke from the turf fires hung heavy in the air.

Once the shadowy figure had hobbled round the corner, neared the entrance and stepped up to the building's large and windowless door, he turned towards a brass plate fixed to one of the columns standing sentry either side of the porch. He tugged the top of his hoodie back a little, leaned in and screwed up his eyes to get a better look. A quick squint confirmed that this was indeed the home of The Order of the Sisters of the Immaculate Conception.

Encouraged that this was the correct place, he pressed the doorbell and stepped back. He wasn't sure if the bell had rung and soon lost faith when nobody came. Impatient, he moved forward and grasped the heavy iron ring hanging from the door and knocked it hard against the wood making a loud clang.

Before long he heard faint footsteps tip-tapping towards him from within. A short pause was followed by a creaking as a small flap halfway up the door was slowly prised open. The top of a nun's head rose up behind the vertical bars set in the aperture. Tottering on tiptoe, her features were lost in the depths of her wimple. He could barely make out the twinkle of her eyes in the shadows.

"Hello. Can I help you? Do you have an appointment, young man?" the nun asked. Her voice high-pitched and frail.

"No, sorry, sister. It's just I believe that my mother was or is residing at this address. I was hoping that if she still lives here, I might be able to see her."

"Your mother? I'm sorry, young man, but there's no mothers living here now."

"Please, sister, it's taken me ages to find this place. It's been a long journey. Can't you help me? I'm pretty sure she was, or is, living here."

"Here – your mother? I'm sorry, but I can assure you that you are mistaken."

"No, I don't think so," he said pulling a dog-eared piece of paper from his pocket, unfolding it and holding it up. "In fact, I'm sure of it."

"But, as I've already told you, there are no mothers living here."

"Please, look at this. It gives this place as my mother's address," he said rolling up the scruffy document and thrusting it towards the nun.

The sister raised a skeletal hand, snatched at the notepaper and yanked it through the bars.

"I take it you are not from around these parts, young man?" she said as she scanned the wrinkled note. "If I'm not mistaken, yours is not a Dublin accent."

"My accent might not be local, but as you can see from that letter, it appears that I *am*. It states quite clearly that I was born at this address. According to what I've been told, your order has been running this laundry and taking in disadvantaged women for many years. So, if my mother *is* here, I would be grateful if you could fetch her for me."

"If the woman who wrote this letter were still in residence, I might inform her that she has a visitor, but, as with all our young ladies and mothers, I'm afraid she no longer lives here and hasn't for quite some time."

"Why? Why is that, sister?"

"Unfortunately our order no longer takes in girls or offers them refuge. All our young women have left. And that would include your mother."

"So what happened here?"

"I am sure if you were to do a little research, you would find plenty of stories about this place in the newspapers. But I, we, the sisters, wouldn't recommend that you do. You see, we earnestly refute all the scurrilous allegations that have been made against our order over the last few years."

"I'm sorry but none of that is of any interest to me. I've simply come here to try and trace my mother."

"As I have already told you, young man, if she were here, I could help you, but, I'm sorry, only the Lord himself knows where she is living now."

"Don't you have forwarding addresses?"

"No. I'm sorry."

14

"No details at all? No records? No files?"

"No, I'm afraid not. We're not allowed to divulge such information, in any case. You see, all the personal details of our residents are protected by law these days."

"You're a nun – surely you can understand why a son would want to find his mother? Is there nothing you can do to help me?"

"Contact the government's adoption department. The address is easy enough to find. I'm really very sorry but there's nothing more I can say or do to help you. Thank you for your interest," the nun said passing back his note.

"Wait! Please, wait!" the dark figure shouted in vain as the old woman lifted her hand to close the flap.

"I hope you find what you're looking for, son, but, sad to say, you won't find it here. Goodbye," the nun said in a shrill voice, then slammed the flap shut and bolted it.

The young man lurched forward and swung a boot at the bottom of the door. The kick made a powerful thud but left no mark or impression on the thick wooden panel. Cursing and wriggling his toes to relieve the stinging, he took two or three steps backwards until he was standing in the road tottering on the wet cobbles again. He stared up at the front of the building desperately searching for a face, a silhouette or any other sign of a human presence in the windows. There was none.

As his hood fell back over his shoulders his face became fully exposed to the rain. He wiped his brow on the sleeve of his hoodie as the water trickled into his eyes to mix with the tears already welling there.

3

Six months later – Friday, 15 June 2018

"Ladies and gentlemen, please be upstanding for your bride and groom!"

A pause. A second or two of silence and then mayhem as feet were stamped and tables thumped; the function room erupting with applause as an elderly couple struggled to stand, nodding to all around them in appreciation of their ovation.

"Speech! Speech!" friends and family chanted with a carnal ferocity that startled the youngest of the children and had one of them in tears.

The husband of the ancient couple raised a shaky palm to restore order before clasping his wife's fingers in his other hand to ease her back into her chair. Stretching to his full height he turned to his audience and took a deep breath.

"As you know, I am a man of few words—"

"Thank God!" someone shouted from the back of the room but was quickly silenced. Some tittered.

"But on behalf of Philomena and myself, I would like to thank you all for coming to celebrate our golden wedding anniversary and for your many cards and presents. You're a great bunch and we love every one of you dearly and are very glad you can be here with us today. Now, that's enough talk. Please, go and enjoy the free bar, sing your songs, dance your dances, behave yourselves and then, in a wee while, I think our Patrick would like to say a few words," the old man concluded before sitting down, his final words followed by a short pause and then a generous round of clapping.

A loud hubbub reverberated around the room but soon abated when, from the bar, a voice rose above the din singing in a plaintive soprano. The song was soon taken up by one or two others and then joined with enthusiasm by the rest who belted out the traditional ballad as if it were a family anthem:

"Her eyes they shone like the diamonds
You'd think she was queen of the land
And her hair hung over her shoulders
Tied up with a black velvet band ..."

The Richmond Green Hotel in Surrey catered for family occasions to celebrate every stage in life from christenings to weddings to wakes. Today was the turn of Patrick McDade's parents, Philomena and Brian, who were celebrating fifty years of long and happy marriage. The couple were both in their early eighties, native of Holywood, County Down, but now resident in South East England where they'd moved on retirement to be nearer their grandchildren.

*   *   *

Mr Bartram, the hotel's function manager, had been monitoring events from a discreet distance since the start of the party. Two hours in and he was beginning to wilt under the strain of having too little to do and too much to worry about. His shoulders were hunched and beads of sweat were forming on his brow.

"Are you OK, Mr Bartram?" his genial assistant, Barbara, enquired, growing worried for his mental stamina.

"NO I AM NOT, BARBARA!" he suddenly yelled above the din. "I'm worried, extremely worried," he moaned from behind tightly folded arms and without making eye contact.

Mr Bartram had expected that the McDade party would be a sedate affair when he had taken the booking. The family's representatives – Patrick's younger sisters – gave the impression of being decent, respectable people. They were well dressed and appeared to be well educated, well mannered and well spoken. They had South West London accents and South West London addresses. But now the signs for a peaceful conclusion to the evening's festivities were not looking favourable. Many of the guests were drunk and there was singing in the bar, plus musicians, dancing and spillages. And those guests who weren't singing or dancing were whooping and hollering encouragement to those who were.

"Barbara, how many people are in here, for God's sake?"

But Barbara didn't answer – she couldn't hear. Mr Bartram couldn't hear himself speak either and felt that he had lost control of the situation. He could only watch in horror and cringe at the implications for health and safety and insurance claims. Worst of all, since the hotel's residents had started to complain, he feared for the negative posts that were sure to appear on Tripadvisor.

*   *   *

"Oh, please get me out of here, Kat!"

"What the hell's the matter, Patrick? I thought you were having fun. And you're the one who's always saying that there's no one like the Irish for throwing a party."

"No, that's what you always say, Katrina."

"Everybody else is enjoying themselves, Patrick, so why can't you? Your parents are and, let's face it, that's all that really matters today."

"How do you do that, Kat?"

"Do what?"

"Be right all the bloody time. Couldn't you slip up and be embarrassingly wrong just for once?"

"Calm down, fat boy – it's why you married me."

"Why? Because you're perfect?"

"Maybe, Patrick, maybe."

"Ha bloody ha. One thing, though, whenever we celebrate

our golden wedding anniversary, please promise me there'll just be you, me and a crate of champagne. Oh – and a packet of pork scratchings. Yes, pork scratchings would be nice, Kat."

"You should be so lucky."

"The champagne or the pork scratchings?"

"Both. I'd only give us about another twelve months or so anyway, the way things are going, Patrick."

"You've been saying that every year for the past two decades."

"It's a good job that you're tall and reasonably handsome then, isn't it? It's a pity you're not dark too, but then I suppose a girl can't have everything."

"Mum, Dad! Have you seen Milo?" Cerin, the elder of their two girls, gasped as she hurried over to join them.

"Why, what's he wearing?"

"Not funny, Dad. I haven't seen him for ages and he doesn't know a soul here."

"Perhaps he's slipped out for a fag."

"He doesn't smoke, Dad."

"Maybe he's gone to the loo?"

"How would I know?"

"Patrick, go and check."

"Check what, Katrina?"

"The men's toilets! Go on, go! Go and check them NOW!" Katrina barked.

*   *   *

Patrick McDade's extended family was equal in population to that of a small country. Andorra, perhaps. It seemed that way anyhow. There might not have been seventy thousand in Patrick's branch of the McDade family (that being the total of people native to Andorra according to Google) but their number ran into the hundreds. By ancestry they were Northern Irish, and while a minority were still home-based the majority had migrated across the water to become part of the great Irish diaspora in the south-east of England.

Why Patrick's parents had chosen to celebrate their golden wedding anniversary with a full-blown family party in a four-star hotel in Richmond was beyond Patrick. A natural claustrophobe, the idea of partying in an overcrowded function room gorging on piles of finger food and gulping gallons of cheap fizzy wine was his idea of bourgeois hell.

Patrick was happiest at his office high up on Richmond Hill, which he shared with his diminutive Italian business partner Luca Salvatore and their team. There he worked alone for much of the day in his own studio – a space where he could create a calm atmosphere playing jazz on Spotify and glugging coffee. Apart from his home, a few miles away in East Sheen, the smoked-glass open-plan office felt like his natural habitat.

*   *   *

"I expect Milo will be snorting something powdery off a toilet seat by now," Patrick whispered into his wife's ear before heading off in search of Cerin's new best friend.

"Patrick!"

"Where did Cerin find him?"

"She met him online apparently."

"What?"

"Oh, wake up, Patrick – it's what they do these days!"

"So what does Cerin see in him?"

"He makes her laugh."

"Is that all?"

"Isn't that enough?"

"I guess so. But what's with those glasses, Kat? Can he see anything through those lenses? They're very thick."

"Milo's got impaired vision, Patrick!"

"Oops, sorry."

"I wouldn't worry too much. *She* wouldn't exactly be *his* cup of tea if you know what I mean."

"Oh ... right!"

"Now, shut up and go and find him. Do it for Cerin."

A few minutes later Patrick reappeared through the throng of guests crowding the bar and produced Milo as if he were a rare species of marmoset rescued from the depths of a rainforest.

"Here's your man," he said looking pleased with himself.

"Milo!"

"He was stuck at the bar buying a round of stout for my uncles, the chancers. Getting fleeced, he was. It's a free bar, you numpty. Never trust a McDade, Milo."

"Oh, shut up, Patrick," Katrina scolded.

"Don't take any notice, Milo. I know Dad's very fond of you really," Cerin added with a reassuring smile.

"Thank you for that, Cerin. And she's right, Milo, but a word of advice – watch out for the McDade women too. They're a fierce bunch, all right," Patrick added.

"Well, don't include *me* in your character assassination please, darling. I'm not really a McDade woman, Milo, I'm a Wyatt-Browne. We're English and old money. We go back centuries. William the Conqueror and all that. We've got superior genes and good breeding."

"Or is that inbreeding? We all know what you English toffs are like, Katrina."

"Patrick!"

"It would explain your sticky-out ears and lazy eye. Actually, it would explain rather a lot, Katrina. Oh, thank God! Here's Luca – LUCA!"

"*Buongiorno*, Patrick," Luca bellowed as he walked over from the bar, his continental accent turning heads. "*Buongiorno*, Kat, Alice, Cerin and ...?"

"Milo. This is Cerin's friend, Milo, Luca."

"*Buongiorno*, Milo."

"*Buongiorno*, Luca."

"Enjoying your parents' party, Patrick?"

"What do you think?"

"He's having a great time, Luca. And thank you for coming."

"No problem, Kat. I kind of had to, didn't I? But what's up, Paddy? You look like you've seen a ghost."

"Two words – family and parties."

"Come on, it can't be that bad," Luca said smiling.

"What about you, Luca? Are *you* having a good time?"

"Yes, I've been having a great time, thanks, Katrina. I've been chatting to your mum and dad, Patrick—"

"Mmm lovely, I'm sure," Patrick mumbled.

"However, I'm afraid I'm going to have to head on now."

"What, you're leaving us already, Luca?"

"Yes, Kat. I'm going to pop outside, have a sneaky fag and then go on."

"You can't leave this early – the party's just getting started."

"I have to, Katrina. I've got to prepare something to show the folks at the meeting in Plymouth."

"Plymouth?"

"Yes, we've got a major presentation on Wednesday, Kat," Patrick said, straight-faced.

"Of course you have, of course ..."

"It's with the guys from the Emirates Investment Office?"

"Yes, yes, Patrick. I'm sorry, I forgot."

"It's with the directors of their UK property arm, Katrina," Luca added.

"But, shit, Luca, do you really have to go into work now?" Patrick interjected.

"I've no choice."

"Shouldn't I be coming in with you?" Patrick said, leaning forward and whispering into Luca's ear.

"No. No need. Don't worry, I can get the design visuals together on my own. The brief was pretty straightforward," Luca replied in a suitably hushed voice.

"Are you sure, Luca? You sound a tad overconfident to me."

"Don't worry, Paddy. Trust me. How many years have we been doing this?"

"Too many. And that's all fine and dandy just as long as you remember to smile during the presentation too. And be deferential. And—"

"And what, Patrick?"

"Listen to whatever they're trying to tell *you*, and don't get huffy and argue the point if there's anything they don't like about your design."

"Why are you telling me all this?"

"Because I know what you're like."

"You *are* coming to the presentation, aren't you, Paddy?"

"Of course! I know how personally you take criticism and how easily you lose your rag, Luca."

"Who – me? I'm just passionate. Anyway, as long as you do all the talking, Paddy, we'll be fine. You can always give me a kick under the table if I start getting emotional. You usually do.'

"Good! That's that sorted, then."

"Patrick, I've really got to get going."

"I'd call you later to see how you're getting on, Luca, but there's not much point since you never have your bloody phone switched on or charged."

"I love the peace and quiet, Paddy. You should try it."

"Very professional, Luca. Very professional."

"I've got to go, Patrick – really got to go!" Luca said springing up and down on his toes.

"Go on, then, go! Get out of here!"

"*Arrivederci*, Katrina. *Ciao*, girls ... Milo," Luca Salvatore voiced in theatrical fashion before kissing them all on both cheeks, spinning round and making a dash for the door.

"Oh, my God, Patrick, here's your—"

"Mum! Hello! Are you having a good time, sweetheart?"

"Of course I am, Patrick. And how are my favourite granddaughters?"

"We're great, thanks, Gran."

"You're not thinking of leaving already, are you, Patrick?"

"Just because I'm standing in a doorway, Mother, doesn't mean I'm about to leave. It makes me feel a little more secure and a lot less like fainting, that's all. It's also a structurally safe spot to stand should someone decide to drop a bomb on this place, which if they did, would almost be an act of kindness and certainly forgivable."

"I know your game, Patrick McDade."

"Do you, Mother?"

"Yes. Anyway, as your father mentioned earlier, we would both like you to say a few words to mark the occasion."

"Really, Mum?"

"Yes."

"He'd love to, Philomena. You would, wouldn't you, darling?"

"Err, yes. Would love to."

"Thank you, Katrina. Thank goodness someone can control my wayward son. It's beyond me!"

"But not for want of trying, eh, Mother?"

"Yes, Patrick. And once you've got everyone's attention please remember, don't mention the you-know-what. You know how it embarrasses your father."

"The what?"

"You know."

"No, I don't."

"The oil business – the forecourts."

"Why would I? That would be *so* tacky, Mum. I'm sure they're all sick to death of hearing about your blooming petrol stations. I bet they'd rather hear a funny story about our childhood or your courting days. I know! How about I tell them about the time Granda went after Dad with his shotgun when he thought he'd got you in the family way?"

"Patrick, please! Please promise me you won't be telling them anything like that! It's not true, in any case."

"OK, Mum, don't worry. I'll just say a few nice words about you and Dad, tell everyone how much we love you both and then shut up. After that Cerin and Alice are going to dance a two-hand reel to entertain everyone."

"Dad!" Patrick's daughters gasped in horror.

"Or not. Only joking, girls. Right! Let's get the show on the road. Thank God Luca isn't going to hear this. He'd never let me do a presentation again. Now, where's the cake?"

"It's on the other side of the room on the long table in front of the windows. I'm sorry to say but you're going to have to step away from that doorway, Patrick."

"Wonderful, Mum, just wonderful."

"Patrick," Katrina hissed into her husband's ear whilst pulling him back by the arm.

"What, Kat?"

"Here, I've got a clue from tomorrow's crossword for you."

"Oh, go on, then," Patrick said, leaning in and bowing his head to concentrate on the words.

"It's 12 across, four letters – *brave warrior. He takes half of Italian city.*"

"Jesus! No, hold on, hold on ... Yes, got it! *Hero*! Yeah, it's 'hero'! So is that how you see me?"

Katrina blinked and looked bashful.

"Why, thank you, sweetheart. I didn't know."

"Och, you're very welcome, Patrick."

Patrick McDade pecked Katrina on the cheek then shuffled through the minefield of aunts, uncles, nephews, nieces and cousins between him and the far side of the function room, enduring hefty slaps on the back along the way. The anniversary cake sat resplendent on a table by the windows. It featured two sugar-crafted petrol pumps with intertwining hoses and the initials B and P set in a pink heart on each.

Three or four taps on his champagne flute with a spoon and Patrick McDade had the guests' attention, then immediately became aware that while *he* was holding a champagne flute the rest of the menfolk were grasping pints of stout. Patrick's cheeks flushed and he could feel his stutter threatening to erupt at the back of his throat – his speech likely to explode into a spluttering shower of consonants and vowels.

There was a hush.

He began.

"L-l-ladies and gent-gent-gentlemen, what a p-p-pleasure to see you all here t-t-today ..."

4

Saturday, 16 June 2018

A doorbell rings with the familiar chimes of Big Ben, but synthetic and synthesised. The bells are barely audible outside in the porch of the large Arts-and-Crafts-style house. A man in a red fleece and cargo shorts is hovering on the step; a bundle of post tucked under one arm. A woman comes scurrying down the hall towards the door and immediately recognises the blurred figure looming in the frosted glass.

"Sam, come on in!" the woman exclaims excitedly as she swings the door open. "What have you got for us today?"

Sam Healy had never envisaged spending his working life walking the streets of South West London as a postman when growing up off the Shankill Road in Belfast. His boyhood dreams had centred on emulating his hero, George Best. Like George his footballing talent was prodigious from an early age and like George he was lucky enough to be spotted by a scout for Manchester United. When Sam was signed up and packed off to Old Trafford as a seventeen-year-old, his future seemed assured.

Within a month or two of arriving in Manchester, however, Sam ruptured the cruciate ligaments in his right knee in training. Sadly his football career was over before it had even begun. Following his recuperation he discovered another game: golf. Armed with his insurance payout and accompanied by his fiancée, Sam moved south where he imagined he wouldn't be hounded with questions about his time at Manchester United and where he found an occupation, the demands of which complemented his new sporting passion. Working for the Post Office proved to be stress-free, secure and sociable and provided plenty of free time for playing eighteen holes in the afternoon.

While delivering post over the next thirty years, Sam grew to respect the dull ache in his knee. A constant companion, it was a reminder of his first love and the fame and fortune that he might have achieved as an elite professional footballer.

Sam's demeanour was suited to his new profession. He liked that he was a purveyor of news, a conduit for celebrations and commiserations – a de facto Angel Gabriel. His winning smile and easy, outgoing manner quickly established him as a popular personality on his round.

But today was an exception. Today's deliveries, the last of the week, brought him no joy. It was Father's Day tomorrow; one of Healy's least favourite days of the year. Every greetings card delivered was a painful reminder of another, sadder loss. For Sam, Father's Day was a day of regret.

"*Down, Simba*! Sorry, Sam!"

Sam Healy smiled as the golden retriever came charging down the hall and started spinning in circles before him.

"Here you are, Mrs M," he said smiling broadly as he handed over a bundle of post, his Ulster accent still clearly discernable.

Sam was fascinated by Katrina McDade. She was just so damned eccentric – an anthropologist's dream. He would never forget the time their paths first crossed when the McDades moved in a few years before. It was her voice that had startled him – so loud, so shrill, so upper crust. That and her colourful turn of phrase.

"What the fuck are *you* doing hanging around on *my* fucking doorstep like you own the fucking place?" was her opening gambit the first time he arrived with a delivery that required a signature and had rung the bell a little too persistently.

But Sam loved her directness and decided then and there that this – that she – was a challenge to be won over. And while he hadn't failed to be entranced by her piercing green eyes, he always thought of her, and respected her, as a friend.

"Looks like the girls' Father's Day pressies have arrived," Katrina McDade gushed when she spotted a couple of small Amazon packages in Sam's bundle. "Oh, good, they will be pleased. *Get down, Simba*! Sorry, Sam."

"It's OK, Katrina. I think Simba's more likely to lick me to death than take a bite."

"Yes, but all the same, I bet you fucking hate dogs, Sam."

"No, not really. Anyway, Simba's different, aren't you, Simba?" he mewed in a soppy voice while patting Simba's head. "As it happens, I've only got to put up with mad dogs and Englishmen until the end of next week, Katrina."

"What?"

"I've received confirmation. I'm entitled to take early retirement from next Friday."

"That's very sudden."

"I've been negotiating my package for months, Katrina."

"You kept that quiet."

"Sorry."

"But shit, Sam, you can't. Please, don't stop. Please, don't abandon us!"

"A postman's working life might be a hard one but it doesn't go on forever, thank God. So, Katrina, that's me, I'm afraid. One more week and I'm hanging up my postbag."

"But you're no age, Sam."

"Flatterer!"

"And who's replacing you? Some knobhead, I bet."

"Whoever it is, you go easy on them, Mrs M. Don't be giving them a hard time."

"Me? Would I?"

"Yes! And you know you would."

"Tea, Sam?" Katrina asked, changing the subject.

"I shouldn't, but I'm sure a quick one won't do any harm. Is Patrick here?"

"He's still at work."

"On a Saturday?"

"Och, you know what he's like. He's just popped in for an hour or two. He'll be disappointed to have missed you though."

"And how are the girls?"

"They came back with us last night. Naturally they're both still in bed – you know what students are like. Come on, come through to the kitchen, Sam, and I'll get the kettle on."

The McDade's home was halfway along Fife Road – round the corner from the main gates of Richmond Park in East Sheen – one of South West London's most exclusive addresses. The sprawling detached properties in Fife Road sold for millions whatever the financial climate. Healy wondered how *anyone* could afford to buy one of the huge houses without winning the EuroMillions or smuggling large quantities of coke into the country. In an idle moment he had calculated that it would take him at least two hundred and fifty years to save anything like the amount required, and only then if he didn't spend a single penny of his salary on anything or anybody else in the meantime. Things might have been very different, he imagined, if he'd had a successful career at Manchester United followed by a lucrative transfer to the likes of Real Madrid.

The post for the residents of Fife Road took the longest to deliver on his round as the houses were set so far back off the road. These were also the properties where there was the least likelihood of a chat or the offer of a cup of tea. The home of the McDade family was different, though. To Sam it had become an oasis. He always timed his run to be there at around eleven – the perfect time for his tea break, even on a Saturday.

"I see next-door-but-one is sale agreed."

"God, they've done well what with the Brexit effect."

"Indeed," Sam Healy murmured, while perched on a stool at the kitchen island sipping a mug of tea.

"Do you know what they got for it, Sam?"

"Yes, I had a peek online."

"And?"

"Four and a half, Katrina."

"Million?"

"Naturally."

"Bloody hell, I don't know where people find that kind of money."

"Venezuela? Bogotá?"

"You probably wonder how the hell Patrick and I afforded *this* place."

"No, not at all. It's none of my business, Katrina."

"Actually, it was after my brothers sold the estate in Cornwall. We had no choice, really ... I mean, to sell the whole caboodle. The death duties when my parents passed away were horrendous. There was no way we could keep the house on. We were very lucky to find a buyer."

"Big, was it? The house, I mean."

"Huge, Sam."

"As big as Blenheim, say?"

"No, not that big but a stately home all the same. And there was land too."

"How much?"

"Five thousand acres."

"Blimey! Was your father the duke of something or other?"

"No, just a baronet."

"What does that make *you*, then?"

"Nothing at all. My eldest brother inherited the title."

"I guess you were sorry to lose the estate, though?"

"A bit. But in some ways it was a blessing. Running this place is a piece of piss in comparison – no employees, no staff, no wage bills, no stress. We were lucky to find a buyer and cash in."

"Fair enough."

"And sod the ancestors – sod the history. You can't eat history, Sam."

"So how did the do go?" Sam Healy asked, nodding over to the invitation stuck to the fridge door.

"Och, you know what family parties are like. It's a pity you couldn't come." Katrina McDade replied, pouring more tea.

"Yes, I'm sorry about that but I hope you and Patrick had a good time."

"It was all right but I'm not sure if it was really Patrick's bag."

"He must have enjoyed it a little bit."

"Mmm, maybe. Now, tell me, Sam, will you be getting a Father's Day card this year?"

"That's still a bit of a sore point, Katrina."

"Of course! I'm sorry."

"It's OK. But I don't expect anything from him any more, to be honest. And I've kind of got used to it now sadly."

"How old is Stephen, Sam?"

"He's twenty-three in September."

"And, you never hear from him?"

"Sadly not. We've no contact at all these days. It's his mother. I think she puts ideas in his head."

"Are they still up in Manchester?"

"Yes. They're living somewhere near Altrincham."

"And you never think to visit?"

"No. I've kind of given up."

"Sam!" A loud voice suddenly filled the awkward pause.

"Patrick! I thought I heard a car door. How did the party go?"

"Don't talk to me, Sam. If I could have got out of it, I would have."

"Still it must have been nice to catch up with your family and friends?"

"Nope. There's no two ways about it – it was hell."

"He doesn't mean that," Katrina interjected.

"Oh, has my *Architects' Journal* arrived, Sam?"

"Yes, I think so."

"Oh, good."

"It's over in that pile by the microwave," Katrina said, waving a hand. "But I don't know why you bother with it, Patrick – you never read the bloody thing."

"I don't know that that's true," Patrick McDade replied, wandering through the kitchen and giving his wife a peck on the cheek as he passed.

"I guess you need to keep up with current design trends, eh, Patrick?"

"There you are, Kat! Quite right, Sam. Now, if you'll excuse me for a mo, I have to go and get changed. Kat, we'll need to be leaving soon if we're going to meet Mum and Dad for lunch. It's just another tragic act in this weekend's melodrama, Sam," Patrick McDade said, glancing down at his tatty jeans and trainers.

"What time's the taxi picking us up, Patrick?"

"Half one."

"When do you get your driving licence back, Patrick? It seems ages already."

"Not till the first week of August, Sam," Patrick replied, avoiding eye contact.

"Silly fool. I hope you've learned your lesson."

"Yes, Katrina. As you keep reminding me. But then we can't all be as saintly as you. Sam would understand. He's a wee bollocks from Belfast like me."

"Speak for yourself, Patrick, you're from the posh end of town."

"Touché, Samuel!"

"Sorry, but I've got to head on now, guys," Sam said, making for the front door. "Oh, and here comes trouble!" he added, nodding towards the two bleary-eyed millennials blinking into the daylight as they waddled down the stairs tightly wrapped in their dressing gowns.

"Hi, Sam," the first mumbled, yawning.

"Hi, girls. Back from uni?"

"Not really. Term ended weeks ago. We've been staying in town. We're house-sitting for friends."

"Cerin and Alice are living in a squat, Sam."

"No, we're not, Mum!" the younger of the sisters, Alice McDade, countered.

"They've yet to invite me round for a visit, so what else am I supposed to think?"

"I guess I'm best left out of this one, Katrina."

"Yes, let's leave Sam alone. He's only popped in for a cup of tea, poor guy," Patrick McDade said retreating upstairs. "If I don't see you before, see you tomorrow week, Sam!" he called before disappearing across the landing.

"Next Sunday? What's happening, Sam?"

"I'm picking Patrick up for a round of golf, Katrina."

"Early?"

"Yes. Very."

"I guess you'll have plenty of time for playing golf soon."

As Kat opened the front door, Sam Healy paused, turned, raised his hands, flapped them in a beckoning motion, grinned and offered a quizzical frown in the exaggerated manner of a clown. The gesture brought a smile and pre-empted a group hug beneath the spread of Sam's long arms.

The moment was not lost on the dark figure staring up at the house from the picket fence bordering the front garden and who had been standing still, silent and unseen since Sam's arrival. The elfin figure's frozen expression and fiery eyes were left unmoved by the happy scene, the culmination of which caused him to turn and stomp off stamping and kicking the ground whilst muttering curses, unnoticed.

*　　*　　*

Mid-morning the next day and the McDades were gathering downstairs in the lounge.

"Happy Father's Day, Dad. Aren't you going to open your presents?" Alice asked, slumping down beside Katrina and

Cerin on the large L-shaped settee and gesturing towards the small pile of presents and cards on the coffee table opposite.

"Are you sure we've got time, Alice? Our taxi's due soon."

"Come on, it'll only take a minute, Dad."

"OK, sorry. Things have been a bit hectic this weekend but I guess we might as well do it as we're all here," Patrick replied as he strolled across the room having changed for Sunday lunch with his parents and sisters and their families.

"There's a small pressie from each of us," Cerin added, snuggling up to her father as he sat down on the sofa.

"Thank you! You're both very sweet. I had no idea."

"You say that every year, Dad."

"Come to think of it, I haven't done anything for your granda – not even a card. We didn't bother with Father's Day much when I was your age. I don't think it even existed back then. *Damn*! You know, I probably should have said something about it in my speech at the party – for your granda, I mean. What an idiot."

"Why don't you bring a card with you at lunchtime, Patrick. I'm sure he'd love that."

"Would he, Kat? As I say, I doubt he even knows that it's Father's Day. But, no, you're right."

It cheered Patrick McDade that his family were all together and at home for the weekend. He loved having his daughters around him; loved it when they filled the house with their chatter. He'd missed them since they'd moved away to art college. Cerin had recently completed her second year of a degree in marketing at Goldsmiths, while Alice had just finished her second year studying fashion at St Martins.

"Great speech at the party, by the way, Dad."

"God, my stutter was terrible. It only seems to rear its ugly head whenever your grandparents are around."

"Don't worry, Dad. People love a good stutterer. All that vulnerability and pathos brings a tear to the eye. It makes you appear sensitive and loveable."

"What, like the Elephant Man, you mean, Alice?"

"Yes, but better that than sounding like some egocentric arsehole," Cerin replied in a deadpan voice.

"Oh, thanks very much for that, girls. You really fill me with confidence and pride," Patrick McDade said with a smirk, before opening the first of the gifts bearing his name.

"There appears to be a CD inside. Mmm, I wonder what it is? What can it be? Ah, *The Best of Louis Armstrong*! Brilliant! What a lovely surprise! And there's a card. Thank you, that's exactly what I wanted. How did you know, Cerin?"

"Because you told me to get it when I called you last week."

"Ah, yes, of course. But thank you very much all the same. That's very sweet of you. Nice card too!"

"You're welcome, Dad."

"And this one must be from you, Alice. Yes, here we are. Ooo, another CD! Chet Baker with Bill Evans. *The Complete Legendary Sessions*. Wow! How did you know?"

"Same. I called you, Dad."

"Ah, right."

Patrick McDade leaned over and embraced his daughters. "Thanks, kids. You spoil me!"

"Just a second, what about this one, Patrick?"

"What is it, Kat?"

"I don't know. I didn't notice it earlier. It must have come with yesterday's post. It's addressed to you. It looks like an invite."

"Who do we know who'd send us an invite in a lemon yellow envelope?"

"Yeah, right enough."

"You never know, Dad, maybe it's another Father's Day card!"

"Don't be daft, Cerin."

"Hey, Dad, there isn't something you'd like to tell us, is there?" Alice said laughing.

"Don't be such a smart-arse," Patrick mumbled, turning the card round in his hands and checking the postmark. It was illegible.

"Come on, Dad, get it open!"

"OK, Cerin, there's time enough," Patrick moaned as he slipped a finger beneath the flap.

The room fell silent as he tore along the top edge of the envelope, paused and glimpsed at the three women before delving inside.

"Stop stalling and get on with it, Dad!"

Patrick pulled a greetings card from the envelope and opened it with the dexterity of a croupier. It was a crazy typographic treatment in bold flat colours. He tensed and slowly raised it up in one hand, bemused.

"It's a bloody Father's Day card!"

"Told you, Dad."

"Oh, my God!"

"What, Patrick?"

"There's a message, Kat."

"A bit of verse – a rhyming couplet?"

"No. I mean, yes. Naturally, there's the usual preprinted tosh, but there's also a message. Same hand as on the envelope."

"What does it say?"

"*To Mr McDade. Happy Father's Day.*"

"Is that it?"

"Yes," Patrick replied flapping the card about. "Weird or what? Is this one of your daft pranks, Cerin?" he asked, sounding stern.

"No!"

"It's probably a silly mistake, Patrick," Katrina said, leaning forward and touching her husband gently on the arm.

"How the hell can this be a mistake, Kat?"

"I-I-I don't know."

"And if this is someone's idea of a joke, I don't think it's very funny. I mean, who the hell would pull a prank like this?"

"Oh, Patrick, it's probably just a bit of fun."

"Fun? It's sick!"

"OK, calm down. Perhaps this'll help ..."

"What?"

"I've got a clue for you."

"Oh, God, here we go. More of your cheap diversion therapy, Kat. Go on, then, what is it?"

"26 down, four letters – *it's fake when embarrassment's not complete.*"

"OK. OK. Wait a minute ... Ah, yes! Got it! *Sham*? Yes, it's *sham*, Katrina. Got to be! The answer's *sham*. That one was a bit too easy, even for me, but very appropriate. Katrina, the card ..."

"What about it?"

"It can't be a mistake. It was addressed to me and has a bloody handwritten message inside."

"Forget about it, Patrick. It's more than likely from one of your stupid drinking buddies. Who knows? Maybe it's from Luca. Yes, it's probably from Luca! It's typical of the stupid pranks he likes to pull."

"Yes, I suppose that could be it."

"What about the handwriting, Patrick? Do you recognise it?"

"No, not at all."

"Here, pass it over."

"What do you think, Kat?"

"Mmm, I don't know. I don't recognise it either. But then if it is from Luca, he'd get someone else to write it for him, wouldn't he? I mean, he's not stupid and he's got an eye for detail."

"Do you think you can tell how old they are from that scrawl, Kat?"

"No, except it's obviously not the handwriting of a child. I'd say it's an adult's hand."

"Agreed."

"I'm sure it's just a prank, Patrick."

"Either that or you've got a secret family you've been hiding from us, Dad."

"Yes. Very funny, Alice. A secret family? Ha bloody ha. As if my family's not big enough already," Patrick said smiling. "Right, you two! You'd better go and get dressed. The taxi's due any minute," he added, clapping his hands.

5

"What the hell's the matter, Patrick?"

"Uh?"

"Could you please stop fidgeting!"

"Wha?"

"Please, Patrick, you're driving me nuts. I need some sleep, for fuck's sake!"

"Sorry. I'm having trouble sleeping myself."

"Yes, that's fucking obvious, but please stop rolling around the bed."

"Wha?"

"Stop rolling around the fucking bed ... PLEASE!"

"But I can't get to sleep, Kat."

"Why? It's three o'clock in the fucking morning!"

"Tell me about it."

"Aren't you tired?"

"Bloody exhausted."

"Then what's wrong?"

"What do you think, Kat?"

"Not the fucking card again?"

"Of course."

"Oh, for Christ's sake, Patrick, it's just a silly card. As I said earlier, it's probably one of Luca's stupid pranks."

"Luca's daft but he's not that daft. Anyway, he's flat out at work. He's got our presentation to deal with. He hasn't got time for playing silly buggers."

"But it's clearly someone's idea of a joke. Come on – who? Who do you think?"

40

"Don't know. I really don't know. I can't think of anyone. It's kind of creepy, though, isn't it?"

"Yes, very creepy."

"And there's no simple explanation I can think of."

"Unless you *do* happen to have a secret love child hidden away somewhere."

"None that I know of, Katrina. I mean – NO! Of course I bloody haven't!"

"Good. Then please please go to sleep," Katrina McDade murmured before pecking her husband lightly on the forehead, rolling over and dragging the duvet with her.

"Patrick?" Katrina mumbled a few minutes later.

"What?"

"I've been thinking."

"Oh, God! What now?"

"One last thing."

"What is it?"

"Illegitimate children."

"Eh? What about them, Katrina?"

"Don't worry. There's no disgrace."

"What? What do you mean?"

"We've probably had hundreds of bastards in our family down the years."

"What the hell *are* you talking about, Kat?"

"The Wyatt-Brownes. We're aristos. I'm sure my ancestors spent half their time shagging each other and the staff. If you DNA-tested my brothers and me, I'm sure you'd find we're related to the whole of North Cornwall."

Patrick McDade sighed, turned his pillow, rolled in the opposite direction and stared into the dark whilst scrolling back through the years, riffling through his history of relationships, recalling the faces, names and the personalities of the girls he'd dated from his teens onwards. He repeated this three or four times before dropping off to sleep at some point in the late eighties, picturing himself prancing round a dodgy nightclub in

Newquay to The Human League while sporting a floppy quiff and flouncy shirt.

*   *   *

Patrick McDade had been glad to get to work on the Monday morning and find something useful to do to distract himself from the ups and downs of the weekend – the presentation on Wednesday being his major focus.

It was a struggle. He felt jaded from the lack of sleep and couldn't help yawning every couple of minutes.

Shortly before lunch Patrick's mobile rang.

"Hi, Kat."

"Have you got something to tell me, Patrick?" she barked down the phone.

"Sorry? Are you OK?"

"Is there something you'd like to tell me?"

"Why? What's the matter?"

"There was a fucking message!"

"A message?"

"When I got home from the park with Simba."

"From whom? Where?"

"On the fucking answerphone. Apparently it was from your son – someone claiming to be your fucking son, anyway! You know, the one that sent the fucking card. Unless there's two of the bastards now. I picked up the message as soon as I came in. This joke has gone too fucking far."

"Shit! Did they leave a name, Kat?"

"No."

"God, that's freaky. Did you dial 1471?"

"Yes, of course."

"And?"

"Number withheld."

"Christ! I knew that card wasn't a prank – I just bloody knew it! I had a weird feeling, like someone was walking over my grave or something."

"Well, it's shocked me too, Patrick. I really don't know what to say."

"You didn't seem so worried last night when you were banging on about being related to the entire population of the West Country."

"That was just to shut you up so I could get some sleep."

"Oh, thanks very much. So what did he say?"

"Here, I'll play it back for you."

"What?"

"I'll play you the fucking message."

"Jesus, Katrina! Please. You can't. I'm about to go into a team meeting. It's a dress rehearsal for the presentation on Wednesday. Everyone's waiting for me in the conference room. There's a lot at stake here. The hotel development in Plymouth could be the difference between our being in profit or making a loss this year. There's at least six people's livelihoods on the line here – mine and yours included."

"Fucking hell, Patrick! Call me as soon as you've finished, then. This has put the willies right up me."

"Eh?"

"Oh, you know what I mean. I'm worried that this weirdo's not only got our address, but has also got our fucking phone number. I mean, how did he know we wouldn't be in and wouldn't pick up the phone when he called? It's all getting a bit too close to home and creepy."

"Katrina, I'm sorry but I really do have to go. *Now*, I mean. Right now."

"What time are you coming home tonight?"

"I'll be home by six. Six sharp. We'll sort it out then. Look, got to go. Like, right now. Sorry! Got to—"

Katrina McDade replaced the handset on the base unit in the hall and sloped back to her stool in the kitchen. She gawped at the ebony worktop for a minute trying to get her head round the answerphone message, bursting with questions. Unable to relax she wandered out to the answerphone again and stood staring down at the base unit for a second or two before pressing the play button.

The message replayed and ended with a bleep, the machine rewinding in a manic whirr. Katrina returned to the kitchen island and sat contemplating the call and the caller, her head in her hands. She imagined that the caller was a youngish man, possibly of a similar age to Alice and Cerin – in his early twenties maybe. She shook her head feeling disoriented, scared and vulnerable. This scenario just didn't ring true. Katrina felt tears coming but stopped herself abruptly lest someone might find her crying.

Christ, the girls!

Cerin and Alice had enough worries of their own. There was so much more pressure associated with being a student these days what with coursework, student debt and the lack of accommodation to cope with.

The doorbell rang.

"Sam!"

"Hi, Katrina. I hope I haven't caught you at a bad time."

"No, not at all. Come in, come in. I'll make you a coffee."

"Thanks, I've only got time for a quick one."

"That's OK. Come on through, Sam," Katrina McDade said, turning to walk down to the kitchen and being sure to wipe her eyes along the way.

"Are you all right? You don't quite seem yourself today?"

"You're very perceptive, Sam."

"Is there anything I can help you with?"

"No. No, thank you. You're very good. It's something and nothing. Anyway, how's your golf, Sam? Patrick tells me you've been winning competitions left, right and centre."

"Och, it's not bad but I don't harbour any great ambitions. I'll not be making the Ryder Cup team any time soon."

"Patrick's really looking forward to golf at the weekend. Where are you playing – Strawberry Hill?"

"No. We're playing on the public course in the park."

"Of course! I'll make sure he books a tee, Sam."

"You know you've got a good one there, Kat."

"Oh, I hope so, Sam. I do hope so."

*   *   *

True to his word Patrick McDade arrived home promptly, his taxi pulling up at six on the dot. Katrina was sitting in the kitchen. She'd been reflecting on her life with Patrick to see if there was anything that stood out that might help make sense of things.

She thought about how their relationship had progressed from their first encounter at the wedding in Rye. She was still living at home in Cornwall and working locally then. They dated at the weekends driving hither and thither in his battered Golf. Katrina had found Patrick a bit coarse at first. That he was from Northern Ireland made him an unknown quantity to her. She found that an attractive feature however – that and his natural charm. He thought her a little stuck-up, a little too horsey, but there were sparks and laughter.

Meanwhile, her parents bit their lips and hoped for the worst, but while they bit and waited they slowly grew fond of their future son-in-law. His irrepressible humour and devotion to their daughter gradually won them round. Marriage, followed by children, sealed their approval. Their trust in him was a generous act of faith he was keen to repay. Patrick was devastated when they died.

"Patrick? Oh, thank God!"

"I'm sorry I didn't get a chance to call you back, Kat. Thought it better to come straight home," Patrick gasped.

"Did you get the presentation finished?"

"Yeah. All done."

"And you're both off to Plymouth tomorrow?"

"Yes, we're going by train. Back Wednesday evening."

"Not too long, then?"

"No. But, shit, are you OK, Kat?" he asked, giving Simba a

quick pat on the head in passing before sweeping his wife up in his arms.

"No, I'm bloody not. It was just so fucking weird hearing that bloody voice on our answerphone," she replied, wriggling free of his grasp.

"I'm sorry about this, Kat."

"And so you fucking should be!"

"I know, b-b-b-b-but ... but ... all the same—"

"BUT WHAT!"

"But I haven't done anything wrong, have I?"

"That's what you say, but my stepson seems to think otherwise."

"Sod him – whoever he is! He's made a terrible mistake."

"Except *he* obviously doesn't think so."

"Well, *he* has. And I should bloody know! I wouldn't mind so much, but when someone you don't know starts calling your house with a crackpot story you're bound to start feeling a bit threatened."

"*You* feel threatened?"

"Yes! And, as I keep saying, as far as I'm aware, I haven't done anything wrong. Nothing. Absolutely nothing."

"So now it's 'as far as I'm aware'. You were a bit more sure of yourself earlier."

"You're twisting my words. In any event, there are proper channels to go through with things like this. There are agencies that adopted children have access to that can help them trace their birth parents with care and consideration to both parties."

"How do you know?"

"I've seen it on the telly – on *Long Lost Family*, on programmes like that. You should know. You've watched them with me often enough."

"Still, I never thought you'd be the type to have trouble keeping your dick in your pants, Patrick."

"I'm not. I have ... Kept it in my pants, that is. OK, let's

46

calm down and take a step back for a moment, shall we, Kat? Remember, I haven't heard the message yet."

"Do you want to?"

"Yes, of course – like right now. Is there anyone else here?"

"Only Simba. The girls are up in Hoxton."

"Good. Right, let's go and listen to the bloody thing, then."

Katrina and Patrick ambled into the hall.

"Good morning, Mr McDade,
I hope you liked my Father's Day card.
Erm ... You don't know me ... obviously ... but, err ... I believe you knew my mother. I hope you don't mind me calling you. It's just I wanted to make contact as I have good reason to believe that I am, in fact, your son.
I know this must come as a bit of a shock, but I would very much like to meet up with you some time, you know, if that suits.
I think we've got quite a lot to discuss and catch up on. And so, until then."

"Shit, Kat. That's quite a shock to the system," Patrick said, blowing his cheeks out.

"Tell me about it."

"Really creepy. What about his tone of voice?"

"What do you mean, Patrick?"

"Do you think he sounded aggressive, for example?"

"His voice was quite muffled. It's hard to tell, but, no, not aggressive. I think he sounded pretty deadpan."

"Yes, I agree, Kat – unemotional and deadpan. Not particularly friendly but then not unfriendly either, just very deadpan. A bit robotic."

"Yes, a bit like a satnav, perhaps, or a male version of Alexa. He doesn't sound like a very happy bunny, though, Patrick."

"I've got a feeling he was reading from a script."

"You think?"

"Yes."

"What about his accent, Patrick? I thought it had a bit of a West Country twang earlier, but now I'm not so sure."

"West Country, Welsh, English, Scottish, Irish ... I don't know. It's hard to say, the sound quality was so poor. And you reckon he's in his early-to-mid twenties?"

"Yes. I think so. But again, it's quite hard to tell."

"It's strange that he didn't use my name, Kat – my Christian name, that is."

"Yes, same as on the Father's Day card."

"A bit odd, that. A bit formal, don't you think?"

"Yeah, I bet you've never called your dad Mr McDade."

"No, never. But then I don't call him Brian either, and, anyway, I'm not this guy's father."

"Shit, I find this all so fucking weird, Patrick. It's like someone's trying to burst our bubble. It's not funny and if this is someone's idea of a joke, they're sick bastards."

"What do you want me to do, Kat? Call the police?"

"How can you? What are you going to tell them? So far he's sent a greetings card, made a phone call and left a message. That's hardly a hate crime."

"And it's not as if we can get a court injunction without a name and address."

"All right, so what *do* we do, Patrick?"

"I don't know. I'll think about it. We'll just have to wait, I'm afraid. But if he's been in touch once, I expect he'll get in touch again."

"Creepy. And what then?"

"Dunno. As I say, we'll have to wait and see, Kat."

"If he really does want to get in touch, meet up and discuss this, then it's a bit odd he didn't leave a contact number. It's a bit like he's toying with us. I mean, he even blocked his number with a 141. Isn't that a bit strange?"

"Of course – and bloody annoying!"

"And you're sure you have absolutely no memory of any

careless behaviour that could have caused this, Patrick? You don't remember those occasions when you didn't take precautions? Are any of your ex's single parents? I mean, what about that girl you were with the day I met you?"

"At Sean's wedding?"

"Yes, her – the one who threw up over my Jimmy Choos."

"Natalie? But we didn't go out for more than a couple of months."

"It just takes one prick and a quick squirt to get someone pregnant, Patrick."

"I think we only slept together a couple of times, Kat. It was the early nineties. We were off our faces most of the time back then."

"There you go, then."

"Look, we might have been young but we were pretty careful. HIV and Aids were a big thing. We took precautions when we needed to."

"Well, we'll see."

"Do you think we should tell the girls about this, Kat?"

"No. Absolutely not. Not yet. Not till we find out more about this guy and what this is all about. If we don't react, you never know, he might get bored and go away."

6

12.30p.m. Friday, 22 June 2018

Patrick and Luca were having lunch in the Roebuck Inn at the top of Richmond Hill; as traditional an English pub as traditional English pubs can be. Georgian and characterful, the Roebuck overlooked the Thames and was only a short walk from their office. They had brought the rest of the team with them. An office lunch – a rare event.

Patrick and Luca were sitting on a separate table from the others and talking in hushed tones. The bar was busy with lunchtime drinkers. Glasses clinked and chatter reverberated around the dark wood panelling of the downstairs bar while the two partners leaned in conspiratorially.

"You must be fucking joking, Patrick. *You*? You've got an illegitimate son?" Luca spluttered, nearly choking on his Guinness.

"No. And that's the point. Anyway, haven't you been listening, Luca?"

"So you haven't?"

"No! And I'm not bloody joking. This goes way beyond a joke, Luca!"

"Positive?"

"Yes!"

"You're sure?"

"Yes!"

"Really?"

"Yes! Of course I'm bloody sure. You'd think I'd know if I'd got someone pregnant and fathered a son, wouldn't you? It's not as if I've ever slept around. I mean, I'd know if I'd sired a son. And I think that anyone I've ever been out with would have told me by now if they'd happened to have given birth to our love child."

"I suppose the colour of the child's hair would be a dead giveaway."

"Yes! According to statistics only one per cent of the world's population have red hair, Luca. We're an endangered species, apparently."

"What, like the white rhino?"

"Yes, up to a point, but we're not as highly prized and there's no one trying to trophy hunt us as yet."

"So why didn't you tell me about this before, Patrick?"

"Today's Friday, Luca. I got the Father's Day card last Sunday. Then we had the presentation in Plymouth to keep us busy. It's not like I've been hiding it from you or anything. You've been working flat out and I didn't want to distract you. I wanted to catch you at the right time."

"Fair enough."

"But the whole thing's got me really spooked, Luca."

"I'm sure it has."

"At the moment it feels like we're being attacked by something unstoppable, unseen and virulent, you know, something like the Spanish flu. Apart from work it's practically all I can think about right now."

"Shit, Paddy!"

"At first I thought it was some kind of prank. I thought it might be one of those practical jokes *you've* become famous for."

"Hang on! I can see where this is going. You thought that I sent you the card. Oh, I bet you did, though, didn't you?"

"Well, Luca, you have developed a bit of a reputation for this kind of thing," Patrick said in hushed tones.

"*Oh, grazie mille*, Paddy."

"Anyhow, that's not really why we're here, is it?"

"Oh, thank goodness for that. So why *are* we here?"

"As I hinted in the office this morning, I just wanted to say ... C-c-congratulations, everybody!" Patrick stammered, getting to his feet, turning to face the rest of the team, raising his voice so that they could all hear and thrusting his pint glass in the air. "CONGRATULATIONS! We've only g-g-gone and won the b-b-bloody hotel c-c-contract!"

Everyone from the office gasped, paused then cheered.

"I got confirmation in an email from our new clients this morning. And we haven't even done a f-f-full costing and technical spec for them yet!" Patrick McDade enthused as he chinked glasses with each of the team in turn. "Cheers, everybody! And cheers, Luca! Bloody well done!"

"Cheers!" they all yelled back in unison.

"There's p-p-plenty of hard work still ahead, but for now let's celebrate our success. And, just for once, guys and gals, the lunch and the drinks are on me!" Patrick bellowed in Churchillian fashion.

The speech over, the team returned to chatting in their separate groups on the adjoining tables.

"How the hell did we swing that one, Patrick?"

"Because, Luca, with us the developer knows that they will get a very personal service. We might not be the biggest practice in London, but they know that they will be our biggest client," Patrick replied, before downing his pint to quell his nerves.

"Agreed."

"It's that and our portfolio, of course. The quality of our work speaks for itself," Patrick mumbled leaning in to talk in hushed tones. "And what's more, they know that when they pick up the phone they can speak directly to you or me without having to go through layers of admin and a host of account handlers first," Patrick whispered.

"Good point!"

"And they loved everything about our presentation, Luca."

"What you're really trying to say is that they loved my design drawings."

"Naturally!" Patrick replied before taking another large gulp of Guinness. "They certainly liked your design concept and I think they liked you too, Luca."

"And you know why that is, don't you, Paddy?"

"No, I don't, but I'm sure you'll tell me."

"It's because I'm Italian."

"And?"

"We are the best designers in the world."

"Are you sure about that, Luca?"

"Of course! Who designed Saint Mark's Square, The Ponte Vecchio and the Colosseum in Rome, for fuck's sake? It wasn't Christopher Wren or Richard bloody Rogers, was it?"

"Richard Rogers is half Italian, Luca."

"Are you sure?"

"Yes!"

"There you go, then. Proves my point."

"Pint, Luca?"

"Why not? *Grazie mille.*"

Patrick and Luca's design partnership had been forged at college when they realised that they worked far better together than on their own. Once they had acquired their final qualifications, the launch of their own practice was the obvious next step. Over the years it had proved to be a shrewd move but never more so than now.

"So what about the costing, Luca? The outline budget's pretty generous."

"It's oil wealth, Paddy. If they like what they see, I'm sure they'll go for what we propose."

"They want a site meeting on Monday."

"Monday coming?"

"Yes. They want us to go through some figures and discuss our initial concept in more detail, Luca."

"Shit!"

"Come on, it's nothing we haven't dealt with before. Sure I'll work on some projections over the weekend," Patrick said before tucking into the steaming portion of shepherd's pie that had just been plonked down in front of him.

"So it's back to Plymouth, then?"

"Yes, Luca, we'll set off early on Monday morning."

"Actually, it might come in handy for you to be heading down to the West Country again, Paddy. There's someone down there I think you should go and see."

"Who's that?"

"Who do you think?"

"I don't know, Luca. Who?"

"Jenny."

"Jenny? Not Jenny Harris from college?"

"Yes, Paddy. I mean, how many Jennys do you know?" Luca asked as a gargantuan plate of lasagne was placed in front of him.

"Why the hell do you think I should talk to Jenny, Luca?"

"Jesus! You know why!"

"To ask her about my stalker, you mean? Really? That would be an odd conversation."

"She might know something, Patrick. It's worth asking her. Perhaps she'll remember something from your time together at college. She knew everyone you hung out with back then too. She might have heard some gossip about one of the girls."

"Girls?"

"Och, you know, she might have heard something about one of the women you associated with."

"What 'women'? There were no *women*, plural."

"OK, but maybe you should check out what *she's* been up to all this time. You know ..."

"Based on what?"

"That you knocked about together for at least a year."

"You don't think this has anything to do with her, do you?"

"I've got no idea, Patrick! Let's hope not. But if you really want to trace your stalker, maybe talking to Jenny would be a good place to start."

"Maybe, Luca."

"Good."

"But it's only a maybe – talking to Jenny, that is."

"I take it you've not kept in touch with her, then, Paddy?"

"No, I haven't spoken to her for years. You?"

"No, hardly. I wasn't exactly one of her favourites back then."

"Oh, yes, I'd forgotten about your night of passion, Luca."

"I don't know what you're talking about. Can't remember."

"I can. At least we – she and I – had some kind of meaningful relationship."

"Congratulations, Patrick! I'm very happy for you both," Luca said frowning. "So where does she live now? Do you know?"

"No, but I imagine she's still in North Cornwall somewhere. I'll see if I can track her down online."

"Would you like me to come along with you?"

"Yes! It'd be handy. I could do with some moral support and you might as well since we'll both be down that way anyway."

"How far's Plymouth from North Cornwall?"

"If she's settled anywhere near where she's from—"

"Where's that?"

"She's from Wadebridge. It's no more than a fifty-mile drive from Plymouth."

"And how are we going to get about without transport, Paddy? You can't drive. I don't drive."

"Good point."

"Taxi?"

"A bit pricey."

"Bus?"

"You mad?"

"Would anybody drive us?"

"Don't know, Luca."

"Oh, well."

"Hang on, Sam might!"

"Sam?"

"Yes! Sam! He's taking early retirement. Stops work today. He's got wheels. I'm sure he'd help us out."

"Actually, that might not be as daft as it sounds, Patrick."

"Yeah, he'll probably welcome a little driving job in exchange for some beer money. I'll ask him when I see him on Sunday. I'm sure he'll do it. I think he'll enjoy it too."

"*Saluti*, Patrick! Good luck to you. And here's to our brilliant presentation, eh?" Luca said raising his pint of stout.

"*Saluti*!" Patrick responded, clinking glasses with him. "It's not often we get a chance to have a beer at lunchtime. We should do this more often."

"Yes, going to the pub at lunchtime's very old school. But shouldn't we be quaffing champagne, Patrick?" Luca teased.

"This is a pub not a bloody wine bar, Luca. You're lucky I've agreed to sign off on an extravagance for once."

"Lunch? Everybody needs to eat lunch, Patrick, except perhaps you," Luca said laughing.

"Piss off, Luca! Are you inferring that I'm putting on weight?"

"Would I? You six-footers can get away with carrying an extra pound or two. Anyway, what about this son of yours? When did you say he left the message on your answerphone?"

"Monday."

"Monday just past?"

"Yes."

"And you've heard nothing from him since?"

"No, nothing," Patrick replied looking stern.

"And you don't know his name, age or where he's from?"

"No, I don't know anything about him at all. I've only heard his voice. He's got a bit of an accent. Katrina thought it might be West Country but I'm not so sure."

"If he *is* from the West Country, that could tie him in with Jenny Harris."

"But his voice *was* very muffled. There was only a vague hint of an accent. It's a hard one to pin down, Luca."

"And you have no memory of getting anyone pregnant?"

"No, Luca, because I didn't. I haven't – except Katrina, of course."

"And who knows about this, Patrick?"

"Katrina and you. Oh, and I also mentioned it to Sam."

"Do the girls know?"

"No, not really. They know about the Father's Day card but not the phone call."

"Are you going to tell them?"

"No, I don't think I need to. There's no reason to worry them with this at present. And with any luck this guy's buggered off back to wherever he crawled out from."

"Unless he wants something."

"Like what?" Patrick said shrugging.

"Did he ask for money?"

"No."

"That could just be a matter of time. You do realise that this could be a scam? He probably thinks you'll pay him off once he threatens to tell the rest of your family and friends – you know, expose you online, etc., etc. I bet he does this kind of thing all the time."

"I don't know, Luca. That seems a little far-fetched to me. I mean, most people in my position know whether they've fathered an illegitimate child or not, don't they? I do. I know – I know I haven't!"

"Maybe you wouldn't be so sure if you were from Italy, Patrick. You know what we Mediterranean men are like."

"Is that supposed to be funny, Luca?"

"Sorry."

"It's all right, you big eejit. It's just that I'm feeling a bit shaken up by the whole thing."

"Is there anything I can do to help, Patrick?"

"Only if this *is* one of your practical jokes. And, if it is, *now* would be a good time to own up and stop effing about."

"Patrick! Not even *I* am that sadistic. Not even *I* would go to those lengths. I'm your best friend. Why would I want to scare you half to death? I have to say it's given me ideas, though. I think I'm going to send a sackload of anonymous Father's Day cards out next year. It'll create havoc."

"Do you celebrate Father's Day in Italy, Luca?"

"*Pensi che siamo pagani*, Patrick? Of course we bloody do. It's St Joseph's Day – nineteenth of March."

"I might have guessed. You Latins have got nearly as many saints as you've got people. Are there any saint's days you don't celebrate in Italy?"

"No, not many."

"Right!" Patrick said abruptly, standing up, pocketing his phone and stowing his iPad.

"Where are you going?"

"Why?"

"It's only lunchtime, Paddy."

"Well, I've been away from home quite a lot this week, Luca, and I'm going to be away for most of next week too, so I'm going to get a cab home and spend some quality time with my gorgeous wife before she divorces me."

"I imagine that Katrina is quite high-maintenance, Paddy, but I'm sure she's worth it," Luca said with a warm smile.

"She is, Luca, she is."

7

Sam Healy couldn't recall dropping by the McDade house as early before. It was precisely 7a.m. and, at that time on a Sunday, there was little to disturb the peace save for the occasional jet making its final approach into Heathrow Airport a few miles to the west. The din of low-flying planes could be thunderous over Fife Road at any time of day, but as Sam Healy climbed out of his car there was complete silence. No wind. No birdsong. No people. Not even the usual traffic hum from the South Circular down the hill. The sounds of the suburbs had, for now, abated.

Healy left his VW Beetle at the bottom of the drive and trod the familiar path up to the McDades' front door, crunching as quietly as the gravel would allow but with a spring in his step born of the sense of freedom that comes with early retirement. As he approached the house Healy could see that the ground-floor lights were on through the frosted panes to the side of the door and, as he neared, caught sight of a shadowy figure moving about in the kitchen.

Good. Patrick must be up and ready, he thought. This was encouraging since Healy was excited about the morning's activity and didn't want to be late for their seven forty-five tee-off at the public course in the park.

As Healy reached the porch his eye was caught by what appeared to be a sheepskin rug dumped by the bins round to the side of the house. The discarded rug surprised him as the grounds and gardens were usually immaculately kept. Aware of the time, Healy was of a mind to ignore the bundle of sheepskin but hesitated when he noticed a dark liquid trickling down towards the drain at the foot of the gable wall. Curious, he wandered over, crouched and leaned forward. He gasped the second he recognised the rug for what it was.

*   *   *

"Ah, Sam, you're here. Well done – seven on the dot. Do you fancy a quick cuppa?"

"Patrick, Patrick, I'm sorry, mucker, but you really need to come and take a look at what's out here!"

"What? Why? What are you on about, Sam? Why are you whispering?"

"Please, Patrick, come outside. You need to come outside with me, now. Right now."

Healy grasped Patrick McDade firmly by the forearm and marched him through the front door. He paused in the porch and raised a finger to his lips to urge Patrick to be quiet, then screwed up his features whilst raising his palms in warning. Patrick shrugged and fired Healy a wide-eyed quizzical look.

When they reached the bundle of fur, Patrick took a quick glance and then immediately leant on Sam for support as his legs buckled.

"I felt for a pulse, Patrick, but I couldn't find it. None – nothing. There's no hope, I'm afraid. Absolutely no hope," Sam Healy murmured placing a hand on Patrick's shoulder.

Patrick McDade sunk onto his haunches staring at Simba's carcass, his shoulders slumped and tears gathering in his eyes.

"You OK, Patrick?"

"Oh, fuck! Fuckedy, fuck, fuck! Poor old Simba," he sobbed, wiping away tears.

"When did you last see her, Patrick?"

"Shit, Sam! I-I-I let her out for a pee last night at about eleven o'clock and then d-d-didn't see her again. She didn't come back in as she usually would. Katrina had gone to bed. I-I-I was watching an old Bond movie. After a while I got worried and went to check to see if Simba was in the garden somewhere but couldn't find her. I gave up after about twenty minutes or so. I didn't tell Katrina because I didn't want to worry her. I-I-I was going to call round to the neighbours' houses this morning but ... Do you think she's been hit by a car, Sam?"

"No, Patrick. I can't be sure what's happened to her but I definitely don't think it was that. She's got a laceration to her throat. It's a deep one. Look at the trail of blood. I think she bled out. I definitely don't think she's been hit by anything."

"Do you think it could have been a fox? We get a lot of foxes round here – I see them all the time. Some of them are huge! There's rich pickings for them in the bins all along this road. They thrive here."

"Patrick, it's not a tear – it's a cut. I think someone's cut her throat with a knife of some sort."

"Oh, God, no! Poor Simba. Who the hell would do a thing like that?"

"I haven't a clue but, as we all know, there are some sick bastards out there these days."

"Yeah. I remember reading about all those cats killed in Croydon a year or two ago. Did you hear about that, Sam?"

"What – oh, the Croydon Cat Killer story?"

"That's the one."

"Didn't they decide that that was the local wildlife having a go at cats that had already been run over – you know, foxes feeding on roadkill? I think they eventually ruled out the involvement of a human predator."

"But you think this is different?"

"It's a cut – a deep laceration. So yes, and, as I say, it looks deliberate to me."

"Oh, shit!"

Sam knelt down beside Patrick McDade to comfort him. Could sense that there were more tears to come.

"I-I-I don't know what to tell Katrina! What *do* I tell her?

And what do I tell the girls? They'll be heartbroken. What am I going to tell them, Sam?" Patrick sobbed.

"Do you have any idea why anybody would do this?"

"No, none whatsoever. I mean, why the hell *would* anyone do this? Who the hell could be this cruel? Unless ... unless ..."

"What?"

"Shit! The Father's Day card, Sam – the phone call ..."

"Oh. The boy who's been giving you grief?"

"Yeah, the weirdo who called on Monday."

"Bloody hell, Patrick. Don't you think it's time to go to the police?"

"Report him?"

"Yes!"

"Well, I do, but God knows how interested they're going to be. It's a tragedy for me, for us, but to the police, you know, there's not much of a case to follow up."

"Have you still got the Father's Day card?"

"No, I binned it the day it arrived and the sodding bin's been emptied since then."

"Pity, there might have been some of his DNA on it."

"I know. Stupid, but there we are."

"What about the postmark?"

"Good question, Sam, but unfortunately it was illegible. I couldn't make head nor tail of it."

"OK, can I suggest something, Patrick?"

"Please do."

"Obviously we're not going to play golf this morning, and of course that's not a problem, but, tell me, what time is Katrina likely to surface?"

"It's Sunday. Not until about nine or half past, I guess."

"And the girls, are they here?"

"No. They're at a friend's place in London, thank God."

"Right, so why don't we get Simba here buried before Katrina gets up? You know, somewhere nice and discreet and mark the grave. Then, if you're worried about how she's going to react, why don't we tell her that Simba was knocked down by a car? A hit-and-run. I mean, does she really need to know that Simba's been stabbed to death by a madman?"

"Yeah, I think you're right, Sam. There's no need to scare the bejesus out of her – her or the girls. But what if this was more than a random killing? What if we *have* been targeted by my weirdo? And another thing, if we call the police, wouldn't they prefer Simba to be left lying here as we found her?"

"It might sound a little heartless, Patrick, but if needs be, she can always be dug up again. For now, however, maybe it's for the best."

"You think, Sam?"

"Yes. Definitely."

"Let's face it, it's bad enough losing a dog, but losing one in these circumstances? Right, Sam, you stay here. I'll go and gather up some tools."

*   *   *

The two of them rolled Simba up in a blue plastic tarpaulin and dragged her through the back gate and across the garden to the rear. They picked a clearing behind some bushes at the bottom of the lawn and started to dig.

After five or six minutes Patrick glanced up, dropped his shovel and took off towards the house. By the time Sam Healy stopped to check what he was doing, Patrick had already sprinted halfway down the lawn. Healy gulped when he saw that Patrick was dashing across the grass to intercept Katrina who was striding towards them at pace – her dressing gown billowing out behind her like a cloak flapping in the wind.

"What the fuck's going on, Patrick?"

"Nothing. It's nothing, sweetheart."

"Nothing? Then what the fuck are you two up to? Is that ... is that ... ?"

"Yes, it's Simba. I'm so so sorry, sweetheart. I think she's been hit by a car."

63

"Is she ... is she ... dead?"

"Yes, I'm afraid so, Katrina."

"Oh, Patrick! Fuck – I had a feeling something was wrong!"

"I know, I know. Poor old Simba."

"And you're sure she's dead, Patrick?"

"Yes, there's no doubt about it, sweetheart."

"Absolutely sure?"

"Yes. I'm so so sorry, Katrina."

Patrick held Katrina close. She rested her head on his arm, her shoulders heaving and tears starting to flow.

"H-h-how did you find her?" she sobbed.

"Sam found her when he arrived. There was no pulse. There was nothing we could do. She's quite cold, we think she's been dead a good while."

"I want to see her, Patrick."

"I don't know if you should do that, Kat," he said fighting back tears.

"I want to see her."

"I really don't think you should, Kat."

"Patrick, she's my fucking dog! I want to see her!"

"OK, OK," he said, looking at Sam and frowning.

Patrick took his wife's hand and led her down the lawn to where Simba was lying wrapped in the blue tarpaulin. He lifted the tarp in the manner of a forensic scientist revealing a murder victim for the next of kin to identify. Katrina gasped, dropped to her knees and extended a hand to stroke Simba's head – tears spurting down her cheeks.

"You know who did this, don't you, Patrick?" she murmured, sniffing to hold back her tears.

"I-I-I really don't know, Katrina. Unfortunately I didn't see anything."

"Didn't see what?"

"The driver."

"Do you think I'm stupid, Patrick? Do you genuinely think that I don't know what's going on here?"

"Going on? I'm sorry, I don't know what you mean, Kat," Patrick said nervously.

"It was him, wasn't it? He did this, didn't he?"

"Who, Katrina?"

"Your bastard son, Patrick! Your fucking weirdo! It's him, isn't it? This is his handiwork. He did this, didn't he?"

"I don't know. We can't be sure, Kat."

"This is getting very fucking serious, Patrick. I don't think we've been left with any option but to go to the police. What do you think, Sam?"

"Totally! I agree, Katrina. If it's him, he's seriously overstepped the mark here. Sending a silly card is one thing, but this!"

"Killing our fucking dog, you mean, Sam?"

"Yes, killing your dog. Of course it's time to get the police involved, Kat."

"And in the meantime, Sam, I guess we'd best not put poor old Simba six feet under just yet."

"No. On second thoughts, Patrick, perhaps not."

*   *   *

DI Baxter liked Sunday shifts the least. Unlike Saturdays there was rarely anything that occurred on the final day of the weekend that called upon her extensive experience and training. Sunday mornings might bring the odd complaint of domestic violence – no surprise in the aftermath of many a boozy Saturday night – but otherwise very little actual crime. Shoplifting, fare dodging and vandalism were not the kind of criminal activities to which she believed her finely honed skills as a detective were best suited. Minor misdemeanours didn't really do it for Detective Inspector Edith Baxter.

At least the police station was close to the town centre where she was spoilt for choice when it came to coffee shops and places to grab a sandwich on her break or when the telephone lines fell silent.

DI Baxter had just returned to the station, an Americano in hand, when she got a call from the desk sergeant asking if she could attend a serious incident in Sheen. He'd teased her by saying that he'd received a report of a fatality at the address. DI Baxter immediately took the bait, which had her firing back questions before the hapless sergeant had the opportunity to set her straight. She wasn't best pleased, therefore, when she was informed that the victim wasn't a local resident but a ten-year-old golden retriever.

Sending the desk sergeant to Coventry, Baxter slurped down the last of her coffee, stomped through the station door, marched round to her navy blue Vauxhall Astra and drove off towards East Sheen at speed. By the time she arrived at the McDades' house in Fife Road, she had composed herself and was ready to treat the case with the gravitas it deserved.

*　　　*　　　*

"Mr McDade?"

"Yes, that's me, Patrick McDade."

"Good morning, sir, I'm Detective Inspector Baxter. I believe you rang about your dog?"

"Hello. Yes, that was me. Thank you for coming so promptly, Detective Inspector. This is my wife Katrina and our friend, Sam Healy," Patrick said, making the appropriate gestures.

They had congregated at the side of the house near the spot where Simba was found and close to where she was now lying, having been dragged up from the garden on the tarpaulin.

"I've been informed that you've had a nasty scare and believe someone has attacked your dog?"

"Yes," Patrick said in a mournful voice.

"I take it that this is the victim?" DI Baxter asked, stepping towards Simba.

"Sam found her here about an hour ago. We're pretty sure that whoever did this cut the poor dog's throat, DI Baxter," Patrick replied calmly.

"Mmm, quite. And so I see," DI Baxter mumbled as she bent down to take a closer look carefully rolling Simba's head to one side. "And do you have any idea who might have done this to Simba?" DI Baxter asked as she got back to her feet having inspected the wound.

*   *   *

A little while later the four of them were sitting around the kitchen island, tea in hand.

"Clearly this is a difficult and worrying situation, Mr and Mrs McDade. The message on the answerphone seems innocent enough. I can't detect any malice in that voice. It's not hostile or threatening. I can't see that an offence has been committed there. Same with the Father's Day card. Conversely, if these are linked to your dog's untimely death – if, say, there is a link between this person claiming to be your son and what's happened to Simba, then things are becoming rather more sinister. But we can't be sure of that yet."

"Well, I'm sure of it, Inspector. I'm sure there's a link."

"Of course you are, Mrs McDade, and I can understand why that would be so. This would be a worry for anybody in your situation, but, as I am sure you are also aware, we have very little to go on at present. There is nothing to prove a definite link between the killing of your dog and the phone call and the card."

"Have there been any other attacks on dogs in this area of late, Detective Inspector?"

"Nothing significant that I'm aware of, Mr McDade. No, no incidents of note. There hasn't been a rash of them reported recently if that is what you're asking."

"So what do you recommend we do, DI Baxter?"

"Be vigilant. Be careful. Make sure your house is secure at night. Ask your neighbours to keep their eyes open."

"I'm sorry but there's fat chance of the neighbours doing much to help around here."

"Yes, well, I can assure you that before I leave today *I* will be paying a visit to your immediate neighbours to ask them a few questions and see if they've seen or heard anything. Look, I know it's an obvious question, but have *you* seen any strange people hanging around here recently?"

"No, no one. Have you, Sam?"

"Sorry, no, no one or nothing out of the ordinary, Patrick."

"You say you have two daughters, Mr McDade?"

"Yes, they're in their early twenties."

"And where are they now?"

"They're staying in East London. They're house-sitting for some friends. It's a short-term thing over the summer."

"Mmm, I'd explain the situation to them and advise them to be vigilant too if I were you."

"Oh, God! Do you think they're in any danger?" Katrina asked, frowning.

"No, not necessarily, Mrs McDade, but it always pays to be vigilant. Let's face it, we don't really know what's going on here, do we? It is quite possible that you won't hear from this person again and that these incidents are unconnected, but it always pays to be alert."

"Apart from that what do you suggest we do?"

"If this person gets in touch with you again, do everything you can to get their name and a mobile phone number. If you can arrange a meeting, let me know immediately. Be smart. Be clever. Try and get something we can use to trace and identify this person. On the other hand, and with luck, it is possible that you may never hear from them again too."

"God, let's hope so," Patrick said.

"However, I'll record this incident back at the station in case we hear of similar attacks in the area. In the meantime, if any of you need to speak to me further, or if you remember something that you've omitted to tell me today, you can get me on this number," DI Baxter said, handing out her contact card as she got up to leave.

Patrick walked DI Baxter to the front gate leaving Katrina and Sam staring down at Simba, lost in thought and silent.

"Mr McDade, are you sure there's nothing else you would like to tell me?" DI Baxter asked in a hushed voice.

"Like what?"

"Like if there is the slightest possibility that you have fathered a child out of wedlock. And if you have, I would suggest that now is a good time to inform me. I can assure you that nobody else need know."

"I can assure *you*, Detective Inspector, that my conscience is clear on that score. Completely clear."

"Good. Thank you for your candour. Even still, if I were you, Mr McDade, I would think long and hard about your past relationships. You never know, something might twig."

"Detective Inspector, I can only assure you again that I have been thinking hard along those lines and there's nothing."

"With luck this will blow over, Mr McDade, but in the meantime please keep your eyes peeled."

"Thanks for the advice, Detective Inspector, and thank you very much for coming to see us."

"It's what we're here for, sir."

"Oh, one final question. Are we OK to bury Simba, or do you need to check her over for forensic clues? Do you need to perform an autopsy?"

"No, that won't be necessary, Mr McDade, thank you. We are not in the habit of performing autopsies on family pets and it's pretty much impossible to leave fingerprints on fur. No, you carry on. It's safe to bury your dog now."

8

"Do you really have to go to Plymouth, Patrick?"

"Oh, sweetheart, yes, I have to! We've got to meet the client on site at eleven. I have to be there. Can't miss it – can't. They'll have a heap of questions that need answering and, at this stage, we can't appear to be uncooperative."

"You do realise that I am shit-scared, Patrick, don't you? Really shit-scared. I don't want to be left here on my own without Simba to protect me."

"I'm only going away for a couple of nights. Why don't you go and stay with the girls, Kat?"

"What – kip on their floor? Are you joking?"

"I'm sure they've got a sofa. It's two nights! It'll be fun and it'll be safe and it might help take your mind off things. I won't worry quite so much if you're all together."

It was first thing Monday morning and Patrick and Katrina McDade were sharing an early breakfast at the kitchen island.

"When's Sam picking you up?"

"I told him to be here for seven sharp."

"Poor sod. God knows what time he's had to get up. And what about Luca?"

"We're picking him up outside Richmond Station at seven thirty."

"And you're driving all the way to Plymouth in Sam's orange Beetle?"

"Why not? It's a classic. Those things go on forever."

"What's the client going to think when you rock up in that heap of shit?"

"Sam's kept it in showroom condition, Kat. It's mint. You've seen it – it's a beauty. Very stylish. Quirky and stylish. I think they'll be impressed."

"Are you sure?"

"Clients don't like seeing their suppliers driving around in flash motors or having to visit them in flash offices. They'll presume they're footing the bill for the extravagance. They'll think our profit margins are too high and will want to negotiate lower rates."

"And Sam's happy enough to wheel you about Devon and Cornwall in search of your ex-girlfriends?"

"You make that sound very tawdry."

"Isn't it?"

"No, not at all, and it won't take any longer than it has to. I plan to be back in the office by Wednesday lunchtime and then home at teatime at the very latest."

"What's wrong with bloody social media? Why do you have to go and visit her, them or whoever in person?"

"There's nothing wrong with social media, Katrina, but I'm not going to contact everyone I've ever had a relationship with on Facebook and enquire if, by any chance, I might have got them pregnant in the last twenty-something years and, if I did, did they have the child and then somehow forget to let me know. No. Not on Facebook, Twitter, Instagram, Snapchat or any other social media platform, come to that."

"Social media's a communication tool, Patrick. Nothing more and nothing less."

"It's so superficial. Trying to write something meaningful on Twitter or Facebook is like trying to reproduce the *Mona Lisa* on an Etch A Sketch. Social media's great for sharing photos of what you've made for your dinner, showing off your latest jumper or for a rant about Brexit, BoJo or Donald Trump, but not for debating unwanted pregnancies."

"Why the fuck not?"

"Because, like me, those I need to contact – my ex-girlfriends, that is, and there aren't that many of them – have probably acquired husbands and families by now."

"You haven't acquired a husband, Patrick."

"Och, you know what I mean! And it would hardly be fair to any of them, or their families, for me to go barging in asking awkward questions out of the blue. We could open a can of worms for some poor woman who has absolutely nothing to do with this. I mean, we don't know, Kat, maybe one of them *has* had an illegitimate child at some time in their lives? And, who knows, maybe that child was taken into care and their current partner knows nothing about it?"

"That's a bit far-fetched."

"Perhaps, but I'm sure it happens and I'm sure you know what I mean."

"You keep saying that, Patrick, but do I? I don't know if I know much about anything any more. In fact, all this has made me question whether I know *you* or ever knew you very well at all."

"Oh, come on! That sounds a tad overdramatic. I think you've started to panic a little."

"I don't fucking think so, Patrick."

"Katrina, I have no memory of any of my ex-girlfriends ever getting pregnant. I'd have known, wouldn't I? I would! Of course I would! There's nothing to worry about, Kat."

"That's easy to say!"

"Look, we've just got to work out who this maniac is and get them collared before they do something truly regrettable. And part of that is to eliminate all possible suspects. It's simple."

"Really?"

"Yes. And I can assure you that before this I haven't wanted to, needed to or have had any contact, let alone sexual contact, with any of my old flames, or with anybody else for that matter, for *at least* twenty-five years. Not since I met you and not since we've been married."

"Really?"

"YES ... REALLY! Why would I want to? I've been happily married to you all that time."

"Happily married. Are you sure?"

"Yes! Very happily married."

"And there's nothing I don't know about? Nothing you haven't told me? There's nothing you want to share with me now? There's nothing you're hiding?"

"No, nothing."

"No illicit affairs, no one-night stands, no knee-tremblers in the stationery cupboard at work?"

"No, I wouldn't do any of that stuff and you know it!"

"So apart from there being some weirdo out there claiming to be your child, I have absolutely nothing to worry about, Patrick? There's just some random boy running around claiming to be your long-lost son, and who, *if* you are telling the truth, is the result of a virgin birth. I have to say, he didn't sound much like Jesus on the answerphone, and Jesus wouldn't be the type to cut our dog's throat, would he?"

"How do you know what he sounds like?"

"Jesus? Easy. He was a Middle Eastern Jew. I believe he spoke Aramaic – a Galilean dialect. I can imagine his voice."

"Have you ever been to Galilee, Katrina? Have you heard the local accent?"

"Oh, fuck off, Patrick!"

"All right, then, with the benefit of hindsight, how old do you think the little creep sounded?"

"Young."

"Younger than Cerin and Alice?"

"I don't know. And regardless of what the policewoman said, I want to keep them out of this, Patrick. There's no need to worry them with this."

"I know. It's all starting to get a bit out of hand. But how do we know that this isn't simply some kind of devious con, Katrina? There's plenty of that going on."

73

"We don't. And you're right – this *is* getting entirely out of hand. And probably more so now you're planning on driving around the country looking up your ex-girlfriends."

"It's a start, Katrina. We need to find out who the hell this guy is, get his details and pass them on to the police. If he's killed Simba, God knows what else he's capable of."

"So where do they all live?"

"Who?"

"Your exes."

"This is where social media *does* come in handy."

"Hang on, are you telling me that you've been stalking your exes on social media, Patrick?"

"No, not stalking."

"Corresponding with them, then?"

"No, not directly. There's a college Facebook page for our year. I might give the odd post a like or wish someone a happy birthday every now and then but nothing more."

"Bloody hell, Patrick!"

"Well, don't you, Katrina?"

"What?"

"Keep in touch. I'm sure you've shared a photo or two with that Hooray Henry you used to go out with – what's his name?"

"Hamish Hargreaves-Darling?"

"That's the one. What a name? I bet your parents liked him, though."

"Of course they did. He's more like one of ours. His family own a large chunk of Scotland. And, yes, I do keep in touch with him. Anyway, he doesn't count in the context of this conversation, I'm afraid."

"Why not?"

"He was never that keen on me."

"Why not?"

"Use your imagination."

"Oh."

"Yes, Patrick. Nevertheless, you haven't answered my question."

"Which one?"

"You're right. There's two."

"Go on. I can handle it. Spit them out, Kat."

"First, exactly how many girlfriends did you have before you met me, and secondly where do they live?"

"You want to know right now?"

"Why not?"

"Exact figures?"

"To the nearest hundred, say."

"OK, let me think. Mmm ... wait for it ... yep ... six!"

"Six or six hundred?"

"Six."

"Six! Is that all?"

"Yes, there *were* six, but one died."

"Who was that? What was her name?"

"Dorothy. Dorothy Mawhinney."

"Oh, yes, poor Dorothy. I remember you telling me about her. Could it have been her?"

"Hardly."

"Why not?"

"Kat, we went out with each other for about a year. We were very young. Schoolkids in our teens. She was my first proper girlfriend, for God's sake. I think we only had sex once and that was right at the very end. She'd just turned seventeen. It was the last time I saw her. The night before she was packed off to boarding school so she could concentrate on her A-levels. Actually, the true story is that she was expelled from her grammar school for stealing."

"Stealing what?"

"Anything she could lay her hands on, apparently."

"And you had sex with her?"

"Yes, but it was a bit of a non-event."

"Why?"

"Why do you think?"

"I don't bloody know."

"Because we were both virgins. It was a bit of a fumble in her parents' living room when they'd gone to bed. We didn't really know what we were doing."

"So why didn't you try before?"

"I've just told you – we were young, too young. I think I was her first proper boyfriend. It was something we didn't think about that much."

"How old were you when you met?"

"I was sixteen, nearly seventeen."

"How old was she?"

"Sixteen."

"Oh, is that why—"

"Yes, that's why. It didn't seem right at the time. And I was scared, to be honest. I didn't want to get locked up."

"Could that have happened?"

"YES! The age of consent was seventeen in Northern Ireland then."

"What happened to her?"

"Leukaemia."

"How awful."

"We'd lost touch by then but I heard."

"Shit! That's terrible."

"Yes, tragic. I liked her very much. She was very talented."

"What at?"

"She wanted to be an illustrator. She was always very good at drawing. Never stopped. She showed great promise. Wanted to go to art college in London."

"Oh, shit, how sad. I'm so sorry, I didn't know."

"That's OK. Why would you? It was a long time ago. It's not something I ever talk about."

"It couldn't be her. Your mystery son would be in his thirties by now if she'd been the mother, Patrick."

"Congratulations, Miss Marple. And how do you know that he isn't, Katrina?"

"Because of his voice."

"That isn't conclusive. It was very muffled on the tape."

"I know, but I've got a hunch."

"Oh, that's very helpful."

"OK, what about all the others?"

"*All* the others? Bloody hell, Kat. There's only five. I'm sure I've told you everything there is to know about each of them at one time or another. Do you really want me to go through all that again?"

"Maybe, maybe not – oh, I don't know."

"Well, the five others comprise a couple of girls I knew at college, a couple I know from work placements in London and then Natalie, of course."

"Yes, I remember her all right!"

"As far as I am aware, one of the girls from college, Jenny, is still living down in Cornwall somewhere, the two from London are still there or thereabouts, and Mairead, the other girl from college, has gone back home to live in Northern Ireland."

"Northern Ireland?"

"Yes, Portaferry, I think."

"Did you ever go over there with her?"

"No, I didn't get a chance."

"Too scared? Weren't the Troubles still going on then?"

"Yes, but that would hardly have bothered me – I was born and brought up there. Even when we moved over here we used to go back at least twice a year to visit my grandparents on the North Antrim coast. You know, when they were still alive."

"So what are you going to do?"

"Go and see them. Talk to them. See what they know. Someone's made a terrible mistake. Perhaps one of them might know something. We'll see."

"You hope!"

"Yes. And who knows, there might be something or

someone I've overlooked too. There might be an incident or a bit of gossip they remember and that I've forgotten that could be relevant. I think I need to see them in person to cross them off the list."

"A process of elimination?"

"Exactly."

"Just remember that this is all perfectly fine if your mystery son happens to be older than twenty-four. If you find out he's any younger, it'll mean that at some time since our wedding you've been a total bastard and betrayed the girls and me."

"Except I'm not and I haven't. I haven't done anything wrong."

"As far as you know."

"Yes, as far as I know."

"But you don't really know, do you? You don't. You don't really know for sure, Patrick, do you?"

"Well—"

"No. No, you don't."

"Whatever – I'm going to find out who the hell this person is and stop them bothering our family."

They were suddenly interrupted by the chimes of Big Ben.

"Ah, there's the doorbell, Patrick, and right on cue."

"I hope that's Sam."

"It must be. I'm pretty sure I heard a car backfiring and the sound of a wing mirror falling off."

"Oh, stop it, Kat!"

Katrina scampered down the hall to the front door.

"He's through in the kitchen, Sam. You do know what you're letting yourself in for on this trip, don't you?"

"It's a pleasure to be able to help out, Katrina."

"I'm surprised he hasn't kitted you out in a peaked cap and a uniform, Sam. Whatever you do, don't be calling him 'Sir'. His head's big enough as it is."

"Katrina, leave the poor man alone," Patrick called over from the island. "Hi, Sam! Did Jan get hold of you? I asked her to put you on a monthly retainer."

"Yes, but really, Patrick, there was no need to do that. I'm your mate, you shouldn't have bothered."

"You might as well get paid for driving me about, Sam. It'll just be for a month or two until I get my licence back."

"OK, but only if you're sure and you can afford it."

"Don't you worry, Sam. He can afford it all right, believe me," Kat whispered into Sam's ear.

"Right, Sam! Time's moving on. Shall we hit the road? We're due to pick Luca up in about twenty minutes."

9

The drive down to the South West was slow and dreary and exacerbated by thick cloud and drizzle. The site meeting was to be the first of two appointments with the team from Cygnet House that day. The location of the proposed development was easy enough to find: a green-field site off a major carriageway heading west of the city. The route was familiar as it was less than a week since their last visit.

After the site meeting they were to move on to the Regent Palace Hotel in Plymouth where Patrick had booked a room for a second design presentation and a detailed discussion on budget and scheduling. They were then going to stay on at the hotel for another two nights so that Luca could do some groundwork at the site while Patrick hooked up with a couple of his girlfriends from college before Sam drove them back to London on the Wednesday.

"What do you want me to do when you're having your meeting, Patrick?" Sam asked once they'd passed Exeter and were heading across South Cornwall.

"It would be handy if you could hang around and wait for us, Sam. We shouldn't be too long. I agreed with the client that we'd only spend about an hour on-site before heading over to the hotel at twelve. I've arranged for a buffet to be available during that meeting, Sam, so when we get to the Regent, why don't you park up and take a stroll around the city and find somewhere nice to get a bite to eat? Put it on expenses. I'll give you a buzz when the presentation's finished so you can join us for a drink in the hotel bar."

"Sounds good to me."

"Perhaps you could entertain our guests with some stories about your time at Man United. Remind me, who were your contemporaries – Beckham? Butt? The Neville brothers? Cantona?"

"Very funny, Patrick – bloody hilarious. By the way, am I allowed to swear at you while I'm employed as your driver?"

"Give me a wink and a nudge and I'll be happy to do that for you," Luca said leaning forward from the back seat. "Anyway, you're the head honcho today, Sam. You've got the car keys."

The journey grew more pleasant the further south and west they travelled and, as the clouds cleared, the rain eased.

"Tell me, Luca, where were you coming from when we picked you up this morning? Where do you live?" Sam asked to break the silence.

"Has Patrick never told you?"

"No."

"I live on the Regent's Canal, Sam."

"On it?"

"Luca lives on a houseboat, Sam. It's a refurbished wide beam canal barge, to be precise."

"Really? And why's that, Luca?"

"Because I love it, Sam! It suits me perfectly. It's all I need."

"I think Luca must have been a Venetian boatman in another life. He says he enjoys the simple life and that it stops him from thinking about fixtures, fittings and foundations when he gets home from work."

"Thank you, Patrick, but I *can* speak for myself!"

"Yeah, but that's about the size of it, though, isn't it Luca?"

"If you say so, Patrick. But it also minimises my carbon footprint, Sam."

"I guess it's hard to leave any kind of footprint when you're living on a houseboat, Luca."

"Exactly."

"That's also why he doesn't drive a car, Sam. He's pretty much carbon-neutral now – except for today, obviously. But he'll be planting a small tree when he gets home to compensate. I guess it'll have to be a bonsai tree, though."

"Fuck off, Patrick, you plank!"

"Sorry, Luca."

"What I love about being on the houseboat is the idea that if I leave my mooring and meander down the canal network to its furthest point to the south, I can escape into the Thames Estuary and then on out into the North Sea and freedom. Not that I would, of course."

"And you live alone, Luca?"

"Yes."

"You've never married?"

"He claims he's never had time, Sam."

"Is he gender-neutral too, then?"

"Hey! Am I not allowed to speak for myself?"

"Apparently he's got lots of lady friends, or so he tells us. Says it's in his blood."

"Oh? What flavour's that, then?"

"Chianti. He claims he's Italian."

"Well, I didn't think that was an East End accent, Patrick."

"Hey! Am I not allowed to speak? My parents moved to South West London when I was fifteen, Sam. I could barely speak a word of English when I arrived."

"No change there, then!"

"Thanks very much, Paddy. Anyway, what about you, Sam?"

"What about *me*, Luca?"

"Where are you moored?"

"I live down the road from Patrick."

"Really?"

"Down the hill and on the other side of the high street. Don't get the wrong idea though, Luca. My accommodation's on a wholly different scale to his. Nothing as grand as Paddy's mansion."

"Careful!"

"Sorry, Patrick."

"But, I love your place, Sam!" Patrick McDade enthused.

"I suppose it does have a certain charm. Actually I'm bloody lucky that I bought it back in the eighties before the first property boom."

"Luca, it's a bachelor's paradise. It's a little two-up two-down terraced cottage in Sheen Lane. It takes ten minutes to clean, Sam's got a coal fire in the downstairs knock-through that heats the whole house and it's only two hundred yards from the nearest pub, twenty yards from a Spar shop and just up the road from the station with main line trains running to Waterloo every fifteen minutes."

"You sound jealous, Paddy."

"Almost, Sam, almost."

"Paddy?"

"What, Luca?"

"Do we have time to stop for a coffee?"

"No, Luca."

"A fag?"

"No, Luca."

"A pee?"

"No."

*　　　*　　　*

They arrived at the site twenty minutes early – the location easily found with the benefit of Google Maps. They parked, wandered over to the site entrance and stared through the mesh fencing at the huge expanse of earth littered with an eclectic mix of broken bricks, rusting metal, an old mattress and numerous discarded shopping trolleys. The site offered a broad view of the sea at Plymouth Sound. The sun blazed out of the heavens.

"You're right, Patrick."

"About what, Sam?"

"This. It's about the size of four football pitches."

"I guess you would know, Sam. Do you like the view?" Luca asked, staring towards the horizon.

"It's stunning on a clear day like this, Luca, but for someone like me it's hard to visualise a hotel on this site in its current state. What was here before?"

"A large detached house. I understand it was last used as an old people's home. The site's about eight acres."

"What happened to the old people's home?"

"It was knocked down – not by us, I hasten to add."

"Who, then?"

"The previous developers. They were going to build apartments but they pulled out and sold it on."

"Why was that, Patrick?"

"No idea, Sam. The Brexit wobble and the downturn in the property market maybe, who knows?"

"So how do you tackle something like this, Luca? I mean, where do you start with designing a hotel?"

"How long have you got, Sam?"

"We'll show you the presentation we put together for the clients later. That should explain what we have in mind. Well, I bloody well hope it does."

Standing around waiting they soon ran out of conversation. Half an hour passed and there was still no sign of their clients. Sam walked back to the car and returned with a plastic football tucked under one arm.

"What the hell are you going to do with that?" Patrick asked with a nervous frown.

"Watch!" Sam yelled as he lobbed the ball in the air, tilted his head forward, arched his spine and caught the ball on the back of his neck. He let it roll off one shoulder, drop and then trapped it between his right foot and ankle, balancing it in mid-air as he swayed on the other leg.

"I thought you'd hung up your football boots, Sam."

"I have, Patrick, but I can still do my skills and tricks," Sam replied before commencing a juggling routine built around a multitude of deft kicks, flicks and keepy-uppies.

Sam had the other two spellbound for the next three or four minutes of his routine, which ended as neatly as it had begun when he headed the ball high in the air and caught it in one hand. They clapped loudly and smiled with enthusiasm.

"You wouldn't find that level of skill at Juventus, Luca."

"What the hell would you know about football, Paddy?" Luca sneered.

"So you're a Juventus fan, then, Luca?" Sam asked, grinning.

"Juventus? Sure am, Sam. It's Juventus and England for me."

"Why Juve?"

"It's where my family are from."

"And England?"

"Er, why not?"

"I think it's to keep the Border Force at bay," Patrick said with a smirk.

Suddenly remembering the business at hand, Patrick McDade checked his watch.

"They should be here by now, Luca. I'm getting worried."

"Patience, Patrick. They're only five or ten minutes late."

"Still, we've a lot to get through this morning."

"Do you think they're having trouble finding it?"

"No, Sam, I doubt it. It's their site, after all," Patrick replied, reaching into his pocket for his phone. "I'll give Jan a call at the office and see if she's heard anything. I don't want to be late at the hotel if they've forgotten that they're supposed to be coming here first and are waiting for us there. Just a sec ... Jan? Hi, it's only me," Patrick said, speaking to his PA, January White in a soft and friendly voice. "Could you check our diary entries for today, please. We were to meet the team from Cygnet House on-site at eleven, weren't we? Yep, I thought so. Has anyone called from ... no. Oh, OK, then. Thanks, Jan. Yeah, please call me if you hear anything from them. Yes, cheers, thanks. Yes, and you. Bye. Thank you!"

"All good, Patrick?" Luca asked as Patrick ended the call.

"Yes. *We're* in the right place at the right time but I've still got no idea where *they* are."

"Do you think they've gone straight to the hotel?"

"I don't know, Luca, maybe."

"I thought you were the master of logistics, Patrick."

"I am and it's as I thought. Jan says the first meeting was to be here at eleven o'clock. I'll call their MD's PA and see what they're up to. Failing that, we'll just head over to the Regent and see if they're waiting for us there."

Patrick rang Marcus Creed's PA. The call went straight to answerphone. Patrick shook his head.

"No good?"

"No good, Luca. I'll try the MD himself."

Patrick looked up Marcus Creed's number, tapped and waited, mobile pressed to his ear. Within a few seconds he shook his head again.

"No?"

"No. Straight to answerphone, Luca," Patrick said, wiping sweat from his brow.

"Perhaps we'd better scoot over to the hotel. We don't want to miss them if they're already there."

"Agreed."

As they turned to go back to the car, Sam casually tossed his plastic football into the air and began juggling it on his head as he walked. He'd only taken a few steps when there was a loud crack followed by a sudden hissing. The ball flopped to the ground, spinning round on the spot with dizzying speed, then decelerating and deflating into a lozenge-shaped lump. Within seconds there was another loud crack after which Sam clasped a hand to his neck and collapsed to the pavement beside the ball.

"Fuck! Get down! Quick! Get down!' he yelled. "There's a nutter firing at us from those bushes. Get down!" Sam repeated, a trickle of blood seeping through his fingers as the sound of automatic gunfire started to zing and ping around them.

The other two threw themselves onto the path beside him, speechless and ashen-faced.

"Get to the car. Use it for cover! Come on, NOW!" Sam shouted. "Come on ... GO! GO! GO!"

"Sam! Are you OK?" Patrick whispered breathlessly as they huddled against the side of the Beetle.

The shooting stopped briefly.

"I'm fine, but let's get the hell out of here before someone gets killed."

"Can you move, Sam?"

"You just watch me! Come on, let's get into the car and get the hell out of here while he or she – or whoever they are – are reloading. Come on, NOW! Quick ... quick ... NOW!"

The three scrambled in through the driver's door as pellets peppered the far side of the car making tinny clangs. Sam stabbed the keys into the ignition and accelerated off, blood trickling down his neck and eyes peeping over the steering wheel just enough to keep the car on the road. The other two ducked down on the back seat keeping well below the line of the windows. Within a few yards the storm of pings and tings ceased. Sam drove a few miles up the road before pulling over so they could sit up, take stock and get their breath back.

"What the hell was that?"

"It's just some twat with an automatic air rifle, Paddy."

"Shit! And how the hell do you know *that*, Sam?"

"Because like you, Patrick, I'm from Northern Ireland."

"So?"

"So I know the difference between the sound of a bullet and a bloody air rifle pellet."

"Well, I don't."

"Maybe that's because you were brought up in the posh part of Holywood, Paddy. I'm from up the Shankill and we've had stray bullets flying up and down our streets for years. I should know the sound of a bloody air rifle pellet when I hear one – I used to fire them at the peelers every now and then."

"You what? Are you nuts, Sam?"

"To be honest, yes, I was a bit of a tearaway when I was a teenager. Firing air rifles at the police was a bit of fun at the time. You should have seen them panic. Fucking hilarious it was, or so it seemed back then."

"Bloody hell, Sam, are you completely off your rocker?"

"As I say, I probably was when I was a kid."

"Jesus, Sam. I wish you hadn't told me that story. I don't think I'll ever see you in quite the same light again."

"That's Belfast in the seventies for you, Paddy."

"But still …"

"Come to think about it, I wish I hadn't told you that story either. Can we pretend that conversation never took place?"

"Fair enough, but who the hell was that firing at us?"

"Kids. It's the kind of moronic thing they do when they bunk off school in the summer. He or she couldn't have been firing from too far away. Air rifles only have a range of about fifty to sixty yards."

"I guess you would know that too, Sam."

"Indeed, Luca, indeed."

"How's your neck?"

"Not too bad, thanks. It was only a graze. I think it's stopped bleeding. I'm more upset about my bloody football."

*   *   *

It was a relief to arrive into the relative calm and refined atmosphere of the Regent Palace Hotel after their hasty departure from the construction site, even though their scratched and pockmarked Beetle raised an eyebrow or two when they pulled up on the front concourse. Patrick and Luca had no time to dwell on the shooting and just hoped the property company's team would show up at twelve as arranged. Once Sam had dropped them at the entrance he drove round to the hotel car park at the rear and walked off to explore the city centre in search of some lunch, as suggested.

Patrick and Luca checked in at reception. They had no more than ten minutes to prepare and went straight to the conference room to set up their presentation. They nodded approvingly at the welcome sign in the foyer that the hotel had arranged for their guests:

The Regent Palace Hotel welcomes
Cygnet House International PLC
and Quantum Design Associates

Within a few minutes they had linked Luca's laptop up to the conference room projector, clicked on Luca's updated presentation file and made sure the pages were showing up on screen and could be scrolled through easily enough, and then spread the sets of bound documents they'd brought with them out around the large oval table for their guests. Sandwiches and soft drinks had been left on the sideboard as requested.

With barely a moment or two to spare before their guests were due, they sat down, breathed a sigh of relief and buried their heads in their hands.

"I guess it would be better if we stood up, Luca. We don't want to be slumped across the table when they come in, do we? We need to appear keen and be on our toes and look them straight in the eye."

"If they're coming, that is."

"Of course they're coming."

*   *   *

Time crawled, the windowless meeting room growing stuffier, their eyes fixed on the wall clock above the projection screen with its second hand that seemed to sweep more slowly with every passing minute.

"Jesus, Patrick, is there no air conditioning? It's suffocating in here," Luca whined, throwing off his jacket and loosening a couple of shirt buttons.

"There's a control panel over there. I'll try and turn the cold air up," Patrick said, fiddling with the programmer.

"Oh, God, thank you. *Grazie*! *Grazie*!"

"Better?"

"Yes. But where the fuck are they, Patrick? They're fifteen minutes late already."

"Calm down, Luca. I'll call Jan and see if she's heard anything," Patrick muttered, lifting his phone. "Jan, we're sitting here like lemons. Yes, the hotel. The clients haven't shown up yet. They're late. Have you heard anything from them? No. OK. Could you check our emails, please? OK, good. Ah, you've received one? Could you forward that to me, please. Great. OK, got that. Thanks very much, Jan. Yes, I'll speak to you later. Better get on, thanks. Bye," Patrick glanced up at Luca. "Here, this might be something. Jan's just forwarded me an email. It's from Cygnet House."

Patrick paused to read the correspondence.

"Bugger! The bastards! I don't bloody believe it!" he shouted slamming his iPhone down on the conference room table.

"What is it?"

"Bloody hell, Luca! Take a look at this," Patrick said, passing him his mobile phone.

Dear Patrick,

I am sorry that this comes at such short notice but I wanted to let you know that my team and I won't be able to attend either of the meetings scheduled for today.

I would like to thank you for the interest you have shown in our hotel development scheme for Plymouth Sound, but regret to inform you that, after much careful consideration, we have decided to award the design contract elsewhere.

Thank you again for your input to date and for your excellent presentation. I hope we can embark on other exciting projects together in the future.

Yours sincerely,

Marcus Creed, MD, Cygnet House International PLC.

*   *   *

Half an hour later and Patrick and Luca caught up with Sam Healy in a gastropub near the seafront. Two pints down and they finally felt capable of discussing their calamitous morning.

"God, I'm so glad to be out of that fucking conference room. Have you ever experienced anything more depressing, Paddy? No windows, just cheap strip lighting, magnolia walls, a projector and a ton of egg sandwiches wilting in the heat. If our clients *had* come to the meeting, we'd probably have poisoned them with our fucking buffet lunch."

"Except they're not our clients any more, are they, Luca?"

"No, it would appear not."

"Why the hell did they let us travel all this bloody way if they were going to screw us over when we got here?"

"Didn't they make a commitment to us, Patrick? What about the email they sent suggesting we'd got the job – doesn't that count for anything?"

"Not binding, I'm afraid, Luca."

"Shit!"

"Exactly. So thank you very much, Cygnet House International PLC. That's us well and truly shafted. And you know what this means, don't you, Luca?"

"What?"

"Unless we can pick up another sizeable project quickly, we're going to have to scale down our operation."

"How, Paddy? What do you mean?"

"We'll have to lay people off, Luca."

"We can't!"

"We might have to. We might not have any choice."

"So what happened?" Sam Healy asked tentatively.

"That is a very good question, Sam, and one I'd like answered," Patrick replied.

"Well I'm going to find out, Paddy. We had them in our pocket. They loved my design, they loved everything about the projects we've worked on previously and seemed to like us.

We could have signed a fucking contract last week if we'd wanted. Signed it right then and there at the last meeting. And that *would* have been binding."

"I'm sorry, that's my fault, Luca. I thought there was no need to hurry and that it would be better not to rush into anything – that we could deal with the detail today. Oh, what a total idiot!"

"So why have they changed their minds?"

Patrick shrugged, was speechless.

"Someone must have got to them, Patrick. Someone must have slipped them a bung – a brown envelope or two."

"Oh, come on, Luca. These people represent a Gulf state. They're hardly going to be swayed by a few quid. It's something else. Something else has put them off."

"Perhaps it's something they've heard, then," Luca suggested, leaning back in his chair.

"What do you mean?"

"Maybe they've heard something about our company that they don't like."

"Eh?"

"Maybe someone has planted an idea in their heads. You know, fake news."

"Who the hell would do that, Luca?"

"You don't know? You really can't imagine, Patrick? You can't think of someone who's got it in for you?"

"The weirdo? But what could he possibly have said? There's nothing we've ever done professionally that a prospective client could hold against us. There's nothing. Nothing at all."

"There's plenty of accusations you can make these days. Use your imagination, Patrick."

"Oh, my God, Luca! That's a truly terrible thought. You really think our weirdo could have said something?"

Luca stood and sloped off to the bar to order another round.

"Maybe killing your dog was just for starters, Patrick. If he could do that, then I'm sure your friend would be capable of doing this too – you know, queering your pitch with a nasty little story or rumour. It also wouldn't surprise me if he's a hotshot with an air rifle too," Sam said before downing the last of his pint.

"The air rifle, Sam? Oh, come on! You've got to be kidding? How the hell could he know where we'd be this morning and at what time?"

"Perhaps he followed us."

"No, I think that's a little far-fetched. And the business with Cygnet House – there's plenty of competition out there. I'm sure we've got plenty of rivals who'd stop at nothing to snatch this brief out of our hands. This hotel development's worth millions, Sam."

"Yes, but as Luca says, there's plenty of accusations you can make against individuals these days that will stick. You read about it in the papers all the time. I'd give that detective a call, Patrick. You can never be too sure. And I'd call Katrina."

"I can't tell Katrina about this, Sam! I don't want to panic her. She's scared enough as it is – especially after what happened to Simba."

"I'd still give her a call to warn her to be careful and to keep her eyes open."

"You don't have much luck, do you, Paddy?" Luca said as he wandered back from the bar.

"Eh? What do you mean, Luca?"

"Most people who have an illegitimate child turn up on their doorstep get to invite them in for a cup of tea and a nice chat. There'll probably be tears, a lingering hug and a conversation about how sorry they both are and how the parent need no longer feel guilty, and then they'll go their separate ways. Perhaps the parent will get a Christmas card every year and a birthday card if they're lucky. Maybe they'll meet at the occasional family wedding or funeral. But, no, that's not for you, Paddy. Your long lost son is an evil bastard who'll cut your dog's throat and try and shoot you given half a chance. A psychopath intent on wreaking havoc and turning your life upside down."

"You really think so?"

"Yes."

"Thanks a bunch, Luca. Thanks for that comforting insight."

"*Prego* – you're welcome! Better luck next time."

10

Fife Road. Katrina felt uneasy as she pulled the front door shut, turned the key in the deadlock and stood listening to the alarm beeping through its setting mode. It was the kind of discomfort that comes with a sense of having forgotten to pack something vital like a passport or wallet, or that maybe the oven has been left on or the freezer door left open. But once she'd filed her crossword for Saturday's paper she had been meticulous in making a final check around the house; a routine that took on board all and any eventuality that might encourage a break-in, fire or flood. She'd even taken the precaution of hiding her laptop in the oven – the last place she imagined that any burglar would look for something of value – but she still couldn't shift the strange sense of foreboding enveloping her.

Katrina was only planning on being away for two nights – the couple of nights that Patrick was going to be in the West Country – but as she stared at the closed door the nagging feeling persisted. She blinked hard, stamped her foot and took two or three deep breaths to try and reset her focus while entertaining pleasant thoughts of the food and drink she was going to enjoy with Alice and Cerin once they were out and about in London. She sighed and turned to head off down the road for the train station.

*   *   *

Katrina was climbing the stairs at Old Street tube, no more than a four-minute walk from the bar where they were to meet, when her mobile started to vibrate accompanied by the sound effect of a roaring motorcycle engine: it was Patrick calling. She thought to glance at the battery icon – seventy-five per cent charged – which was fine, but put her in mind to rummage through her shoulder bag to double-check that she'd remembered to bring her charger – she had – which just left her time to swipe the screen on her iPhone to take Patrick's call.

"Hello, darling, how are you getting on?" Katrina panted.

"Yes, all good here. You?"

"I'm at Old Street. I'm walking over to meet the girls in Shoreditch. We're going to get something to eat and then go back to their place for a girly night in. Let's hope that they really aren't living in a squat."

"Yes, very funny. Nonetheless, please take care when you're running around town, Kat. And don't be talking to any strange men, and no hanging about in dark alleys."

"Why the concern?"

"Och, you know. Just be careful, sweetheart."

"You almost sound like you care, Patrick."

"Well, that's good, isn't it?"

"OK, call me later when I'm with the girls. I'm sure they'd love to talk to you. Mwah," Katrina air-kissed before ending the call.

*   *   *

Patrick McDade had phoned Katrina hunched up against a wall in the lobby of the gastropub in Plymouth.

Three pints down and early afternoon had drifted into early evening. It was an old, traditional pub, the ceilings ribbed with wooden beams, but had evidently been given an expensive makeover. Comforting wafts of woodsmoke meandered through the bar while Al Green's, "How can you mend a broken heart?" played at a low volume on the vintage jukebox. All was calm.

From where he was standing Patrick could see Sam Healy and Luca Salvatore slumped side by side on a pew in a quiet corner of the saloon. They were nattering furiously in between glugs of Guinness. It was beginning to look highly likely that the three of them would be in residence till closing time judging by the number of empties on the table and their steadily improving demeanour.

When Patrick McDade ended his call to Katrina, he reached into his pocket to retrieve the contact card that DI Baxter had given him and tapped in the number.

"Detective Inspector Baxter? Hi, it's Patrick McDade."

"Hello, Mr McDade! Can you hear me OK? I'm in the car on hands-free."

"Yes, yes, no problem."

"Good. So how can I help you today, sir?"

"I'm not sure where to start, Detective Inspector."

"Has this something to do with your dog, Mr McDade? Sorry, what was her name? Simba, was it? The incident has been logged onto the PND."

"Sorry, the what?"

"The Police National Database. I'll be monitoring the PND to see if there are any similar incidents involving dogs reported in your area in the coming weeks."

"That's great, thank you. But I'm also calling to let you know that there have been further developments."

"To do with Simba?"

"No, not specifically, Simba, as such. It's just that there's been some strange stuff going on today that's really got me stressed out and that I think could be linked to the guy who's been bothering us."

"All right, Mr McDade, please, go ahead and tell me what's been happening."

"So far today we've been shot at with an automatic air rifle and fallen victim to what I perceive to be an act of industrial sabotage."

"That all sounds very dramatic, Mr McDade. Where are you now?"

"In Plymouth."

"The shooting – where did that take place?"

"We were inspecting a site overlooking Plymouth Sound and were targeted by some idiot firing an air rifle. They hit one of my friends in the neck. Luckily it only grazed him. I think there's a chance that it might have been our stalker."

"Did you get a clear view of them? Would you be able to identify them?"

"No, we didn't get a clear view – not even a glimpse. We think they were firing at us from the bushes across the road."

"So you think this incident could be linked to the Father's Day card, the answerphone message and your dog's death?"

"Yes, I think there's a possibility, Detective Inspector."

"And what about the sabotage? What's that all about?"

"We've just lost a major contract for no good reason at all. My associate and I travelled all the way here to Plymouth for a meeting with the client today to sign off on a new project, but they didn't show up. Then very late on they sent me an email explaining that they've had second thoughts and don't want to proceed with our firm."

"A sudden change of heart, then?"

"Yes, that's what it sounds like, but I can't think why that could possibly be the case. We had reached a verbal agreement and were about to sign a contract. They were so enthusiastic about our design and seemed very keen to work with us when we spoke at the end of last week. It simply doesn't make any sense."

"But how does this tie in with the lad you think's been bothering you?"

"I can't be sure, DI Baxter, but I think there's a possibility that he's stuck his oar in and queered our pitch. I think he's probably told our clients some kind of nonsense about me or my business partner that has made them run a mile."

"Do you have any evidence to back up your theory, Mr McDade?"

"No, but it's odd that all these things have occurred one after the other since I received the card. It really feels as though I'm being targeted by him."

"But you don't have any actual evidence as such, do you? You don't have his name, a description and, so far, there aren't any witnesses who could link him to these episodes either? No one has been spotted hanging around your house or office, for instance, have they?"

"No."

"Mr McDade, was Simba in the habit of barking a lot?"

"She was a dog. She barked. Not very often, but, yes, she barked. Why?"

"It's just that it's not uncommon for noisy dogs to be bumped off by unscrupulous people – burglars, for instance."

"What, you think that someone is or was trying to burgle our house?"

"It's a possibility, Mr McDade, but then again it's only a possibility. You see, there are plenty of other plausible explanations for what happened to Simba too."

"Such as?"

"Aggrieved neighbours, Mr McDade."

"Eh?"

"It is not unheard of for aggrieved neighbours to be driven to taking extreme measures. I have come across instances where people have become so annoyed with their neighbour's pets that they have taken matters into their own hands, if you follow my drift."

"What about the other things that have happened?"

"How does your supposed stalker know your movements? How does he know where you work? How did he know you were going to be in Plymouth today for a business meeting?"

"Perhaps he's hacking our work emails. Perhaps he's been scavenging through our bins. I'm sure there's plenty of stuff that we throw away that gives details of where we'll be and what we're up to."

"That's a very imaginative proposition, Mr McDade."

"Yes, but it's a possibility."

"'Possible' is a word you seem very fond of, Mr McDade. What I need are hard facts because in my professional opinion there's no obvious link between the events you've described. Some might say that you're experiencing nothing more than a run of bad luck. It could be that the Father's Day card has upset you to a degree that you have become oversensitive."

"What! Are you suggesting that I *imagined* being shot at?"

"No, not at all – and I'll come to that shortly. However, as I was saying, it could be that the Father's Day card has upset you to a degree that you have become oversensitive to everyday occurrences. On the other hand, if there is something amiss going on here, that is to say that you *are* being victimised by an individual with malicious intent – the person claiming to be your son – we need to take prompt action to apprehend him. The shooting, Mr McDade—"

"Yes?"

"Regardless of who was responsible for that incident, whether it was your lad or not, it is imperative that you report it to the Devon and Cornwall Police as soon as possible. Unfortunately there is little I can do from here, but you must report the incident to the local police to help prevent whoever was shooting at you doing the same to some other innocent party. And when you report the shooting, ask the local police if they have heard of any other incidences with air rifles in the area recently. If they say that there haven't been any, then please let me know ASAP as that might back up your hunch that your lad was involved."

"Will do."

"Whoever was responsible for the shooting must be stopped before they cause a serious injury. Please let me know when you have spoken to the local force. When are you planning to be back in Sheen, Mr McDade?"

"Wednesday afternoon or evening."

"Good. Why not give me a call on Thursday morning when you're settled and let me know how you—"

"Hello? Hello? DI Baxter?"

Patrick McDade shook his phone but she was gone; the line dead. He tried calling DI Baxter back but there was no reply.

"What's up, Patrick? You OK?" Sam Healy called over from the table in the saloon bar when he noticed Patrick McDade's drawn expression.

"I got cut off."

"Katrina?"

"No, the policewoman, Sam."

"DI Baxter?"

"Yes."

"And?"

"I don't think she's quite seeing things my way yet, I'm sorry to say."

"Eh?"

"I think she thinks I've lost my marbles. She seems to doubt that there's any connection between the events of the last couple of weeks."

"Why's that?"

"Because we've no concrete evidence for her, Sam. We've no proof, mate. We've no name, no description, nothing."

"Do you think she's got a point, Patrick?"

"Well, yes, she's got a point, Sam, but then *she* wasn't shot at by a lunatic this morning."

"What does she suggest?"

"She says we should report the shooting to the local police."

"That's all right. I have to do that anyway, Patrick. I have to report what happened to get an incident number so I can make an insurance claim for the damage to my car."

"Good! First thing in the morning, then, Sam?"

"You two can take care of that while I'm having a lie-in."

"Gee, thanks, Luca!"

"You're welcome."

The pause that followed was the perfect cue for swigging more beer.

"So what's the plan for tomorrow, Paddy?"

"We don't have one, Luca, but once we've finished up here I think we should drive straight up to North Cornwall and see if we can find Jenny Harris so I can ask her what she knows."

"She's definitely someone you need to eliminate from the picture, Paddy. I think she'll be worth talking to. She pretty much knew anyone or anything that was worth knowing back then."

"I'm not convinced, Luca. I'm not confident about this at all. It's a bit of a long shot."

"But it's a shot, Paddy."

"Yeah, I suppose so. I've got to do *something* and I've got to start somewhere."

"Definitely!"

"I imagine Jenny's still in touch with one or two of the others who were on our course, so there's a reasonable chance that she might know or have heard something. It's worth a punt, Luca."

"Well, since we're down here we've got nothing to lose in dropping by, do we? Where did you say she was from, Paddy – Wadebridge?"

"That was her home address when we were at college. That's where she's from and where her parents live. I did a bit of Facebook stalking this week. It appears that Jenny's living in Port Gaverne now."

"Where's that?"

"It's a small cove on the North Cornwall coast somewhere near Padstow, Luca. It's about ten miles from Wadebridge."

"Do you have an address?"

"No, but Port Gaverne's tiny. It's not much more than a cluster of houses and a hotel. If she's living there, I'm pretty sure we'll find her."

"How far away's Port Gaverne from here?"

102

"About an hour by car, Sam."

"How well do you know it, Paddy?"

"Katrina's brother has a holiday house in Port Isaac. Port Gaverne's literally a stone's throw down the road. It's an easy walk from his house. I've had lunch in the hotel there a couple of times. It's lovely! It's very picturesque."

"You could have bumped into Jenny!"

"Could have. But didn't."

"OK, that all sounds doable. And what then, Paddy?"

"Let's see what she says and play it by ear, Luca. But whatever happens I want to be back in Sheen on Wednesday as planned. I really don't like being away from home at the moment, especially when there's a lunatic on the loose."

"And now?"

"I think another round would be very welcome, Luca. And it's your – Oh, hold on, my bloody phone's ringing again," Patrick cursed as he felt a throbbing in his chest pocket. "It's Kat. Sorry, I'm going to have to take this," he added, frowning as he hurried away from the table to find a quiet spot.

"Hi, Katrina. Everything all right?" Patrick asked, as soon as he reached the lobby, bending over to better hear the phone clasped to his ear.

"No, it fucking isn't, Patrick!"

"What's up?"

"It's Cerin. She's disappeared."

"What!"

"She was supposed to meet Alice and me at the pub in Shoreditch and she hasn't fucking turned up."

"Don't worry, she's probably bumped into a friend or something. You know what she's like."

"I thought that too but she's not answering her phone. I've left messages but she's not called back. I'm shit-scared, Patrick."

"When was she supposed to meet you? What time?"

"Seven."

"What time is it now?"

"Eight-o-fucking-clock."

"One hour late? That's not bad by Cerin's standards. I'm sure there's a perfectly rational explanation. And you know how unreliable she can be. Keep trying her phone but if she's coming by tube, you might not be able to get through for a while."

"So what are *you* going to do to help, Patrick?"

"I'm in Plymouth, Kat. What can I do?"

"Come home."

"Can't. Sam's our only driver and he's had more than a couple of pints."

"Oh, brilliant!"

"Don't worry, Kat, Cerin's sure to turn up sooner or later. She always does. I'm sure she'll be fine."

"For fuck's sake, Patrick. I am sick of all this crap."

"Look, if she doesn't show up or get in touch with you in the next hour or two, we'll review our options."

"I'm still not happy."

"I'm sorry, but there's not much I can do from here, Kat. I'm sure she'll turn up. She's always late. I'll call you every hour on the hour to see how things are going."

"Then what?"

"Knowing Cerin there won't be a *then what*. But if you don't see her in the next two or three hours – by eleven o'clock, say – we'll call the police. And in the meantime keep trying to get her on her phone."

"Please come home, Patrick. Please."

"Don't worry. I'll be back on Wednesday evening at the very latest, Kat. Hopefully we'll have a better idea of what's going on and who this person is once I've made a few enquiries."

"Enquiries? Fucking hell, Patrick!"

"We need to trace this person and get them stopped, Katrina. That should be our priority."

"Who do you think you are? Sherlock fucking Holmes?" Katrina yelled into her mobile before the line went dead.

*   *   *

An hour later Patrick was about to phone Katrina as agreed and had walked out into the lobby to make the call when a text came through.

Found her! She's fine X.

Patrick called Katrina immediately.

"It's OK! She's all right, Patrick. She's here. She was only two fucking hours late! Kids, eh?"

"So where was she?"

"Don't ask."

"Where?"

"She'd bumped into some bloke she knows from college and went for a drink and forgot the time. Until she checked her phone and found all my messages, that is."

"Oh, well, I won't say I told you so, but thank God she's all right. And I'm mighty glad you're all together and in one place."

"Yes, but there's something else. After I spoke to you I tried calling DI Baxter on that number she gave us."

"Why the hell did you do that, Katrina?"

"I was in a panic. I wanted to let her know that Cerin was missing. Anyway, you told me to!"

"Well, not quite, and you can't phone the police every time Cerin's late to meet you for a drink, Kat. What did she say?"

"Someone else answered her phone – a policeman. They said she wasn't taking calls."

"Oh, and why's that?"

"They said she'd been involved in an accident."

"What kind of accident?"

"A car accident."

"How did that happen?"

"They wouldn't give me any details."

"Did they say how she is?"

"Not too bad, apparently. She's not in hospital or anything."

"Bloody hell! And I was only talking to her a short while

ago! She was in her car. She sounded fine. Then we were suddenly cut off. Shit, the poor woman."

"I don't know what to say, Patrick. I wish I hadn't bothered to call her now."

"But at least Cerin's with you."

"Actually, she's gone off to see Milo."

"What! She's gone where?"

"She's popped over to see Milo."

"You let her go?"

"It's all right. She's staying over at his place. It's just up the road. She said she'd be back tomorrow afternoon at around five. That's how she is, Patrick. She's very independent."

"And stubborn."

"And belligerent."

"I wonder who she gets that from, Katrina."

"Yes, I wonder, Patrick."

"Katrina, keep a close eye on the girls and please keep in touch."

"Will do!"

"Don't worry, sweetheart, it's not long till I'm back. And I'm not that far away if there's a sudden emergency."

11

"How did it go, then, gentlemen?" Luca asked as he climbed into the back of the Beetle when Patrick and Sam returned from the police station in the morning.

"Seems it was an isolated incident, Luca. But as the desk sergeant pointed out, kids get up to all sorts of madness these days, especially with the start of the warmer weather."

"So they haven't had any other reports of people firing off air rifles recently, Patrick?"

"No, but they said that they get the odd incident from time to time. And it is, usually, kids. They get bored and start taking potshots at pigeons and then it escalates from there."

"But not shooting at people so much?"

"Less so, Luca, but it does happen, apparently."

"What are you going to tell your detective, Patrick?"

"What I've just told you, Luca. That's if she's at work when we get back to London."

*   *   *

The drive to Port Gaverne was straightforward. It was a simple route and the roads were light on traffic. They reached their destination in under an hour.

The closer they got to the north coast the more recognisable Patrick McDade found the landscape. It was a relief when the sea came into view. Soon they were driving past familiar landmarks on the road into Port Isaac – the large car park on the right and then the local Co-op. They continued on past the sprinkling of shops along the top of the village and down the hill into Port Gaverne. Sam pulled up when they reached the parking bays above the beach. It was no more than a hundred yards from the entrance to the Port Gaverne Hotel. Half a dozen seagulls sat gawping at them from a nearby fence.

"Now what, Patrick?"

"I'll pop up to the hotel and ask in the bar if they know where I can find Jenny."

"And you think they will?"

"Look at the size of this place – of course they will."

"And you think they'll tell you?"

"Why wouldn't they? I'm an old friend."

"Data protection law?"

"In North Cornwall? We'll soon see."

"Good luck with that one, then!"

"Aren't you coming with me, Luca?"

"I'd rather leave this one to you, Paddy."

"Sam?"

"Me too," Sam murmured, lost in thought as he gazed down the narrow cove and out to sea.

"We'll go and muck about on the beach till you get back," Luca added.

"Right you be."

"Hey, what's with those seagulls, Paddy? They're pretty intimidating. I've seen smaller dogs!" Luca said, glancing at the seagulls perched beside them.

"They're waiting for you to buy an ice cream, Luca, and then they'll pounce."

"That's never going to happen."

"You should be all right, then. But watch they don't poop in your beer. I've seen them do that before."

"What the fuck's their problem?"

"You. They can tell you're an emmet, Luca."

"A what?"

"A tourist. Cornwall has a natural ambivalence to emmets, especially the four-by-four variety from London."

"Charming."

"Right, I'm off."

"Patrick, if I can get a signal, I thought I might call Cygnet House and see if they'll give me an appointment."

"For Christ's sake, Luca—"

"It's all right. I wasn't born yesterday. I'll see if Creed will grant me a few minutes for a debrief tomorrow, you know, since we're down here. Don't worry, Patrick. It'll be fine. I can handle it."

"Just be careful, Luca. We don't want to burn—"

"Any bridges. Of course! I know!"

"OK, I really am going now. I should only be a minute," Patrick said, clambering out of the Beetle and heading up the hill towards the hotel.

The seventeenth-century inn was evidently a popular spot. It was bunged for lunch even on a Tuesday. The tables arranged outside in the lane along the front wall of the hotel were chock-a-block with diners enjoying the view across the bay. Inside, the bar was quieter. There were places set for lunch but, such was the weather, most had opted to eat al fresco.

The interior met with Patrick's approval – the walls and shelves crammed with an eclectic mix of black-and-white photos of local fishermen, models of boats and a wide variety of oars and blocks and tackle and other seafaring gear.

"Hi, I'm sorry to bother you, but are you from round here?" Patrick asked the barman, employing his most deferential tone.

"No, I'm from Joburg. Can't you tell?" the barman answered with a smile and the appropriate accent. "Why do you ask?"

"I'm looking for an old friend. She's moved to Port Gaverne but I've lost her phone number and haven't got her new address. I was wondering if you knew her and could tell me where she lives?"

"What's her name?"

"Jenny Harris."

"What do you want with her?"

"As I say, we're old friends. We were at college together, that's all. Since I'm here on holiday I thought I'd take the opportunity to call in."

"I'm afraid I haven't been here long enough to be familiar with everybody in the village yet, but hang on ... Chris? Chris?" the young man called in the direction of the small bar on the other side of the counter.

"Yes?" A cheery voice called out, followed by a head popping round the corner.

"Jenny Harris?" the barman asked, as Chris fully emerged.

"Who wants her?" he enquired with a friendly smile.

"This gentleman. He's an old friend."

"Yes, we go back years, but we've lost touch. I know she lives in Port Gaverne but don't have her new address."

"I'm sorry, I can't tell you for obvious reasons, but you'll probably find her up at the church in St Endellion."

"Really?"

"Yes, I should imagine she'll be up there now. I think there's a service on this afternoon."

"Oh, yes, yes, of course, thank you. That's the parish church, right?"

"Yes, that's the one. Drive along the road out of Port Isaac until you reach the junction with the main road into Wadebridge and then follow the signs for Rock. The church is about a mile up on your right. You can't miss it."

"Yes, I think I know it. Thank you," Patrick said backing out the door, nodding and smiling graciously.

By the time Patrick walked down the hill, the other two were waiting by the car.

"What's the story, then?" Luca asked, as they all squeezed on board.

"Apparently she's up at the church in St Endellion. It's back down the road a bit. It's not far."

"Church? Really? What's she doing there?"

"I don't know, Luca. She's probably arranging flowers for a wedding or something. Maybe she's married to the vicar?"

"*Really?*"

"I don't know! I'm sure we'll find out when we get there," Patrick said dismissively.

"Perhaps she's practising the organ, Patrick," Luca said after a short pause. "I remember she was really into music at college. Didn't she play the keyboards in some kind of garage band?"

"Yes, I think you're right, Luca."

"What were they called, Paddy? I seem to remember it was a pretty awful name."

"Weren't they called The Flaming something or others."

"Oh, God, yes – that's it! The Flaming Pussies! How could we ever forget?"

*   *   *

The drive to the church was only ten minutes. When they turned onto the main road to Wadebridge, the panorama ahead, of rolling countryside and the coastline towards the Camel Estuary, said much about the allure of North Cornwall.

"Didn't David Cameron call one of his kids Endellion, Patrick?"

"I think they picked it as a middle name for one of them. I think the Camerons stayed somewhere around here too."

"Didn't he leave one of his kids in a pub once?"

"No, not exactly, Sam. The press put a bit of a spin on it. Made it sound much worse than it was. He and his wife had a lot of people with them – personnel, you know. And were in two cars. One thought the other had the child with them but didn't, kind of thing."

"Left in a pub, then."

"That's how the papers portrayed it, but you know what the press are like. Ah! Here we are!"

Sam braked sharply. Glancing over, their view was partially obscured by the congregation filing out of the church. They parked in the lay-by adjacent to the churchyard gates and sauntered up the stone path towards the line of people, mostly elderly couples, who weaved past them making for the graveyard round to the side. Most were dressed in black, most were hunched over and staring down and most were clasped to the hands of those accompanying them. Ahead of the congregation six pallbearers slow marched a coffin towards its final resting place.

As the boys neared the church steps they could hear a Bach fugue resonating from the organ loft. The choking cloud of incense that greeted them as they reached the doors suggested that the service had been a full funeral mass with all the High Church trimmings.

"Do you think that's her, Paddy?" Luca whispered.

"Playing the organ? Yes, I'd say so, Luca."

They paused before moving inside, then stopped the moment they saw the vicar and four acolytes standing in the central aisle facing the altar. The vicar genuflected, stood and slowly turned round towards them.

"Excuse me," Patrick whispered as the vicar approached. "Jenny Harris – is she here?"

"Well, well, well, who do we have here, then?" the vicar asked smiling.

"Excuse me?" He said, slightly taken aback.

"Patrick McDade, fancy seeing you here!"

"Jenny?" He responded, trying to suppress his surprise.

Jenny Harris, as Patrick remembered her, was a curvaceous redhead in a low-cut T-shirt and micro-mini tottering along on six-inch heels with a plastering of make-up that would befit a geisha. This incarnation of Jenny Harris wore a dog collar and the vestments appropriate for a funeral service. Her hair was cropped, she wore glasses and no make-up and was clasping a red leather-bound Bible to her chest.

"Patrick McDade. I suppose I'm not so easy to spot when I'm in my Sunday best," she said, walking towards them.

"Jenny – is that really you? God! Sorry! I mean … b-b-blimey … I mean, I never imagined that—"

"Yes, Patrick, I'm the Reverend Jenny Harris now," she replied, striding past them and beckoning them to follow.

"Oh, of course, of course! G-g-good for you!" Patrick stuttered trying to keep pace.

"Surprised?"

"Well, y-y-yes. Yes, I am. I-I-I didn't see this coming!"

"Pleasantly surprised?"

"Of course I am. I'm mightily impressed, actually!" Patrick gushed, trying to sound sincere.

"Good. And who's this with you?" she asked whilst ushering them out of the church. "Oh, it's you, Luca. Falmouth's very own Italian Stalli—"

"Don't, please! Please, don't say it!"

"No, you're right, Luca, not in church. But I might have guessed you'd be tagging along."

Luca bowed as he stepped backwards, wishing the ground would swallow him up.

"And who's this smart young man?" Jenny Harris continued, nodding towards Sam.

"This is Sam Healy. He's not one of our alumni, Jenny, but he's an all-round good bloke and much loved by all."

"Welcome to St Endellion, Sam," she said, pausing when they reached the churchyard.

"Jenny, for a moment I thought that was you playing the organ," Patrick continued.

"That's my other half. I've taught them rather well, don't you think?"

"You're married?"

"Yes."

"So who's the lucky guy?"

"That would be Angela."

"Oh, right! I-I-I'm so sorry!"

"Don't be, Patrick. We're not."

"Of course! Of course!"

"So, Patrick McDade, what brings you to Cornwall?"

"That's a long story, Jenny."

"How did you find me – or is this just another of our Lord's wonderous works?"

"I dropped by the Port Gaverne Hotel. They told me you'd probably be up here."

"And are you going to tell me what your visit is in aid of? I take it you're not here for Mrs Clarke's funeral?"

"No. And it's a little bit awkward. I need to talk to you about something quite personal if that's OK."

"What, here? Now?"

"Is that possible?"

"No, not really. As you can see, I've got to get poor Mrs Clarke buried," she said, gesturing towards the congregation gathering at the graveside.

"I'm sorry, that was so stupid of me!"

"It's all right, Patrick. Look, I need to do the committal and make an appearance at the wake in Port Isaac, but if it can keep for a couple of hours, I'll be free later. I could meet you in the harbour there for a quick drink and a chat if you like. You're not in terrible hurry, are you? Can it wait till then?"

"Yes! Yes, of course."

"Good. See you in the Mote Bar and Restaurant, Port Isaac at four. It's down by the harbour at the bottom of the village. You can't miss it," she said before processing on towards the grave.

*   *   *

When Jenny Harris joined them at the Mote Bar two hours later she found Patrick, Luca and Sam sitting at an outside table supping pints of Doom Bar and staring out to sea. She introduced her wife, Angela, who was kind enough to invite Luca and Sam into the bar so that Patrick and Jenny could have a chat in private.

Jenny Harris looked much more like the Jenny Patrick remembered now she had changed out of her vestments.

"So what's up, Patrick? Why *have* you come all this way to see me? It must be pretty serious for you to turn up without contacting me first."

"I'm sorry, I would have rung or emailed you but I don't have your contact details. But, yes, something's cropped up – it's quite a delicate matter."

"Ooo, sounds intriguing! Anyway, how *did* you find me? How did you know I was in Port Gaverne? I'm only in touch with a couple of people from college. I'd say there aren't too many we knew back then who know where I am now."

"I found you on social media. I mean, you haven't fallen too far from the tree, have you?"

"No – North Cornwall's where I belong, Patrick. It's always been home to me."

"How did you come to get married?"

"To a woman, you mean?"

"No! I didn't mean it like that."

"But I bet you're surprised, though, aren't you? I bet you wouldn't have thought I was the type back in the day."

"The type to get married?"

"No, the type to get married to a *woman*."

"I guess it's not something I'd have given much thought to, but things were a little bit confusing for all of us back then."

"Yes, I suppose we were pretty young and immature when we were at college."

"All the same, I hope I didn't cause you any offence. I really didn't mean to."

"It's OK, Patrick. Relax! But I guess it must come as a bit of a shock for you to find that I *am* married to a woman."

"No, not at all. I'm just delighted to see you're happy."

"So am I. And I am. Happy. Very happy."

"Good!"

"I had a pretty rough time at college, though. I really

struggled with the social scene. You must have noticed. 'The college bike', I believe I was described as."

"Who by?"

"I won't name names. Let's just say I heard."

"Are you kidding?"

"No."

"That's terrible, but it really doesn't sound like the kind of thing I'd say."

"No, it would have been out of character for you, but as a first experience of forming relationships with men my time at college was a complete disaster. And people like Luca didn't help."

"Luca?"

"Yes. He was pretty predatorial, as far as I remember. And I do! He was! I hope he's changed."

"I'd say he's grown up a lot since then, Jenny."

"He'd need to!"

"Nevertheless, I'm sorry about your time at college. I wish I'd known and could have been more supportive."

"Didn't you wonder, Patrick? Didn't you wonder why I had so many conquests? Didn't my behaviour seem a bit excessive?"

"With hindsight? Probably ... yes."

"And I bet it was talked about – my libido. My sex life."

"If I'm honest ... Yes, I believe it was."

"I think it was a symptom of my low self-esteem. But that was then. I needed to reinvent myself and, happily, eventually, I did – I have."

"I'm glad you came through that time, and I'm sorry for the way you were treated and any part I played in it."

"Don't worry, you weren't the worst, Patrick. Far from it."

"As far as I can remember, it was *you* who dumped *me* when we had our thing."

"You were too nice, Patrick. Ginger-haired and cute like me, but too nice and too cute. You were very polite, shy and self-conscious. Boyish. All in all, not a very attractive combination to a girl in her early twenties."

"Oh, thanks very much!"

"You're welcome. Anyway, what *are* you doing here? Why have you come all this way to see me?"

"I've got a bit of a problem, Jenny."

"Tell me."

"Earlier this month I received an anonymous Father's Day card. I have no idea who it was from. It certainly wasn't from either of my daughters. It arrived entirely out of the blue."

"Are you kidding? What was it – a joke?"

"No, it definitely wasn't a joke."

"Oh, right. So you received an anonymous Father's Day card and you've absolutely no idea who it's from?"

"Yes."

"And what does that mean? Do you think it could be for real?"

"Yes, I do."

"You actually think you've got an illegitimate child out there somewhere?"

"Possibly."

"That's amazing!"

"Hardly."

"And you're sure it's not a practical joke?"

"No, at first I thought it might be Luca."

"Luca! Yeah, I can see where you'd get that idea."

"But it wasn't. There's been other communication since, but nothing that would identify the person. Whoever it is, they haven't revealed much about themselves. They're holding all the cards."

"You're making this sound really creepy."

"It is. Very creepy. Our dog's been killed and there's other stuff too. The police are on the case. You wouldn't believe the half of it, Jenny."

"So you think an avenging angel could be at hand?"

"Yes, that seems to be the case."

"Someone's playing silly buggers and you don't know who it is or anything about them?"

"Correct. I know nothing. I just know that they're male and relatively young."

"And you've driven two hundred and fifty miles all the way from London – I take it you live in London?"

"Correct."

"Because you think there's a chance I might know something about this?"

"Correct."

"How could this possibly have anything to do with me?"

"The last time I saw you, Jenny."

"What about it?"

"We had sex, unprotected sex."

"I'm sorry but I have no memory of that at all, Patrick. When was this?"

"It was on the master's course ... A party towards the end of the final term."

"But that's well over twenty years ago."

"Yes. We got drunk. I stayed over at your flat in Falmouth."

"Oh, yes, I remember now. You always were a randy little bugger when you'd been drinking. You were all over me like a rash that night but by the next morning I'd hardly woken up and you were gone. There you are, you see, that's what I'm talking about. I got sick of being on the receiving end of that kind of behaviour. I'd had enough of one-night stands. Yes, thanks for that one, Patrick."

"I'm sorry, Jenny. Truly sorry."

"Are you?"

"Yes, I am. I didn't realise what you were going through."

"I wasn't going through anything in particular by then, Patrick. I just didn't like being treated like a blow-up doll."

"I am sorry all the same. I've got daughters of my own now who'd be roughly the same age as you were then."

"Well, anyway, Patrick, you'll be glad to know that I didn't get pregnant at any time when we were at college, so, no, it's not me. I'm not the mother of your mystery child."

"Yes, that's pretty obvious."

"Tell me, how many other women from your dim and distant past do you plan on dropping in on willy-nilly?"

"I don't know. It might surprise you but there aren't many – very few, in fact. I'm simply doing whatever it takes to trace this guy."

"I imagine the first thing you need to do is establish how old this person is – the person who sent the card, I mean."

"Exactly, but that's easier said than done. They seem to be keeping their head well below the parapet. We haven't got a name, address or anything else we can use to trace them."

"You found me easily enough."

"But then you're not hiding from anyone."

"Are you sure?"

"Yes! You're a vicar. You regularly perform in public."

"That can be one of the safest places to hide."

"Where?"

"In plain sight. So, what's your next move, Patrick?"

"I don't know. I'm feeling a bit flummoxed to be honest."

"Maybe you should go and see Mairead."

"Mairead McCullough?"

"Yes."

"I had a feeling you might say that."

"You two were a bit of an item in the last year of the course, weren't you? Didn't things go a bit pear-shaped towards the end, though? I have a vague memory of you being upset about the way things ended."

"She disappeared almost as soon as we'd finished the course – dropped me like a stone. We were pretty close till then. She left without saying a word."

"Why do you think that was?"

"I've no idea. Do you know?"

"I heard a rumour. I don't know if it was true, but I heard a rumour."

"What?"

"I heard that she'd got pregnant, Patrick."

"Bloody hell! Are you sure? When exactly?"

"Towards the end of the final term."

"Shit! And do you think ... you know?"

"That you're the father?"

"Yes! Am I?"

"I've no idea."

"Do you know if she went ahead and had the baby?"

"Again, I've no idea, but, then, I always thought *you* might know the answer to that one."

"Well, you're wrong there. I don't and never did. I knew nothing about this – nothing at all."

"Maybe the pregnancy didn't have anything to do with you, then?"

"But it fits the time frame, Jenny."

"So you think it's possible?"

"Yes, definitely. Tell me, where did Mairead go after college? I always presumed she went home to Northern Ireland."

"Yes, she did. I believe she's been living back in Portaferry ever since."

"You're still in touch?"

"Only through Facebook. A couple of us have got back in touch in the last year or so."

"Shit, Portaferry. Fancy that. I guess it's not wholly beyond the realms of possibility that my stalker could be from Northern Ireland."

"You think?"

"Yes. My wife thought his accent might be West Country, but I wouldn't be so sure."

"You've spoken to him?"

"No, he left a message on our answerphone. The sound was

very muffled, but there might have been a bit of an Irish twang in there. I wouldn't discount it. So who knows? Maybe he is Mairead's son."

"Perhaps that should be your next step, then."

"I wonder if she would talk to me, Jenny."

"Of course she would and for the same reason I'm talking to you now. Curiosity. And who knows, maybe she has more to say to you than me. Maybe she needs to unburden herself of something, if you know what I mean."

"I'd better head over to Newquay, then."

"Why?"

"To catch the next frigging flight to Belfast. I'm not going to do this over the phone. I'm going to have to go to Portaferry."

"What about your mates?"

"They'll be fine. They can drop me off at the airport before driving back to Plymouth. I imagine they'll have plenty to talk about on the journey. But I'd better not hang about here too much longer if I want to get a flight today. I really need to be home sometime tomorrow – tomorrow afternoon at the latest."

"I guess it's easy enough to get in and out of Northern Ireland in a day, though, isn't it?"

"Absolutely. I just hope that I can find Mairead when I get there."

"I can give you her mobile number if you think that'll help."

"What's her married name?"

"It's still McCullough. It's the name she's always used in business."

"It's nice that you're still in touch."

"It doesn't amount to much. We don't communicate very often – once or twice a year at most. I've kind of moved on from my college days. I don't feel a need to revisit the past. I'm happier where I am now."

"Look, Jenny, I *am* sorry. I'm very sorry for whatever

happened when we were at college. We were all a bit thoughtless, young and clumsy back then. We didn't know the half of what we were up to."

"That's OK, Paddy. I'm in a much happier place now and I'm all for forgiving and forgetting. It's what we're trained to do in my line of work, and someone up there has set me a very good example to follow," Jenny Harris said, glancing at the sky.

12

"OK, Patrick, will you be all right from here?" Sam asked as he pulled up opposite the terminal building at Newquay Airport.

"This'll do fine, thanks, Sam."

Patrick hopped out the car and leaned in through the driver's window.

"Thanks for your help, guys!"

"Got your ticket, Paddy?"

"Yep."

"Photo ID?"

"Yep."

"That's you, then, and, you've got plenty of time."

"Good man, Sam. So when are you seeing Creed, Luca?"

"Their offices tomorrow at ten."

"And you're happy enough to handle this on your own?"

"Of course, Paddy!"

"Where are you staying?"

"We're staying at the Regent Palace Hotel tonight and Sam's driving me straight back to London after the meeting tomorrow."

"I guess you're getting to know Plymouth city centre pretty intimately, Luca."

"Like the back of my hand, Patrick. And don't worry – I'll do my best with Creed. I guess we've got nothing to lose at this point – it's definitely worth a punt."

"Tread lightly, Luca."

"Sure. Will do. I'll see you bright and early in the office on Thursday morning, Paddy. We can go through it all then."

"OK. Take care you two and don't do anything I wouldn't do."

"As if!"

*   *   *

Patrick McDade sauntered over to the Flybe check-in desk at the back of the departure hall. It was late afternoon and the airport was buzzing with holidaymakers. There were queues for every desk and every facility. Patrick wanted to phone Katrina as soon as possible to let her know that he was on his way to Belfast but was nervous about her reaction. Nevertheless, he was pleased to hear her voice when she answered the phone.

"Hi, Kat, any sign of Cerin?"

"Not yet, but she's due here any minute."

"Good. And when she arrives, please keep her with you until I get back."

"What time are you getting home tomorrow?"

"Not too late."

"Where are you, Patrick? I can hear people. Lots of them."

"I'm at the airport."

"Which one, for God's sake?"

"Newquay."

"And what the fuck are you doing there?"

"I'm flying to Belfast."

"What!"

"Don't worry, Katrina. I'm still going to be home tomorrow as planned. I managed to book the last seat on the British Airways five-something flight back to Heathrow from Belfast City Airport. I think it lands just before seven."

"Belfast! I might have fucking known!" she yelled. "I need you here. I'm fed up of being on my own – I'm scared!"

"Calm down. Everything's going to be all right, Kat. There's nothing to be frightened of."

"*Calm down*? That's very easy for you to say, you're not stuck in fucking London with a lunatic on the loose."

"It's OK. Relax. I'll be home tomorrow."

"But why the hell do you have to go to fucking Belfast?"

"You know why. And with a bit of luck it'll give us what we're looking for."

"More clues?"

"No, answers."

"Jesus, Patrick, you're not doing a fucking crossword puzzle!"

"I need to track this person down, Katrina. The police don't seem particularly interested in helping, so we'll have to do it ourselves. Once we get a name and, hopefully, an address, then maybe we can get a court order or something to stop them harassing us. We might even be able to persuade the police to press charges and get whoever this is off the streets."

"And what am I supposed to do in the meantime?"

"Where are you?"

"I'm in Hoxton."

"Can you stay another night with Alice and Cerin? Can you stay there till I get back?"

"Yes, if they'll have me, but they'll be looking for rent soon if I stay very much longer."

"Please stay there, Kat. I worry a lot less when I know you're all together in one place. And I promise I'll be home tomorrow evening. With luck we should have some definite answers by then."

"Are you *that* confident?"

"I'm counting on nothing, but I think we might be about to make a breakthrough."

"Really?"

"I can't be sure, but I've got a strong feeling."

"Where are you staying?"

"The Park Avenue in East Belfast."

"And where do you have to go tomorrow?"

"Portaferry."

"How far's that?"

"It's about fifty miles."

"So how are you getting there?"

"Cab."

"Jesus, Patrick! You must have more money than sense."

"Kat, I'm sorry but I've got to go. I've got to check in and get my boarding card. I think my flight's going to be called any second. I'll call you later, sure."

Patrick printed off his boarding card and headed for security. It felt strange being on his own. He'd grown accustomed to hanging out with Luca and Sam over the last couple of days, but whilst he missed their banter he knew he'd see them soon enough back in London. To a certain extent he relished the peace and quiet of travelling on his own, especially after the barrage of questions he'd had to field about Jenny Harris on the dash to the airport.

During the drive from Port Isaac Patrick had seized the chance to fire off a quick text message to Mairead McCullough. He'd toyed with the idea of phoning her but thought a text would be less intimidating and less likely to make her suspicious of his motives. He hoped she wouldn't worry about how he'd got hold of her mobile number.

Mairead it's Patrick McDade!
Hi, long time no see!
I'm in Belfast tomorrow on business.
I've a site meeting in Newtownards.
Do you'd fancy a coffee in the morning if you have time?
PM

As he waited at his departure gate for the final boarding call Patrick kept checking his iPhone, praying for a text from Mairead McCullough to come through, staring at the screen and willing it to light up. He just hoped against hope for a positive response before take-off so that he could be sure he was going to get to meet her in Belfast.

126

Once boarded, he found his seat, switched his mobile to flight mode and braced himself for take-off.

If it wasn't for his family connection to Northern Ireland and that it was familiar territory, he wondered if he'd have bothered to make the trip. But in terms of discovering the identity of his illegitimate stalker, it seemed possible that Mairead McCullough held the key.

While Patrick still possessed enough boyish imagination to embrace the magic of air travel, today he was preoccupied with weightier matters. Leaning back in his seat and resting his eyes, Patrick tried to conjure an image of Mairead as he'd known her at college. She was a keen student. Worked hard. Not that that was unusual on an MA course in architecture. He presumed that she'd have been working in practice in Northern Ireland since graduating and wondered what that must be like. Possibly quite lucrative, he imagined, such had been the volume of redevelopment following the end of the Troubles.

Thinking of Mairead and recalling the feelings he'd had for her worried him. Under any other circumstances Patrick would have doubted the wisdom of flying over to visit her, such was their history. On reflection it was easy to see that it was unrequited passion that had led him to carry a torch for her for so long. It was *she* who had dumped *him* after all and he'd never received, or had the chance to pursue, an explanation. At the earliest opportunity at the end of their final term she had packed up and vanished, never to be seen in Falmouth again. And then, as Jenny had heard, Mairead was rumoured to have had a baby some time after returning home.

Patrick sighed as he remembered their last night. They'd been out partying with their year group, celebrating the end of their final project. They slunked off early when she'd whispered an implicit invitation back to her place, leaving him in little doubt as to what to expect.

As soon as the door to her flat was flung open they'd stumbled through into the hall locked in each other's arms, falling to the floor in a frantic flurry of fumbling fingers and wild kisses. Fired up on alcohol it became a highly charged night that left them physically drained, dazed and breathless when coming to their senses the next morning.

Despite his attempts to make conversation when they awoke, little was said. She seemed aloof and troubled. They went their separate ways. No coffee. No breakfast. She had a last tutorial. He had to pack to go home. And that was the last time he'd seen her.

Turbulence jolted him awake. Patrick opened his eyes and peered out the window trying to get his bearings. He spotted the coastline of the Isle of Man; it wouldn't be long before they'd be landing in Belfast.

When the plane touched down and was taxiing towards the terminal building, Patrick switched his iPhone back out of flight mode to check if Katrina had been trying to reach him. She hadn't. He was in the act of popping his phone back into his chest pocket when a message beeped through.

Patrick!
I've a meeting at the Ulster Hospital tomorrow morning.
Could meet you for a quick coffee there at 11.
See you in the Oasis Restaurant. It's on the first floor.
Let me know if that suits.
Mairead

Mairead McCullough's perfunctory tone pleased him. Patrick had decided that if the tenor of her message suggested she was delighted to have heard from him and ecstatic at the prospect of meeting up, then the chances she had a serious subject to broach were quite low. That her message was quite businesslike suggested the opposite.

Patrick replied immediately, relieved that the coffee date on the outskirts of Belfast would save him an expensive hundred-mile round trip to Portaferry.

Mairead!
That would be great thnx.
See you in the Oasis at 11.
PM

It was a sunny evening when Patrick's flight landed at Belfast City Airport. The giant yellow cranes of Harland & Wolff stood gleaming high above the docks on the way into the city centre. Having disembarked, wandered past the baggage carousels and out into the arrivals hall Patrick paused and was about to call Katrina when his mobile rang.

"Mr McDade?"

"Yes?"

"It's DI Baxter."

"Detective Inspector! Are you OK? I heard you'd had a spot of bother."

"A small accident. I was lucky. Just a mild concussion, a sprained wrist and a little hurt pride. Nothing much to worry about, really."

"That's a relief, I was worried when I heard. Anyway, to what do I owe this pleasure? I thought I was to call you on Thursday," Patrick said, hunching up and pressing the phone tight against his ear.

"Indeed, but I've been considering your case."

"My case? I didn't know we were a case. We're a case now – that sounds like progress!"

"I've had time to reflect since we last spoke. Where are you, Mr McDade? Are you in Sheen?"

"No, Belfast."

"Belfast! I wasn't expecting that!"

"Neither was I, Detective Inspector."

"Listen. Following my unscheduled appearance the wrong way round in the oncoming lane of the A4, and my subsequent visit to hospital, I've had time to consider your predicament and the incidences you reported."

"And what do you think?"

"The Father's Day card, Mr McDade, the answerphone message, your dog, the air rifle, the business sabotage and now my road traffic accident. This number of incidents in one week has had me thinking and brought me to the conclusion that you and your family could be in some sort of danger."

"Oh, my God! So what changed your mind?"

"Well, judging by how my car behaved moments before, I suspect that my car crash might not have been accidental. Due to the unusual circumstances I had the wreckage examined by our engineers. It didn't take them long to report back that the steering mechanism might have been tampered with."

"Really?"

"Yes. It's not certain, but it's possible."

"And you think it could be our guy?"

"I don't know, Mr McDade, but I'm not ruling anything out at this stage."

"Bloody hell!"

"In light of that we have been studying the CCTV footage shot in and around the station over the last while and checking all the people seen passing through our parking lot at the rear of the building. And this is where you could be of assistance, Mr McDade."

"How, DI Baxter?"

"I'd like you to come in and view the footage and see if your man appears on it."

"But I don't know what he looks like. I've never seen him."

"Ah, but how do you know? I simply want you to come into the station, watch the tape and, who knows, maybe one of the faces will be familiar to you."

"OK. I'll call you on Thursday morning when I'm back, as agreed, and arrange a convenient time to pop in. Our office is only up the road from your station."

"Excellent. And in the meantime, where is your wife, Mr McDade? I tried your landline at home. There was no answer."

"She's in East London. She's staying with my daughters."

"Could you please contact her and warn her to be vigilant. We need to be wary of our mysterious young friend."

"Of course, I'll call her as soon as we're off the phone. Is there anything you can do by way of offering us protection?"

"Since your wife's away at the moment I guess we need not worry too much about her personal safety in the short-term, but we'll keep an eye on your house. I'll make sure someone drives by once or twice tonight."

"Thanks, that's very reassuring."

"And you'll be home tomorrow?"

"Yes, tomorrow evening."

"And your wife?"

"I'm not sure what time she's getting back to the house. I'll check and let you know."

"Please do. And may I ask your business in Belfast?"

"I'm following up a promising lead regarding our wee friend, Detective Inspector. I've had a tip-off, as you might say."

"Good. But be careful, Mr McDade, these are strange times. Nonetheless, I look forward to hearing from you on Thursday. And, whatever you're up to in Belfast, I hope it's fruitful."

As soon as Patrick McDade ended the call, his phone rang.

"Hi, Kat!"

"Patrick!" Katrina shouted in a shrill voice that put the fear of God into him.

"Are you OK, Kat?"

"It's Cerin!"

"What about her?"

"She's gone missing again. Milo's with her, but I don't know where they are."

"Are you sure they aren't having a quick drink somewhere?"

"No, they promised they'd be here by seven. They're over two hours late and there's no sign of them. I've been texting and phoning them constantly without any answer. Nothing. Alice has been trying too. We're both extremely worried."

"Are you sure they're not hanging out at Milo's?"

"God, I hope so! It might explain why I can't get hold of her on her mobile. The signal's shite where he lives."

"Still, you'd think she could give you a call to let you know what she's up to."

"What do you think we should do?"

"Give it another hour. If you still haven't heard from her, call DI Baxter."

"What good would that do, Patrick? She hasn't been much help so far."

"I think she's starting to come round to our point of view. I think she's starting to realise we've got a bit of a problem."

"Good! I'll give it an hour, then."

"Phone me immediately Cerin turns up or if and when you hear from her, please."

The call ended. Patrick put his phone back in his pocket.

"Shit!" he said slowly under his breath as he wandered over to the taxi rank.

*   *   *

The journey to the Park Avenue Hotel took no more than ten minutes and cost no more than a fiver, much to the annoyance of the cab driver who'd been waiting for over an hour for a pickup and had probably been hoping for a passenger who'd want to travel a bit further than the hotel round the corner.

Patrick found his room, dumped his stuff and climbed into bed exhausted. He texted Katrina to see if Cerin had shown up. She hadn't.

Kat, pls text me the moment you hear from Cerin.
Any time, day or night.
Paddy XXX

Patrick struggled to sleep – couldn't sleep. Worried about Cerin the whole night, but half expected that she'd be at Milo's.

13

Luca Salvatore made sure he got a good night's sleep and arrived with plenty of time to spare for his appointment with Marcus Creed at the offices of Cygnet House. Once Luca had announced himself at the reception desk, the wait for his audience with the MD seemed interminable.

Twenty minutes later Marcus Creed's PA marched across the foyer. Luca heard her before he saw her – her hard heels click-clacking on the wooden floor.

"Mr Creed will be down to see you shortly. He asked me to apologise for keeping you waiting, Mr Salvatore. He's had to take a conference call but shouldn't be very much longer."

"No problem at all," Luca replied, smiling and maintaining a calm demeanour.

By the time Marcus Creed joined him, Luca's fingernails had been nibbled to the quick. As Creed strolled across the foyer he appeared more subdued than on previous occasions. He spotted Luca perched on one of the half-dozen couches in the seating area but paused to chat to the two women behind the reception desk en route – all smiles, expressive body language and extravagant hand gesturing. His mood defaulted to glum as he turned towards Luca; gone the cordial bonhomie of a moment ago.

"Mr Salvatore, we meet again. How can I help you this morning?" Creed asked, straight-faced and serious, before taking a seat beside Luca on one of the sofas. "I presume you're wondering why we changed our mind with regard to the hotel development?"

"Naturally. We were very disappointed having got so far in the selection process, Mr Creed. We thought we had come to an agreement with you and didn't, and don't, understand what could possibly have gone wrong. We were particularly worried in case you had heard something unsavoury or unflattering about our company that unsettled you."

"No, Mr Salvatore, not at all. I can assure you that that is not the case. In fact, we have only received very positive reports about your practice."

"Oh, good, good. That's welcome news. I do hope you will interpret our disappointment as a compliment and a sign of how committed we were to the project. I know you owe us nothing – no explanations or rationales – and I'm sure there are mitigating circumstances regarding your decision, but we were very excited at the prospect of working with you and your company on the hotel project. I think our commitment was obvious from our dedication to answering the brief in such detail."

"I agree, Mr Salvatore."

"Luca, please."

"I agree, Luca, and everything you say is true, however, I think you will understand a little better if I describe the recent developments that encouraged our change of mind. You see, we haven't so much as changed our mind as changed direction."

"Oh?"

"Yes. You see, after your presentation and our last meeting, we knew we had found the right architects to design our hotel. We were delighted with what you showed us, but, unfortunately for you, Luca, we got a call from another firm of architects – a firm we have worked with before – who were desperate to present their ideas for the Plymouth Sound development. They were very persuasive."

"There's was a hotel design, I take it?"

"No, and this is what made the difference. Unlike you and your colleagues who came up with a design that answered our brief for the three-hundred-bedroom hotel we had originally planned, they took a different approach to, and a totally fresh look at, the project as a whole."

"What do you mean, Mr Creed? Are you saying that they didn't answer the brief?"

"Yes, Luca, they had the *cajones* to rewrite the brief."

"Oh, of course!"

"This is a commercial venture, Luca, and although we have a portfolio of hotel developments that Plymouth Sound would have fitted into very neatly, we haven't delved into retail development in the UK as yet, and while the site is very attractive and, we believe, perfect for a quality, five-star hotel, the other firm of architects pointed out the greater commercial potential of a retail park with a combined development of high-end private apartments."

"I see."

"Yes, they convinced us that a large retail development, along with a raft of residential property – to keep the local planning department happy – would yield a quicker return on our investment. They already have a multinational retailer lined up as a key tenant. And, in the current financial climate, we thought it best to listen to what they were saying. It'll be a very useful pilot scheme for us in this sector of the property market too, Luca. It's an experiment we are keen to try."

"The clever buggers!"

"Exactly."

"Perhaps we took your brief a little too literally, Mr Creed?"

"Perhaps. We liked your design, though, Luca. Your concept for the hotel showed a clear understanding of what we required. You answered the brief perfectly, but unfortunately this is a commercial venture and we are a commercial company investing large amounts of our country's oil wealth."

"So what about the design?"

"What do you mean, Luca?"

"What about the design of the retail park and apartments? Is there nothing we can do for you there?"

"Luca! We have accepted the other firm's proposal."

"Have they signed a contract?"

"I'm afraid I'm not prepared to divulge that information."

"But you like what we do – you've said as much. Is there nothing we could help you with at Plymouth Sound?"

"No, Luca, there's nothing. I'm sorry, but that is a closed book to you now."

"Never mind. It's not that we're desperate for work or anything, more that we were keen to work with you, Mr Creed. I do hope you didn't mind my asking."

"Not at all. And thank you for coming all this way," Creed said, standing, smiling and reaching out his hand.

"You're welcome. I look forward to seeing how things develop and wish you well with the retail park," Luca replied, shaking Marcus Creed's hand firmly.

"Goodbye, Luca, and safe home."

"Thank you," Luca said. He sighed, turned and walked to the revolving doors at the front of the building.

It was a pleasant day out on the street. Luca decided to head to the seafront to enjoy some fresh air and sun before the long car journey back to London.

"Mr Salvatore!"

Luca glanced over his shoulder and saw Marcus Creed striding towards him.

"Have you got a minute, Luca?"

"Absolutely."

"Plymouth Sound."

"What of it?"

"We have just had a bid accepted on a large area of waterfront immediately below the original site. Our initial concept is to build a marina with a development of bars and restaurants. If you can swallow your pride, Luca, do you think you could work in conjunction with the other firm and design some of the buildings we have planned?"

"Won't they object to working with us, Mr Creed?"

"The choice is not theirs to make, Luca."

"Good! Then I can assure you that we are expert at swallowing our pride. We eat, sleep and dream design, Mr Creed, so if your offer is genuine, please count us in!"

"Excellent! Can we talk business, Luca?"

"Here? Today? No, Mr Creed, I'm sorry we can't."

"Pardon?"

"If you appreciate what we do, then I believe it's time to put something down on paper – a proposal. I think we need to have something to sign. A show of good faith, shall we say? When you're ready, that is."

"You're being very bold, Mr Salvatore."

"Indeed, but then we know our worth, Mr Creed."

"You want a contract, then, I take it?"

"Yes, and a retainer."

"I like your style, Mr Salvatore."

"Luca."

"Sorry, Luca. And perhaps, as you say in your country, fortune favours the brave, does it not?"

"Mmm, lets hope so, Mr Creed," Luca replied, smiling.

"Well, please, leave this with me, Luca. I should have something on paper for you to consider by the end of this week."

"A concrete proposal and something to sign?"

"Exactly," Creed replied, exchanging another handshake and a smile.

14

By ten o'clock the next morning Patrick McDade was still taking advantage of the freedom that comes with being away from home. A long lie-in, an Ulster fry and a binge watch of daytime telly were a rare indulgence.

Before long *Homes Under The Hammer* was interrupted by the alarm on his iPhone beeping to remind him that he needed to get up and showered to make his rendezvous with Mairead McCullough at the Ulster Hospital. Easing himself out of bed he tottered forward to inspect the day through the half-drawn curtains. It was grey and cloudy.

Katrina phoned. She sounded like she'd been crying, her voice tremulous. Patrick was mightily relieved when she said she'd heard from Cerin.

"What the hell is she up to, Katrina?"

"I have no idea, but at least we know she's safe. She was pretty vague and short with me for some reason and refused to say where she's been and what she's been doing. She said she was on a train with Milo but wouldn't tell me where they were headed."

"Wouldn't or couldn't?"

"A bit of both, I think. She just said that they had something urgent to do and would call again this afternoon to let me know where they'd be."

"How did she sound?"

"Pissed off. You know, a bit like she used to when she was a moody teenager. It was all a bit strange. One way or another I'm worried, Patrick."

"Did you give her a bollocking?"

"Of course not. How the fuck would that help? She's in her twenties, for God's sake. She's an adult and can do as she pleases. I said to keep in touch and told her that I'd see her this evening."

"Did she sound scared or frightened?"

"A bit quiet, perhaps. Quiet for her, that is, but, no, not scared."

"Kat, I'm sorry, but I've really got to get going. I've got to be somewhere at eleven sharp. Please keep in touch with Cerin as best you can. I wish we knew what the hell she's up to. By the way, did you speak to DI Baxter?"

"I gave her a call last night. She didn't say much, just advised me to be vigilant and to keep in touch. She said that they were keeping an eye on the house, but then you know that."

*　　　*　　　*

Patrick arrived at the Ulster Hospital with minutes to spare. The hospital was only a short cab ride from his hotel and the traffic was light on the Upper Newtownards Road.

The Oasis seemed more like a cafeteria than a restaurant. By the time Mairead arrived, Patrick had already downed a large Americano and was getting stuck into the cryptic crossword in *The Guardian*. Totally absorbed, he didn't notice Mairead approaching until she loomed over his table.

"Patrick McDade! What the hell are you doing here?" Mairead asked enthusiastically and scaring Patrick half to death. He jumped up and gave her a peck on the cheek while struggling to conceal his nervousness.

"Och, y-y-you know, mixing a little bit of business with pleasure. L-l-lovely to see you, by the way, Mairead," he stammered.

"I hope you're not over here to steal any of my clients!"

"Would I?"

"Most probably, yes!"

"S-s-so you're still in practice, Mairead?"

"Haven't stopped quite yet. And you?"

"Yes, still at it, I'm afraid. What are you doing here at the Ulster?"

"I've got a meeting with the hospital administrators shortly. I'm designing a new children's ward."

"Good for you. Oh, I'm sorry! Can I get you a tea or coffee? Would you like something to eat?" Patrick asked, backing towards the food counters.

"What are you drinking?"

"An Americano with milk. I guess it's what we used to call a white coffee, back in the day."

"OK, I'll have one of those too, please," Mairead said with a smile as she eased herself into one of the aluminium chairs at Patrick's table.

"Anything else – carrot cake, a slice of Battenberg?"

"No, thank you, and don't tempt me! It's a bit early for food. I don't eat much. Never did."

"Yes, I remember. Milk?"

"No, thanks."

Patrick strolled over to the counter to order Mairead's coffee. When he reached the till he glanced back and wondered if he would have recognised her if she hadn't approached him first. While her facial features hadn't changed – her face had hardly aged – her taste in clothes certainly had. Her wardrobe at college had been predominantly black – a gothic style typical of design students at that time. Since then she had evidently adopted a more diverse palette. Also, she was wearing a skirt and blouse – girls' clothes. Patrick guessed that that was a necessary evolution that comes with a career: gone the DM boots and in with six-inch heels. And whilst before he might have been aware of the distinctive aroma of patchouli oil, he thought he could now detect the subtler tones of Chanel wafting from her neck.

"So how are you, Mairead? What have you been doing for the last twenty-five years? You're looking great, by the way!"

Patrick said casually as he wandered back to the table with her coffee.

When she peered up he noticed her eyes – as big, bright, blue and captivating as ever – and that her hair was in its usual loose bob; features that he thought gave Mairead a Southern European appearance, Italian or Spanish maybe.

"Thank you, Patrick. Oh, you know, just the usual ... business, work, family."

"Family? You got married, then?"

"Yes, not long after we left college. You?"

"About a year later. Who did you marry?"

"Someone from home. A local guy from Portaferry. I've known him since school – we were childhood sweethearts. We practically grew up together. You know, the same old story. You?"

"A West Country lass."

"Do you have children, Patrick?"

"Yes, two. Two girls. They're both in their early twenties."

"Irish twins?"

"No, not quite, and they're very different in looks and personality."

"Do either of them look like you?"

"I wouldn't like to say. Let's hope not, eh? Here, I can show you," Patrick said, quickly flicking through the photos on his iPhone. "That's Cerin, and the one on her left is Alice," Patrick continued.

"Oh, they're gorgeous, Patrick! I guess they must take after their mother."

"Yes, very funny. Do you have children?"

"Yes, a boy and a girl," Mairead replied, gazing into her coffee to avoid eye contact. Patrick noticed her blushing.

"I bet they're lookers."

"*Lookers*? What does that mean, Patrick?"

"Oh, nothing."

The awkwardness that followed stalled the conversation.

"Well, Patrick. This. Seeing you. It's a bit of a surprise. What made you think of getting in touch? You must have lots of friends in Northern Ireland, so why did you want to see *me*?" Mairead asked, sounding a little defensive, her mood growing more serious. "And how did you get my number? We didn't have mobiles the last time I saw you."

"I got it from Jenny Harris. I was planning to be in Newtownards today and thought that if you were still living or working in the area, you might fancy a quick cuppa."

"I hope you don't mind me saying this, but I thought it a bit odd when I got your text. Let's face it, things were a little weird the last time I saw you, Patrick."

"That was a long time ago."

"Yes, but it makes me wonder what you're really doing here. I mean, what business have you got in Newtownards, for God's sake? It's a bit off your beaten track, isn't it?"

"Och, you know," Patrick muttered, shrugging.

"No, I don't. Tell me."

"It's hard to explain. I'm not going to lie to you."

"Good, cos you were never very good at that. You make a terrible liar, Patrick. It's your face. It's so open. I can read you like a book – a children's book. We all can."

"Oh."

"So why *are* you really here, Patrick?"

"Nothing in particular. I'm from here. I've got family here. I don't need an excuse, do I?"

"You haven't come searching for answers or anything enigmatic like that, then?"

"Answers to what exactly?"

"I don't know. Maybe you're still wondering why I disappeared back here so suddenly at the end of our course."

"I was a bit thrown by that at the time, but it's not something I've dwelt on since. Life goes on."

"And there's plenty more fish in the sea."

"Oh, I've always hated that expression, Mairead!"

"Me too."

There followed another lull in the conversation and the longer it lasted, the harder the awkward pause became to fill. Patrick began to panic when he realised there was a danger he might not get the answers he craved if he couldn't shift the brain freeze that was impeding his ability to ask the questions needed to obtain them.

"How old are your kids?" Patrick finally asked, hoping his question wouldn't arouse further suspicion.

"Fourteen and sixteen."

"Oh," Patrick replied, struggling to hide his disappointment.

"Why, 'oh'?"

"I'm surprised. It's just that mine are a fair bit older. I must have started earlier than you."

"I doubt it. I started very early, as it happens. You don't know, do you? You obviously never heard."

"Don't know what, Mairead?"

"What happened."

"What do you mean?"

"Something happened not long after the last time I saw you, Patrick. Not long after we left college."

"As you were saying, the last time I saw you things got a bit awkward. I've always wondered why you vanished without saying a word. Why was that?"

"I'm not sure I want to discuss that now."

"What – our night of passion?"

Mairead glanced down with her lips pursed and eyes shut. She sighed and, after a moment or two, slowly raised her head.

"Look, Patrick, I don't want to talk about it but, then again, maybe I should. Maybe it's a ghost that needs laying to rest."

"Maybe, Mairead."

"You see, what you don't know is that I – like plenty of other girls at that time – had a boyfriend at home, a long-standing boyfriend. So I should never have let it happen. I shouldn't have done it."

"Sleep with me?"

"Yes, I'm sorry. It was an error of judgement. And what makes it worse is that – as it turns out – I was pregnant."

"By me!"

"No, it couldn't have been you. I was pregnant before our one-night stand, but I didn't know that at the time."

"You're saying that when you slept with me, you didn't know that you were pregnant?"

"Yes."

"And you're sure the child wasn't mine."

"Yes, I was pregnant by my boyfriend."

"How can you be so sure?"

"The dates."

"And what happened to your boyfriend?"

"I married him. I'm married to him now. He's the long-standing boyfriend I just told you about."

"Wow. I'm glad that worked out for you – truly I am."

"I've never told him about you, though, Patrick."

"Of course! Why would you? And what about the baby?"

"I-I-I can't ..." Mairead stuttered, tears welling in her eyes and trickling down her cheeks. Surprised, Patrick instinctively leaned forward and clasped her hands.

"I'm sorry, Mairead. I am so so sorry. I shouldn't have asked. It's none of my business," he said, shaking his head and squeezing her hands.

"Oh, it's so goddamn awful, Patrick. It's so painful, it's something I don't care to talk about."

Patrick was tempted to ask more but didn't dare.

"The baby. He definitely wasn't yours. For a start, he didn't have your red hair and freckles. He was raven-haired like his dad." Mairead said, placing a hand on Patrick's forearm and laughing a little through her tears, sniffing and dabbing her nose with a tissue.

"*He?*"

"Yes. Gerard. He was called Gerard."

144

"Was?"

"Yes. He passed away," she murmured, taking a deep breath and wiping away her tears. "He's dead."

"Oh, God! I'm so sorry."

"He was only eighteen, Patrick," she said, gazing up into his eyes.

"That is awful, Mairead. I'm so sorry," Patrick mumbled, giving her hands another gentle squeeze. "Please don't feel like you have to tell—"

"He'd been on a night out in Belfast and was walking back to his student flat. He was crossing the Lisburn Road and got knocked down by a joyrider. It was a hit-and-run. Killed outright. They never caught the driver but, who knows, they probably weren't much older than Gerry themselves."

Mairead rattled off the story at a speed that suggested it had been told many times before.

"I'm so so sorry, Mairead. I feel terrible for bringing it up."

"No, it's OK."

An awkward pause followed. Mairead suddenly sat upright and pulled her hands away from Patrick's gentle grasp.

"I still don't understand why you're here, though," she said abruptly, attempting to assume a different mood. "You're pretty transparent, you know. I think there's something you're not telling me, Patrick McDade."

"Oh, God! Do you really want to know?"

"Yes, tell me. Whatever it is, you'll be glad you shared it."

*   *   *

The quick coffee took longer than either had anticipated but was curtailed by Mairead's work commitments.

"Well, I don't know whether to be flattered or appalled that you thought I might be the mother of your stalker, but, seriously, where do you go from here?"

Patrick shrugged.

"It has been strangely pleasant to see you, all the same,"

Mairead said as she rose to leave. "And who knows, had circumstances been slightly different we might have seen a lot more of each other over the years," she added.

"*Strangely pleasant*?"

"Och, you know what I mean."

"Sliding doors, Mairead. I always had the hots for you, you know."

"Yes, I know. You made that pretty obvious. And Patrick?"

"Mairead?"

"What I told you today, please keep it to yourself. I hate the idea of Gerard's story being splashed about on social media."

"Don't worry. Not even I am that stupid."

"Good, and thanks for the coffee. Let me know how you get on. It'd be nice to stay in touch."

They hugged and parted company.

Standing in the hospital foyer Patrick wondered how he was going to fill the rest of the day before his flight in the afternoon. He called a cab and made for the city centre. On board he slumped into the back of the seat, blew out his cheeks and then fumbled through his pockets for his mobile. He tried Katrina's number. There was no answer. He was on the verge of phoning back to leave a message when his mother called.

"Hi, Mum, everything OK?"

"No, Patrick, everything is *not* OK. I've got Cerin here. She's with Milo, and your father is very upset."

"Why is he upset? And what's Cerin doing there?"

"I'm not prepared to discuss that with you now, but what I will say is that I think you've got *some* explaining to do, Patrick McDade!"

"About what Mum?"

"As I say, I am not prepared to discuss that with you over the phone. I want you to come here directly you arrive off your flight. You need to come here and explain yourself. Katrina's on her way. She says she doesn't want to speak to you either, but she's coming here with Alice to collect Cerin. I expect that she'll still be here when you arrive. That's all I'm prepared to say until I see you in person and we can have this out face to face."

"Have what out? What's this all about, Mum? I really don't have a clue what you're talking about."

"I don't want to talk to you right now, Patrick, but, suffice to say, you have let everybody down very badly. Just make sure you come straight here from Heathrow," Patrick's mother said spitting the words out like venom and then slamming down the receiver.

Patrick tried calling Katrina, then Cerin and then Alice. None were answering their phones. He tried Luca.

"Have you heard from Katrina, Luca?"

"No, she never calls me. Why, what's up?"

"Something very strange is going on."

"What?"

"I'm not sure. That's the honest answer."

"OK. How did you get on with Mairead?"

"It was nice to catch up but it was a bit of a dead end as far as the other thing is concerned. It was good to see her but unfortunately my hunch that our stalker might be her child was entirely wrong. I was barking up the wrong tree there. So another trip that was a complete waste of time."

"Oh?"

"It's not her. She's definitely NOT the mother, Luca."

"So how does that leave things?"

"It kind of leaves me with the impression that this guy isn't my son. I mean, no way. There's no other explanation. There's no one else I know or could be linked with who could possibly be the mother."

"And you're sure of that?"

"Absolutely positive. Jenny and Mairead were – are – the only contenders. Any other girlfriends I've had are people I met in London on work placements and there's just a couple of them."

"Catherine and Susie?"

"Yes. And, as you know, I'm still vaguely in touch with them. I'm pretty sure I'd have heard if either of them had got pregnant and gone on to have a child. I mean, *you* know them, Luca. You socialise with them a bit. You'd have heard something, wouldn't you?"

"Yes, probably ... No, definitely. Of course I would!"

"Exactly."

"So how does that leave things, Paddy?"

"Back to square one. DI Baxter wants me to pop into the station to check some CCTV footage. That might throw something up but I doubt it. Apart from that, there's nothing. Apparently I've got to go to my parent's house as soon as I get back this evening. There's something kicking off there. Something to do with Cerin, I think. I don't know. I can't get hold of anybody. My mum called me earlier and ordered me home. I think she's losing her marbles."

"Is there anything I can do to help?"

"Luca – I'm sorry! My God, how could I forget! How did you get on with Marcus Creed?"

"How do you think?"

"Disappointing, I suppose."

"No, quite the opposite, Patrick. Their change of mind had nothing to do with any negative press, gossip or rumour reaching their ears. Clearly your weirdo had nothing to do with their decision."

"Thank God for that! So how did the meeting go?"

"Put simply, I think we can expect to receive a contract to sign by the end of this week."

"Plymouth Sound?" Patrick asked, incredulous.

"Yes, but not the hotel development. It's something new. I'll explain all when I see you in the office tomorrow. But be assured it's good news, Patrick. Really good news."

"Fantastic! Thank you, Luca. You're a mini marvel!"

"*Grazie*! I like to think so, Paddy."

"Right, I'd better give Sam a call and see if he'll pick me up at the airport."

"I can ask him for you if you like. He's here with me now. We're just driving through Richmond."

15

The journey down to Lewes was much less of a hassle than Katrina McDade had expected and far easier than travelling by car she realised as she stared out of the carriage window.

The view offered a reassuring reminder of the swathes of countryside that still lie between London and the south coast. Katrina wondered why there was such a severe housing shortage in the south-east of England when there was so much land still available for development.

While the journey should have been relaxing, Katrina didn't feel relaxed. Alice had noticed. She was sitting opposite her, facing the back of the train. She knew her mother only too well to expect anything less.

"You OK? You haven't spoken for miles, Mum."

"I'm sorry, Alice, I'm just a little preoccupied. I'm sure you can understand why."

About an hour after leaving Clapham Junction their train arrived at Lewes Station. And although the journey was relatively short, their impatience to reach Patrick's parents' house had made the time drag.

Immediately the train stopped Katrina and Alice hopped down onto the platform and dashed straight over to the taxi rank. Within another ten minutes they were being dropped off outside Brian and Philomena McDade's 1930's bungalow on the outskirts of the town. No sooner had Katrina rung the bell than the front door opened to reveal Patrick's parents huddling together in the hall, holding hands and smiling benignly.

"Katrina! Alice! Come on in. You must be tired after your journey," Brian McDade said warmly.

"We're in the sitting room, dear. Can I get you a cup of tea? Are you hungry? Perhaps you'd like something a little stronger, Katrina?"

"No, thank you, Philomena, we're both fine. We had plenty to drink on the train. Anyway, I think we're both pretty keen to hear what Cerin and Milo have to say."

"Come on through, then, we've been waiting for you," Philomena said, trying to sound bright and breezy.

The instant Katrina and Alice walked into the sitting room Cerin sprinted over and hugged them tightly.

"Oh, Mum, I'm so sorry, but you really need to hear what Milo has to say."

"Do I? I wonder about that, Cerin. Hello, by the way! And hello to you too, Milo."

"Hello, Mrs McDade," Milo replied, standing up.

"How many times, Milo? Please call me by my first name," Katrina scolded.

"Why don't we all sit down?" Philomena urged, ushering Katrina and Alice over towards a large paisley-print sofa. "And, Milo, if you're ready, please tell Katrina and Alice the story you told us earlier."

"If you're about to tell us what I think you're about to tell us, Milo, I think it's a pity you didn't come forward with this a bit sooner. It might have saved us all a hell of a lot of worry," Katrina said, struggling to control her mood.

"Well, we're all here now and there's no time like the present, Katrina. I think we should let Milo get on with it so we can hear his story before Patrick arrives," Philomena urged. "Sorry – please carry on, Milo."

Milo paused for a moment before speaking. He moved to the middle of the room, took off his thick-rimmed glasses and gave them a quick wipe on a tissue – his eyes blinking as if exposed to a sudden flash of sunlight.

"I'm sorry, Katrina. This isn't easy to explain and probably won't be what you were hoping to hear, but I'm the one who sent Patrick the Father's Day card, and it was also me who left the telephone message."

Milo looked down and drew a long, slow breath then peeked over to where Katrina was sitting. She said nothing, just sat with a blank expression gazing into space.

"To get to the point, Katrina, I think what Milo is trying to say is that he believes *he* is Patrick's son," Brian McDade said with gravitas – the news inviting a long pause.

"Wait a minute, Milo. Before you start sharing any more of your life story, I want to know why you thought to bring him *here*, Cerin? I'm your mother. Why didn't you two come and see me about this first?" Katrina demanded, leaning forward in her chair and glowering at them.

"Why do you think, Mum?"

"I don't know. I haven't a clue, Cerin. It's why I'm asking you now."

"Because I knew you'd react like this."

"Like what?"

"Like this. Angry. You're always angry. I was worried about your reaction and it seems I was right. In any case, Dad's not around and what Milo has to tell us is extremely disturbing. When he told me I didn't know what to say or do. Then I decided Milo should come and meet his grandparents. I knew they would listen and understand. They've always been there for Alice and I, and I thought they would know what to do."

"I'm sorry, Cerin, but you're not making much sense. None of this is making much sense."

"Katrina, it's OK. Let Milo explain. We're going to get this whole mess sorted out one way or another, and we're going to do it as a family," Brian McDade asserted.

"Fine!" Katrina muttered, leaning back into the depths of the sofa and folding her arms.

"Sorry, Milo. Where were we?" Brian McDade asked politely.

"Katrina, this whole thing, my story, that is, starts with my parents. Well, the couple I had always believed to be my parents. They were both GPs. They ... we ... lived near Kinsale in West Cork."

"Your accent's very subtle, Milo."

"It's flattened out a lot since I've been in London."

"Before, I thought you had a West Country accent, Milo, but then your voice did sound very muffled on the answerphone. How did you do that?"

"I put a hankie over the mouthpiece to disguise my voice. It's an old trick. I saw it done in a Humphrey Bogart movie once."

"But why?"

"At the time I thought it best to take things slowly. You know, take things step by step. I wanted to let you and Patrick get used to the idea that I existed before I made any approaches in person. I also wanted to ensure that you were the kind of people who would give me a warm reception and a fair hearing. I didn't want to turn up on your doorstep and frighten you half to death or have the door slammed in my face."

"Is that why you didn't leave your name and number?"

"Yes. I'm sorry but I wanted to retain an element of control to protect myself from any disappointment. That's why I phoned from a landline – calls from landlines are harder to trace."

"Very odd behaviour, Milo," Katrina said, rolling her eyes.

"Nevertheless, as I was saying, my parents doted on me and I loved them back in spades. I am, was, their only child and for years never had any reason to doubt that things would ever be any different. Then late one night, shortly after my seventeenth birthday, when my father was away at a medical conference, I came across my mother in floods of tears at the kitchen table. She was staring at an old photo of me as a baby. I tried to comfort her, but she was inconsolable and wouldn't tell me what was wrong. Understandably, the experience left me feeling very unsettled. Thereafter I could sense that she was struggling with something. I imagined that that something was guilt. The next time my father was away I took the opportunity to remind her of how she had been that night and told her how it had left me feeling worried and insecure. Before long she started to cry again. And that was when she told me. That was when it all came out."

Milo paused, bowed his head and raised his hands to his face.

"Oh, Milo!" Cerin cried, springing out of her chair and clasping him in her arms. "It's OK, Milo. It's OK," she purred gently while stroking his hair.

"I'm sorry, Cerin. It's all right, I'm fine. All the same, I think you can guess what's coming next," Milo mumbled.

Katrina closed her eyes and rocked her head.

"Please carry on, Milo," she sighed.

"Anyway, my mother confessed that whilst she loved me more than life itself I was, in fact, adopted."

"Good grief! How did the news affect you, Milo?" Katrina asked in a soft voice.

"It was a shock, but in a way I was half expecting her to say something like that, such had been her mood in the days before. And it kind of made sense. It explained a lot of my experiences of, and relationships with, other members of my family – my family in West Cork, that is – and the way they looked at me sometimes, the whispers and some of the things that were said. Also, compared to the parents of my school friends, my parents seemed a lot older. They were both in their early seventies when I was in my late teens. They would have been in their late seventies now."

"*Would have been*?"

"Yes, Katrina. They died a couple of years ago. They passed away within a few months of each other."

"I'm sorry to hear that, Milo. What happened to them?"

"Mum!" Cerin scolded.

"No, it's OK, Cerin. My father had a heart condition and my mother had an aggressive cancer. I guess they were both reasonably old but, still, I was heartbroken. By the time they passed away, however, I had got used to the idea that I was adopted and had come to terms with it. And once they were dead and I was left on my own, I started to wonder about my birth parents. Just occasionally at first, but then more and more as my head started to fill with the obvious questions like – who were they? Where were they from? What did they do? Did I have any siblings? I'm sure you can imagine."

"Yes, naturally."

"When my mum and dad died I inherited their house plus a tidy sum from their savings. I was going off to college in London and thought it best to rent the house out until I had a better idea what to do with it. As part of that process I had to dispose of a lot of their personal effects. It wasn't a very pleasant experience, as you can imagine. I was moving some stuff up into the attic – you know, bits and bobs I wanted to keep, like old photo albums and family videos when I found a manila folder with my name on. Inside were a load of papers, school reports, certificates, and so on – stuff about me that had been stored there for ages. Right at the back of the folder, I found a letter, handwritten on a piece of lined notepaper. It was addressed to me."

"Who was it from?"

"My birth mother."

"Really?" Alice gasped. "What did it say?"

"Judging from the date, she must have written it at the time of my adoption. I would have been a few weeks old. In brief, it said that she loved me very much, was terribly sad to have to give me up, but thought it was for the best."

"What did you think, Milo?" Katrina enquired.

"It blew my mind!" he exclaimed, before pausing and taking a deep breath. "It turns out that my natural mother was an Irish woman called Bernadette O'Sullivan. The note gave an address for her at the time of my birth and adoption."

"What's your birth year, Milo?"

"I'm twenty-three, Katrina, so 1995."

Katrina's expression changed. She looked downcast and close to tears. "That's a good year after Patrick and I married." She sighed, closing her eyes and shaking her head again. "What about your father? Did she name him in the note?" Katrina continued, sitting bolt upright as soon as the question came to mind.

"No, he wasn't mentioned."

"So what makes you think Patrick is your father?"

"I'm sorry, Katrina. I'll come to that shortly, I promise. Anyhow, the address she wrote at the top of the note was a Dublin address. It seems I was born in Dublin."

"Dublin?"

"Yes. As it turns out the address she gave is for an institution run by an order of nuns. It was one of what were known as the Magdelene laundries. A little bit of research told me that right up until the late nineties these institutions took in young girls who were unmarried and pregnant and placed their babies with couples wanting to adopt. This explains how I came to be adopted. And finding the letter only whetted my appetite for more information. Could my mother still be alive? Had she gone on to get married?"

"What did you do?"

"I flew to Dublin and went to find the Magdelene laundry."

"How did that go?" Alice asked.

"Not well. It wasn't a huge surprise that she wasn't there, but, annoyingly, the nun I talked to either couldn't or wouldn't give me a forwarding address."

"Then what?"

"The nun advised me to contact a government agency who could help trace my mother, which I did. Through an intermediary I then made two major discoveries. Firstly that, as far as records showed, my mother was still alive. And secondly, and most surprising, that I have a brother."

"A half-brother? A stepbrother?"

156

"No, a full brother, Katrina. A twin."

"What! You're a twin! Are you sure?"

"Yes."

"That's amazing, Milo!"

"Yes, it was a huge shock. I had no idea."

"Shouldn't you have been adopted together?"

"Yes! But it's probably harder to find couples who are prepared to take twins. The nuns were quite unscrupulous apparently, and from what I've gathered there were quite a number of illegal adoptions arranged by the order over the years. Sometimes they falsified birth certificates recording the adopting parents' names on the certificate rather than the birth parents."

"Really? Why would they do that?"

"I imagine it was a way of encouraging adoptions and to add an air of respectability for the adopting parents. Just shows how little they thought of illegitimacy."

"That's all highly illegal," Brian McDade sneered.

"It also appears the order were in the habit of taking babies away from their mothers and having them adopted whether the mothers liked it or not."

"Bloody hell, Milo! How cruel!" Katrina interjected. "Did the intermediary trace your mother?"

"No. They drew a blank there, sadly, but they managed to find my brother."

"Wow! Did you get in contact with him? Have you met him?"

"Yes, and that is why I sent the Father's Day card and left the message and that is why I am here."

"Why, Milo?"

"Because of what my brother had to say."

"What?"

"We met in January. My twin brother's called Theo, by the way—"

"What's Theo like? Are you identical?"

"No, Katrina. Not at all. And especially not in personality and temperament."

"Before you knew he existed, did you ever sense his presence, that he was there somewhere, somewhere in the background, you know, like twins sometimes do?" Alice queried.

"You mean if he were to stub his toe or something, could I feel it two hundred miles away? No, definitely not."

"How did you get to meet him?" Alice asked.

"The intermediary contacted Theo and told him about me, and since I'd shown an interest in meeting him, they asked if he wanted to meet up with me. The answer to that one, of course, was yes. They gave me his mobile number but explained that he would only respond to text messages."

"Where does he live?"

"At the time we met he was living in Dublin."

"And now?"

"I think he may be lying low somewhere in London or the south-east, Katrina."

"So how did the meeting go?"

"It was a disaster. We met in Dublin. I flew back specially. It was the first time I'd been over following my visit to the Magdelene laundry. Having been informed that Theo was happy to meet up, I sent him a text and arranged a rendezvous in a bar in the city centre, somewhere off Grafton Street."

"Were you nervous about meeting him?"

"Yes, Katrina, because I knew there was a real possibility it could lead to a reunion with my mother. To make things worse, though, Theo turned up half an hour late, which, as it turns out, is typical. However, when he walked into the pub, I spotted him immediately. There's a family resemblance you couldn't miss. He's small and slight like me and he's got similar features. But that's where the similarities end. For a start, I'm polite and sensitive. Theo? He's a bit of a hard nut and macho with it."

"Really?"

"Yes. And communicating with him isn't easy."

"Why's that?"

"He's deaf. Profoundly deaf."

"Since birth?"

"No, it developed in adolescence. It's something genetic, I believe."

"Can Theo speak?"

"Yes, but it's quite hard to understand what he's saying at first."

"Is he literate?"

"Yes, and he's an excellent lip-reader."

"How did you get on?"

"Not too well, I'm afraid, Katrina. I tried my hardest – he was my long-lost brother after all – but he was very agitated. He seemed angry with me, angry with our mother, angry with everyone. Turns out he didn't have the comfortable and caring upbringing I had. He was adopted by a couple in Dublin. Apparently he got it a bit rough. And when I say a bit rough, it seems that his adoptive parents slapped him about a bit."

"Och, the poor wee boy."

"Indeed, Mrs McDade. After that he was taken back into care and passed around from pillar to post. He had no settled home life and was moved from one institution to another. He told me he'd spent some time in a borstal – was caught drug dealing. Sadly that appears to have become his chosen career path judging by the wads of cash he had on him when we met. I think his childhood left a stain on his character. But, here's the thing, Theo had also tried to trace our mother through an intermediary a year or two before me. It turns out that he actually got to meet her."

"So why didn't the authorities put you in touch with her too?"

Milo suddenly became speechless and short of breath, then tears began to well in his eyes.

"I was too late. Theo broke the news in the bar. It was heartbreaking."

"Had she passed away?" Katrina asked, getting up and going over to hold Milo's hands.

"Yes. Theo told me that it wasn't long before our meeting. It turns out that I only just missed her. Apparently she was young – in her late thirties. So young, so very young. Suffice to say, it was a tragedy for her and a massive disappointment for me."

"I'm so sorry, Milo," Katrina said, giving his arm a gentle squeeze.

"What about Bernadette's parents? Did you find out anything about them?" Brian McDade enquired after a long pause.

"No, nothing. Bernadette was an orphan herself. She was orphaned as a child and taken in by the order. She worked in the laundry thereafter. The Magdelene laundries were pretty terrible places. Allegedly the nuns treated the girls in my mother's position like slaves. For them there was only hard labour, little freedom and practically no pay. If they left or ran away the police often brought them back. It was as if there was state collusion. Of course the nuns gave Bernadette a lot of grief when they discovered she was pregnant, but they helped her through the birth and later with the adoption."

"Sounds awful," Alice said.

"Give him his due, Theo was very emotional when talking about it."

"Where did he find your mother? Where was she living?"

"In sheltered accommodation close to the Magdalene laundry. He said she'd fallen on hard times."

"Is Theo bitter about his past, Milo?" Brian McDade asked.

"Yes. As I say, he was very angry when I met him. And that's why I am here – that's why I sent the card to Patrick, Katrina."

"Why?"

160

"To introduce myself and kick-off the process of getting to know you so that I could warn you."

"Warn us about what?"

"Warn you about Theo. I don't know what he's got planned exactly, but when I met him he issued a lot of threats."

"Threats? Why, what did he say?"

"That he wanted to make Patrick suffer like our mother had suffered. That he wanted to make Patrick's life a living hell. Stuff like that."

"When was this? When did you meet him in Dublin, Milo?"

"In January."

"January of this year?"

"Yes."

"So why didn't you get in touch with us before?"

"Because I didn't have any contact details. When we met, Theo simply said that our mother had told him that our father was called Patrick and lived somewhere in London. When I asked him if he had name and address details he said he had, didn't have them to hand but would text them to me later."

"Likely story!" Katrina said, tutting.

"Exactly. I could tell he was stringing me along. When the contact details failed to emerge, I came to the conclusion that he enjoyed being in control and liked the power that withholding the information gave him."

"With respect, your twin brother sounds like he's more than a little unhinged, Milo."

"Indeed, Mr McDade. And, because Theo kept banging on about how he would love to do this, that and the other to Patrick, I kept badgering him to send me the contact details he'd promised. Obviously, I wanted to reach out to you as soon as possible to warn you about him."

"So what happened?" Brian McDade asked.

"Having nagged Theo for Patrick's contact details for what seemed like ages, I eventually received a text message. It came with a couple of picture files attached. They were photos of an old business card. I guess Theo had either had a change of heart or felt he'd tortured me for long enough. The snaps of the business card gave me all the information I required."

"Who did the card belong to?"

"Theo explained in the text message that our mother had passed it on to him just before she died. She'd told him it had been given to her by the man who had slept with her and got her pregnant when she was a teenager."

"Milo, do you still have the photos Theo sent you on your phone?" Alice enquired.

"Yes. Here, I'll show you," Milo said, reaching into his pocket for his mobile and scrolling through the photo library till he found the images.

Milo paused as everyone moved in to get a better look. Brian McDade took Milo's phone and held it close to his glasses, shook his head and then passed it round to the others who stared with mouths agape once they'd seen the evidence for themselves – specifically the name in bold type which read: Patrick McDade, Quantum Design, and the East Sheen address and landline number centred underneath.

"What did you do next, Milo?" Katrina asked, her voice trembling.

"With the information gathered from the business card I went online and searched about a bit. I found Patrick on LinkedIn and then Facebook, which in turn led me to Cerin's profile on Instagram. I made contact with her and we clicked and, since we were both living in London, met up. Meeting Cerin was like finding the sister I'd always wanted – though I didn't tell her about my connection to Patrick, of course. I didn't tell her about Theo either. I didn't want to scare her. I wanted to bide my time, monitor the situation and be around to try and step in and stop Theo from doing anything too daft."

"When did you tell Cerin who you really are, Milo?" Katrina asked.

"Last night. I had to sooner or later. Theo's stopped responding to my calls and texts and there's been no trace of him on social media for weeks, but I'm sure he's in London."

"Do you think he had anything to do with what happened to Simba?"

"I don't know, but when I heard about Simba I was shocked and decided that the time had come to step out of the shadows and warn you about him. Try to get him stopped in case he was planning on doing something similar or worse."

"You left the telephone message *before* Simba was killed."

"Yes. Because of the threats Theo made when I met him in Dublin, I knew I should get in touch, but I was going to do it in stages. You know, so you could get used to the idea that Patrick might have an illegitimate child ... or two! The Father's Day card and the telephone message were the first steps, but the situation became a lot more urgent once Simba was killed."

"So what does Theo want, Milo? What would it take to stop him – money?" Brian McDade asked.

"I don't know, maybe."

"How much do you think?"

"Oh, one moment, Brian! There's the front door!" Philomena said, jumping up.

16

"Taxi for McDade! Taxi for McDade! Oh, but why the long face, sir?"

"Bloody hell, Sam! It doesn't get any easier, does it? I like your sign, by the way," Patrick McDade said, nodding at the piece of card Sam was holding across his chest with *Healy Cars for Mr McDade* scrawled in black felt pen.

At least it was sunny at Heathrow when Sam Healy arrived to collect his passenger, though Patrick's mood was somewhat subdued following three days of bitter disappointment and abject failure. But his spirits were lifted when he caught sight of Sam Healy's warm smile on reaching the exit to the labyrinth of corridors and staircases lying between the plane and the arrivals concourse in Terminal 5.

"So where are we off to?" Sam enquired, as they made for the multistorey car park.

"Sussex, Sam. My parents' place in Lewes. I've been beckoned by my mother. I imagine Katrina's there already."

"Sounds fun."

"I doubt it, Sam. No one in my family's talking to me at the moment. It seems I'm in the doghouse. I don't know what crime I've committed, but I'm sure we'll find out soon enough."

"It wouldn't be a surprise party, would it? When's your birthday, Patrick?"

"Next month."

"There you go, then!"

"If it's a party, you're welcome to come in and join us, but I think it'd be best if you just drop me off and head back to

Sheen, Sam. I don't know whether I'm going to be there for ten minutes, an hour or all night, and it'll be easy enough for me to catch a train back to London when I'm finished."

"It's OK, Patrick, I'll wait for you. I've always fancied taking a stroll around Lewes."

"Why? What's so special about Lewes, Sam?"

"I hear the locals have a long tradition of burning people at the stake."

"They have, Sam, but it's been at least five hundred years since they last set fire to anyone."

"No worries, then. All the same, it's a pleasant evening, Patrick. I'll have a snoop around the town and get a bite to eat. Call me when you want to go home."

*   *   *

By the time they pulled up at Patrick's parents' bungalow, the sun was setting behind the downs and night was falling fast. The downstair's lights were already on in the house.

Patrick tiptoed across the lawn towards the sitting room at the front, confident that his family wouldn't be able to see him peering in from the garden because of the light reflecting back off the windows inside.

The flames from the wood-block fire his father liked to burn at almost any time of year flickered a warm glow across the room. They were all there as expected: Katrina, Cerin and Alice, his mother and father and Milo, who was pacing the room talking ten to the dozen and waving his hands in the air as if giving some kind of pep talk. Patrick tried to gauge the mood from their expressions. They all looked straight-faced and serious. Their body language was easy to read. No one was laughing. No one was smiling. Patrick gulped.

He turned away and crept back across the lawn till he reached the footpath, took a deep breath, stepped into the porch and pressed the doorbell. Rocking backwards and forwards on his heels, he ran his fingers through his hair, straightened his back

165

and waited for the distinctive clomp of his father's footsteps. Shortly, a blurred figure loomed in the frosted glass.

"Ah, Patrick, you'd better come in. We've been waiting. Everybody's in the lounge," Brian McDade said wearily before giving his son a brief hug. Patrick smiled, squeezed past and ambled down the hall without speaking.

Five faces stared up at him, tight-lipped and silent, as he entered the sitting room. Patrick made his way over to the upright piano on the far side, turned and perched himself on the edge of the music stool so that he was facing the others. Brian McDade sat in between Katrina and Alice on the sofa. Cerin and Philomena were leaning forward in the two matching armchairs either side, while Milo remained standing in the middle of the room with his arms folded.

"W-w-would someone like to tell me w-w-what's going on, p-p-please?" Patrick stammered breathlessly, glimpsing from face to face searching for a reaction. "You've got me really worried."

"OK, Milo. I believe it's time for you to introduce yourself properly. I think you've been waiting long enough for this moment," Brian McDade urged in a friendly tone.

All heads swivelled towards Milo. Patrick tried to catch Katrina's eye, but it was as if she were in a trance. She wasn't for paying him any attention or giving him any reassurance, no matter what. There was a long pause as Milo gathered his wits and chose his words. He swallowed hard.

"This isn't going to be easy to explain, Patrick, but I'm the person who sent you the card, the Father's Day card, and left you the telephone message."

Milo glanced down, back up and across to Patrick again, expecting a reaction. Patrick said nothing.

"I think Milo is trying to tell you that he believes he is your son, Patrick," Brian McDade announced grandly.

"I-I-I know, Dad. I kind of gathered that, thank you," Patrick replied, nodding sarcastically. "But why didn't you

166

come and talk to me about this before, Milo? W-w-why did you have to send me that stupid card? It put the fear of God into Katrina and me."

Milo looked down to avoid eye contact, tongue-tied.

"Milo, would you like to explain to Patrick a little more about who you are and where you're from, please?" Brian McDade urged in a genial tone.

"B-b-before you do that, Milo, perhaps you could let us know what happened to Simba!" Patrick said, making a sudden lunge towards Milo. A move that necessitated Brian McDade spring to his feet and get between them.

"Sit down, Patrick! Sit down! You've got this all wrong!" Brian McDade barked. "None of that was Milo's doing. Please, give the lad a chance and hear him out," he added in a calmer voice once he was sure Patrick was backing off.

"What's he doing here, Dad? And why are we doing this in your house?"

"It was my idea," Cerin replied. "I thought Milo should come and meet his grandparents. I thought they would give him a fair hearing. And they have as much right as you do to find out what's been going on, Dad."

"Yes, well, all the same, thanks very much for coming to see me first, Milo," Patrick said, frowning and then stomping back to his seat.

"We might have done, but Milo's story has come as a bit of a shock to us all. Especially when we found out that he is barely a year older than me. I don't think I need to spell out the implications of that, do I? It's left us all feeling more than a little let down, to be honest, Dad," Cerin continued.

"Who by – *me*?"

"Of course! And I felt that the least I could do for Milo was bring him somewhere he could explain his story without interruption or contradiction."

"I see. And this, this gathering, I guess it's supposed to be some sort of intervention, is it? Do please let me know at which point I can argue my case for I know absolutely nothing about any of this and would like to declare myself innocent of all charges. In the meantime, why don't you fill us in, Milo? Please *do* carry on." Patrick said raising a hand and gesturing theatrically.

*   *   *

"Thank you, Milo," Brian McDade said politely when Milo had finished retelling his story.

"Can I see the photos on your phone, please?" Patrick asked when Milo brought up the matter of the business card.

"Of course. But it is yours, isn't it? There's no doubt about that, is there?" Milo said, handing Patrick his iPhone.

Patrick studied the image of the front of the card carefully. Before long he raised his eyebrows, blew out his cheeks and turned to Milo, "How was Bernadette so sure that the man who handed her this card was the man who got her pregnant?"

"I asked Theo the same question. He came right back at me and said that she knew damn well it was the man who gave her the card because she lost her virginity to him. And, it might sound odd in this day and age, but she also claimed that he was the only man she ever slept with. I think opportunities to fraternise with men were few and far between at the laundry."

"Dublin 1995, Patrick. You were there. I clearly remember you going." Katrina sighed.

"So?"

"So you were in the right place at the right time. You were in Dublin. You met Milo's mother, slept with her and gave her your card. You probably fancied going back for more. There's no other explanation, Patrick," Katrina said, with anger rising in her voice.

"But I have no memory of this happening. I'm sorry, but I have no memory of ever meeting your mother, Milo. None.

Since I married Katrina I have NOT had sexual intercourse with any other woman. I've not so much as held another woman's hand. And if she had my card, why didn't she contact me when she found out she was pregnant?"

"I don't know. That's been bothering me too. Though it's possible that she wouldn't have had a mobile phone back then and might not have had access to a landline at the laundry either. Maybe she tried your office number. Maybe she found out you were married. Maybe she found out you already had babies. Maybe she did what she thought was best for Milo at the time."

"OK, Katrina, let's slow things down a bit, shall we?" Patrick said, standing up and striding into the middle of the room as if it were a court and he the counsel for the defence. "Milo, what *are* you doing here? If you are who you say you are, that would make you Cerin's half-brother. Is it just a coincidence that you've been hanging out with her all this time? It seems very odd to me. Can you explain that?"

"It's to do with meeting Theo. As I said earlier, Patrick, my expectations of him were sky-high, but then he put the fear of God into me."

"How?"

"It was what he was saying, Patrick. What he said he planned to do. That he was going to track you down and make your life hell. He said he wanted revenge for what he and our mother had suffered. That's why I felt I had to get in touch with you. It was only after weeks of pestering Theo for contact details that he finally sent me the photo of the business card. And that's why I befriended Cerin on Instagram. I thought it would open a line of communication. I thought it offered a way to get to know you so that when the time was right, I could warn you about him. And that's why I'm here and that's what I'm doing right now."

"OK, Milo. This business card. Please listen carefully as what I am about to say is important," Patrick said, taking a deep breath and pausing for a moment. "As it happens, I remember this card very clearly."

"What?" His father said, cupping a hand to his ear.

"This card. I remember it, Dad," Patrick said, annunciating with care.

"You should do. It's yours, you pillock."

"No, Katrina. I've had heaps of cards over the years and plenty I wouldn't be able to recognise or recall, but I remember this one because of where we were with the business at the time it was printed," Patrick continued, his demeanour brightening a little.

"Actually, I remember it too," Katrina added begrudgingly.

"The reason I remember this card is because it was our first. It's the very first business card we produced."

"So?"

"Well, we'd just started the practice."

"It was only four weeks after our wedding."

"Yes, Katrina, and back then, in the early days, we rented that small office on the Upper Richmond Road in Sheen. It was above one of the shops on the high street. Do you remember, Kat?"

Kat nodded slowly, her eyes closed in thought.

"We were low on funds and bootstrapping the business. Therefore, when Luca designed the card, we decided to save a bob or two by not getting them personalised for all the staff. We did a short print run of a couple of hundred and, since I was doing most of the promotion and client liaison, we only put my name on the first run. Check the address – Upper Richmond Road. We were there for less than two months. It wasn't long after, when we'd completed a couple of commissions and had some money coming in, that we moved to the bigger offices in Richmond and could afford a second print run with personalised cards for everyone."

"Where is this leading us, Inspector Clouseau?"

"The thing is, Kat, there were times in those early days

when other people in the practice needed to carry a business card if, say, they were meeting a supplier or a prospective client or going anywhere where they might need to leave our contact details."

"So what are you saying?" Kat asked frowning.

"That I wasn't the only person using this card – the card with my name on it – at around that time."

"Yes, but you were the only person who went to Dublin in 1995, Patrick. I remember you flying over to do a talk at UCD and staying overnight," Katrina countered.

"UCD?" Brian McDade queried.

"University College Dublin, Dad. They have an architecture course. I was hoping I might get some part-time lecturing hours off the back of my presentation."

"But that's right, isn't it, you made that trip on your own?"

"Yes, Kat. I went alone. I wasn't alone the whole time I was there, though."

"I'm sure Milo's mum would attest to that."

"I doubt if she would, Katrina, because I didn't get to meet her."

"That's rather hard to believe, Patrick."

"Actually, Kat, I have a confession to make."

"Hallelujah! Please, please, just man up and put us out of our misery," Katrina said, throwing her hands in the air.

"No, it's not that."

"Then, what?"

"You know when I said I was going to Dublin to do a talk at UCD? Well, that wasn't the whole story."

"What the fuck else were you doing there, then?"

"OK, I *did* visit UCD, I *did* give my presentation to the students and I *did* make a few contacts with regard to part-time teaching – you know, anything to boost our turnover. So it wasn't a total lie. But, you see, when I was in Dublin, there was an international football match at Lansdowne Road. I was mad keen to go."

"What?"

"England were playing a friendly against the Republic of Ireland. An evening kick-off. It was the first match between them in Dublin for years. It meant staying overnight."

"So you went to a football match and stayed over. That puts you in the right city and at the right time to create young Milo here, doesn't it? That's not much of an alibi, is it?"

"No, it wouldn't be if I'd happened to go to the match on my own."

"Why? Who was there with you?"

"Luca."

"Luca?"

"Yes. He flew over in the afternoon."

"What!"

"It was his idea that we go to the match in the first place. For someone who claims to be Italian, it's odd that he's such an ardent England fan."

"And?"

"There was trouble at the match. England went a goal down in the first-half and also had a goal disallowed. Then it all kicked off when some of the England fans in the upper stands started ripping up the seating and chucking it down on the Irish fans below. The match was abandoned. Luca and I got split up in the melee as we were leaving the ground. I went back to our hotel and waited for him there."

"And?"

"He didn't turn up."

"Didn't turn up till when?"

"The next day, Kat."

"Is that true?"

"Of course it is. I didn't tell you about the football match before because I didn't think you'd approve of the expense when we were a bit strapped for cash."

"Still, why the hell should we believe you, Patrick?"

"Take a look at this other pic on Milo's phone," Patrick

said scrolling on to the next photo. "It's an image of the back of the business card."

"What about it?"

"See there? See those marks – the bold black lines?" Patrick asked, showing Kat the phone. "Hang on, I'll make the image bigger. Can you see them now?"

"Yes! That looks like a one ... And that could be a five. Fifteen, right?"

"They're not numbers, though, Kat. They're letters. I think that's a signature."

"Shit, I guess that could be an L, then, and I suppose that could be an S, Patrick."

"Yes, exactly. They're initials."

"Of course! L S – they're Luca's initials. Luca's! Bloody hell! But what does that mean?"

"Luca was always very arty when he was a student. A little bit affected too, shall we say? He was always fiddling about with his signature. You know, a bit like Prince."

"Prince?"

"The performer – remember? At one point he changed his name to an unpronounceable symbol."

"I don't understand."

"No, I doubt if Prince did either. But never mind."

"But why didn't Bernadette remember Luca's name?"

"A one-night stand? Too much to drink? Perhaps things got a bit hazy the next morning and then there was my name on the front of the card to confuse things. I don't know. So there you go, Milo. Luca, Luca Salvatore. I'm pretty sure *he's* your dad. Come to think about it, I *can* see a slight family resemblance and, like you, he wouldn't be one of the tallest people I know."

"I don't believe it! We shook hands at your parents' party!"

"Yes, I remember introducing you. Anyway, you're a lucky man. He's a good bloke, Milo. I should know, he's been my best friend for nearly thirty years."

"But what about Theo? He's out for blood, Patrick," Milo said, looking concerned.

"Well, we've got a name and a mobile number now, right, Milo?"

"Except I haven't been able to get hold of him on that number for weeks," Milo replied frowning.

"Have you got any photos of him on your mobile? Did you take a selfie when you met in Dublin?" Patrick asked, handing Milo back his iPhone.

Milo fiddled with his phone for a few seconds then held it up, his mobile displaying a shot of two heads nestling together: Milo and a young man who was his near double.

"I thought you said that you weren't identical twins?" Patrick said, taking Milo's phone and leaning back to get a better view. "You look pretty identical to me!"

"Apparently we're not. There are physical similarities, but I can assure you that there are plenty of differences too."

"Do you think Theo could have killed Simba, Milo?"

"I don't know, Patrick, but I don't think so. That could easily have been someone else's random act of unkindness."

"I guess when you're scared it's easy to get a little paranoid and develop a bit of a persecution complex. And by that measure, it clearly wasn't Theo who sabotaged our deal with Cygnet House or who was shooting at us with an air rifle at Plymouth Sound."

"Patrick! You didn't tell me about that!"

"Right, I'll call DI Baxter first thing in the morning," Patrick said, ignoring Katrina's protest. "Even if Theo's discarded his old phone, we should have enough information to help the police track him down. Here's my current business card, Milo, complete with my mobile number. Could you zap me over that photo of the two of you, please," he added.

"No problem," Milo replied tapping away. "What about Luca, Patrick? What do you think I should do?"

"I'll be seeing him in the office tomorrow, Milo. Would you

like me to have a word with him and break the news? I think it might help. I'll give you a call as soon as I've spoken to him. Then we can make arrangements for you two to meet."

"Really?"

"Yes. I'm sure he'll be thrilled once the idea sinks in."

"Do you think so?"

"Yes, of course! He's got a son now – two! Why wouldn't he be? I'll know for sure once I've spoken to him, but he's a soppy individual, Milo. I think he'll be fine."

"Thanks, Patrick."

"Before we go any further, I would like to propose that you all stay here tonight," Philomena suggested. "There's plenty of room and you'll be safe here – we're so tucked out of the way."

"I'm sorry, Mum, but I need to get back to London and I'm sure Katrina will want to come back with me too," Patrick replied.

Katrina nodded.

"Why don't you girls stay here and have a sleepover? You too, Milo," Patrick added.

"That would be lovely," Philomena said gleefully. "And how are you going to get home?"

"Sam's here. He'll drive. But first ... Katrina, don't you have something you'd like to say to me?" Patrick said with a smirk.

"No. Why?"

"I thought you might want to apologise for having doubted me, or are you just too mad at me for staying over in Dublin to go to a football match rather than coming straight home?"

Patrick McDade barely had time to finish the sentence before Katrina jumped up, wrapped her arms round his neck and kissed him full on the lips.

"You go and watch football whenever the hell you like, Patrick McDade," she said with the broadest of grins.

"The football match, Patrick?"

"Yes, Dad. What about it?"

"Who were you supporting?"

"Who do you think?"

"Oh, that's all right, then. And I hope you didn't throw anything back at the English lads."

"No, Dad. I didn't throw anything. I got out of the way pretty damn quick."

"Good. Now, how about a drink before you go – Katrina? Patrick?" Brian McDade asked as he drew the lounge curtains and sighed heavily.

"Is the Pope a Catholic?"

"Patrick!"

"Sorry, Mum," Patrick said grinning. "And what's with the sad face, Dad?"

"Oh, it's only that for a moment there I thought I'd gained a grandson but then, as it turns out, I've just lost two."

"Get on with you! You've got hundreds of grandchildren, Dad. You certainly don't need any more."

17

Sam Healy was sitting in a pub in Lewes town centre sipping his way through a pint of alcohol-free lager, trying to convince himself that he liked the taste.

It didn't seem that long since he'd dropped him off before a text arrived asking him to pick Patrick up again. Sam abandoned his half-drunk beer, happy in the knowledge that he would be able to enjoy a pint of the real thing in a couple of hours when he got home.

It only took Healy ten minutes to retrieve the Beetle and drive round to the McDade's bungalow in its sleepy cul-de-sac. He pulled up alongside the front gate and swung the driver's door open but, in doing so, failed to notice the figure in a black hoodie scurrying towards him from the McDades' front garden. Whomever the dark figure was didn't see the door swinging across his path until it was nearly too late, judging by the surprise writ large across his face. Sam was in the process of clambering out onto the pavement when the figure stalled and sidestepped the car door just in the nick of time.

"Sorry! You OK?" Sam yelled, as soon as he realised that he'd nearly knocked the young man over. The kid didn't reply.

As Sam scrambled out of the car and gathered his wits, he caught a glimpse of the young man's face. The youngster turned away and took off up the street, head down, hands in pockets and shoulders hunched. Sam looked up when he heard a car engine roar into life round the corner and watched as a souped-up Nissan Skyline scorched past the top of the road in a flash of metallic blue.

Never trust a man who drives a car with an aerofoil, Sam thought to himself.

On further reflection Sam thought he recognised the kid but couldn't bring a name to mind. He slammed the Beetle's door, locked it and started walking up to the house whereupon it struck him that the lad in the hoodie bore an uncanny resemblance to the kid he'd seen hanging out with Cerin in Sheen. What was his name? Ah, yes, Milo. That's the one. He looked just like him, but with a harder face and sterner disposition. The kid in the hoodie appeared world-weary and haunted, a face made more memorable by dark, piercing eyes. Sam thought little of it, but wondered what business the lad had at the McDades' house. Sam rang the doorbell.

"Sam Healy!"

"Hello, Mr McDade."

"Come on in, Sam. Patrick and Katrina are ready to go when you are, but would you like one for the road first?"

"No, thanks, Brian. I think we'd better get going, if that's all right with you."

"Sam! Thanks for coming to get us," Patrick bellowed from up the hall as Katrina and he strolled down to the front door grinning and holding hands with the rest of the family following in their wake.

Sam waited patiently as Patrick and Katrina bade their farewells sharing warm hugs and kisses all round.

*　　　*　　　*

"You two look very happy. I presume things went OK?" Sam asked to break a long silence. They were halfway home and conversation hadn't come easily.

"It was touch-and-go for a while back there, Sam, but, yes, in the end everything worked out fine. Turns out Patrick isn't quite the bastard I thought he was," Katrina replied.

"Oh, has this something to do with the Father's Day card by any chance?"

178

"Yes, Sam."

"So I take it you're in the clear, then, Patrick?" Sam asked smiling. "And if it's not you, who *is* the daddy?"

"You won't believe me when I tell you."

"By the way, who was the weird guy in the hoodie hanging about your parents' house?"

"Who?"

"The lad who was leaving as I arrived."

"I'm sorry, Sam – I don't know what you're talking about."

"There was a young guy in a hoodie. I nearly bowled him over as I was getting out of the car."

"What did he look like?"

"It was more *who* he looked like."

"Who's that, then?"

"Cerin's friend. Milo, is it? He's a dead ringer."

"Milo?"

"Yeah, though his face isn't as open and friendly."

"And you think you saw him leaving my mum and dad's?"

"Well, he was *definitely* legging it out of their front garden as I arrived."

"Are you sure, Sam?"

"Yes! I presumed he'd just left the house in a huff or something. He was dashing down the garden path as if he was trying to get away in a hurry. He didn't look very happy."

"Shit, Katrina!" Patrick said, sitting upright and turning towards her. You don't think—"

"No, it couldn't have been, Patrick."

"Couldn't have been who, Patrick? Katrina?"

"Theo, Sam."

"Who the hell's Theo?"

"Sam, you couldn't pull over for a second, could you?"

Sam turned off the dual carriageway at the next junction and stopped at the side of the road.

"OK, Sam, is this him?" Patrick asked, showing Sam the selfie of Milo and Theo.

"I couldn't be a hundred per cent certain. It was dark. But, yes, I'm pretty sure that's him – the bloke standing next to Milo, that is. It's those eyes. They're very dark and menacing. You wouldn't forget those in a hurry, would you?"

"Shit!"

"What are you doing, Patrick?"

"I'm phoning Luca, Kat."

"Why?"

"To warn him."

"Why? What can Theo possibly know?"

"If he was hanging around the house eavesdropping, he probably heard everything."

"How, Patrick? Theo couldn't have heard *anything*. He's deaf, for fuck's sake."

"Yes, but he could easily have been staring in the window."

"So what?"

"He can lip-read, Katrina!"

"How could he have seen what we were saying from outside?"

"We were in a brightly lit room. He was standing in the dark. It's a bay window. He could have sneaked around."

"Shit!"

"Thank God Sam bumped into him or we'd never have known," Patrick said, holding his iPhone up to his ear. "Shit! It's gone straight to answerphone. Bugger, that's typical of Luca. He never has the bloody thing switched on or charged."

"What about his landline, Patrick?"

"He lives on a bloody houseboat, Katrina."

"Does he have any neighbours?"

"Yes, but they all live on bloody houseboats too."

"Shit! What do you think we should do?"

"Head straight for North London. Regent's Park. God knows what Theo's capable of. I'll call DI Baxter and see what she can do."

"What about Milo?"

"I'll call him in a minute, Kat, and ask him to text Theo."

"But he said he can't get hold of Theo on his mobile."

"Yes, but it's worth trying!"

"OK, let's get going. I'll fire up Google Maps. What's Luca's postcode, Patrick?"

"Regent's Park Zoo should do it, Sam."

18

The canal system that runs through North London has created a unique environment – a subterranean world lush in vegetation and free of cars and buses; a rural idyll in stark contrast to the traffic-jammed streets of the metropolis above.

Luca Salvatore's houseboat was moored on the Regent's Canal where it meanders past Regent's Park Zoo before widening out into the Cumberland Turn; the quietest of backwaters and the calmest of havens.

His commute to the office in Richmond was short and simple, courtesy of the North London Railway Line. Luca had granted himself flexible working hours that meant he could avoid the expense of peak-period travel and the hassle of riding in overcrowded carriages. His one-mile stroll to Camden Road Station followed the canal's footpath the whole way and, at his destination, the walk from Richmond Station to the office led him through one of the more picturesque towns of South West London. Often he would take his bike with him should he fancy cycling round Richmond Park at lunchtime.

Luca found the journey life enhancing and one that most days put a smile on his face. It was a lifestyle he had established after much careful planning. Like his buildings, it was designed to be simple, cost-effective and achieved with the minimum of fuss. "Minimalism" was Luca Salvatore's watchword.

*   *   *

As soon as Sam Healy dropped him off at the office on their return from Plymouth, Luca began rustling up projects that he hoped would bring in some quick cash and be a viable alternative should the contract with Cygnet House not materialise. Working late into the afternoon he checked through their client lists and records of old design projects to prompt ideas. He also searched the Internet for invitations to tender and checked the websites of all relevant trade journals to see if there were reports of any building developments that might be of interest.

Around five o'clock he gathered the staff and broke the latest news about the hotel project in Plymouth. Luca also alerted them to the financial implications should events not turn out as expected and set them the task of delving for leads.

He was pretty tired by the end of his first afternoon back at work and glad when he felt he'd done a long enough shift to justify heading for home. Though he'd worked into the evening it was still sunny when he left the office, but by the time he was walking the last mile from Camden Road Station to his mooring night had fallen. It was a somewhat lonely trudge along the towpath in the dark, but one made more bearable by a rolled-up cigarette and the promise of a bottle of his favourite Italian red at home. The moment he got back to his houseboat Luca was going to grab a bottle and scramble up onto the cabin roof where he'd enjoy another roll-up and sip some wine whilst reclining in his lounger watching the comings and goings of the boats and barges along the canal.

His houseboat, *La Pintada*, had become a trusted and much-loved friend. Luca enjoyed the irony of being a designer of buildings built in stone and brick who preferred to live on a floating structure made mostly of steel.

La Pintada was a classic wide beam canal barge extensively restored and much cared for. The porthole windows evenly spaced along each side created a strong nautical flavour. A spartan bachelor pad, the living space was uncluttered being bereft of knick-knacks and with only a few pictures on view. The large sliding door to the aft let in plenty of daylight.

Luca's was a permanent mooring and although he thought of his houseboat primarily as a floating apartment, it was fully navigable and had, in its time, tackled various stretches of the Thames in good weather.

That Luca's barge was moored next to a public footpath had never left him feeling vulnerable to vandalism or crime. There was little to steal, in any case, since he bought and hoarded nothing. His simple routine and minimalist home were complemented by a disinterest in all things material. Luca liked to think he was refugee-ready for any emergency or eventuality. His escape plan comprised but two simple steps: slip the mooring and away.

Although Luca lived on the canal, the iron footbridge just behind gave easy access to Regent's Park Zoo on the nearside bank and the warren of streets leading up towards Chalk Farm on the other. Here the small parade of shops and a local pub, all within easy walking distance, served most of his needs. And although Luca might not have been able to hear or see the traffic up at street level, the road was only about a hundred yards away.

Luca would have been oblivious to the metallic blue Nissan Skyline parked in Princess Road on the far side of the bridge as he ambled the final stretch of his journey home, and that the car's driver, Theo Salvatore, had boarded *La Pintada*, picked the lock of the sliding door and gained access to the main living area.

Luca would also have been unaware that Theo had been riffling through his possessions in the dark for the last ten minutes in a frantic attempt to learn a little more of his quarry before their return from work. Luca would also have been unaware that Theo, unable to find anything of any value by the light of his iPhone's torch, was intent on carrying out a random act of vandalism to scare the living daylights out of him.

Theo rushed over to the cooker in Luca's galley kitchen and tried to switch on all four rings and leave the gas running with the intention of flooding the houseboat with propane – a noxious and heavy gas. But, like all modern cookers, the hob was equipped with the standard safety feature that doesn't allow the rings to be left on without being lit. Thinking quickly, he searched the galley area, found a sharp knife, yanked the stove forward, squeezed in behind and sliced the pipe where it connected to the oven from the gas cylinder, before shoving it back against the wall.

As the cooker quietly hissed and the room started to fill with propane, Theo took a last scavenge around the forward end of the living area looking for a souvenir of his visit before leaving. He paused when his eyes came to rest on a framed photo. Black-and-white, it featured a couple with a small boy sitting between them. He imagined the couple were the child's parents. Theo thought the boy looked like him. Yes, there was a definite resemblance. It stunned him for a second when he realised that the people in the photograph were probably his grandparents and the small boy – the man who he now believed to be his father – Luca Salvatore.

Rather than pacify him, the photograph filled Theo with renewed rage. He could feel the blood pumping in his ears, his fingers tightening into fists. He smashed the frame on the sideboard, pulled out the print, stuffed it in his pocket and turned to leave, growing nervous lest he be caught on the premises. Suddenly, he heard feet clomping on the deck outside and the door being slid open. Theo ducked down behind the nearest armchair but found that he had to gasp as the propane gas, which had been flooding the room from the floor up, had already reached knee height. At the sound of a first footstep stomping inside the room he cursed that the kitchen knife wasn't to hand. Shutting his eyes, he waited for the lights to be switched on and gulped when he realised the disastrous consequences should this create a spark. Then the lights were on and nothing happened. Theo sighed with relief. But a momentary respite.

Gathering his wits, he rose onto his haunches and glimpsed over the back of the chair wincing the moment he saw Luca trying to strike a match to rekindle his roll-up. Before Theo could shout a warning, the match was alight, the roll-up was lit and the match was being waved about to extinguish it, but too vigorously, as, still aflame, it slipped from Luca's grip and fell to the floor. The effect on the propane cloud was instant and explosive.

The last Theo remembered of being on the houseboat was the surprise of being able to hear the sound of the blast and of the blinding brightness of the flames. That he was braced and standing behind a heavy object allowed him to resist the initial shock wave. Luca, however, was standing in closer proximity to the source of the explosion and was fortunate that the blast threw him backwards with such force that he was hurled through the open door and into the canal; the water dousing his burns and bringing him round.

Theo, on the other hand, was engulfed in a fireball of burning gas. Transformed into a tottering inferno with his clothing and hair in flames, he staggered through the smoke-filled cabin with his arms outstretched heading towards the opening where the sliding door had been and from where he could now sense fresh air and the possibility of escape. Theo kept lurching forward until he toppled over the edge of the houseboat, plunging into the canal and creating a tall column of steam. It wasn't long before pandemonium broke out along the canal; the cutting soon reverberating with the sound of sirens, screams and shouts.

*   *   *

"Shit!"
"What, Sam?"
"Fire!"
"Where?"
"Over there! Towards the canal, Patrick!"

186

"Christ almighty! What the hell's that?"

"I don't know, but it doesn't look too good," Sam replied as he reached the top end of Princess Road, pulled over and parked. "Fuck! See that car? I think that's Theo's," Sam added, nodding towards the blue Nissan Skyline.

"You sure?"

"Yes, I saw him drive away from your mum and dad's in it earlier. Drove right past me, he did. I'm sure it's the same one. They're pretty distinctive."

The three of them ran across Prince Albert Road and down towards the canal. As they approached the footbridge, Patrick grabbed Katrina by the wrist, stopped her in her tracks, puffed out his cheeks and raised his palms as if to gesture for her to slow down and take care.

"Patrick, I know I'm not Wonder Woman, but there's no need to be so fucking patronising," she snarled before brushing past him and running on towards the bridge.

By the time Patrick caught up with Katrina and Sam they had paused at the far end of the footbridge and were staring down over the canal and the remains of Luca's houseboat – a flickering ruin. There was little left of the superstructure above the waterline and what there was was still smouldering. DI Baxter was standing on the footpath below them, her right arm in a sling. She was watching as a team of paramedics attended to the two dark and bedraggled figures stretched out on the bank beside her. The medics' faces were illuminated by the last of the flames, while nearby a fire crew directed a water hose onto the embers.

From the road beside the zoo up above, emergency vehicles flashed bright blue light across the canal in intermittent sweeps, both macabre and dramatic. The scene reminded Patrick of the portrayal of the Mekong Delta in *Apocalypse Now*. He half expected Marlon Brando to rise from the water murmuring, "*The horror! The horror!*" but didn't care to share the thought.

"I-I-I don't bloody believe this!" Patrick yelled.

"Do you think it was Theo?"

"Who else, Katrina? Of course it was him. He couldn't have arrived long before us. Shit, we could have stopped him if only we'd got here sooner."

As they hurried down onto the towpath to check on Luca, DI Baxter turned towards them.

"Mr and Mrs McDade," she mumbled in an emotionless monotone. "We heard it, we saw it, but unfortunately didn't get here in time to prevent it."

"Luca?"

"Your friend on the houseboat?"

"Yes. How is he, Detective Inspector?"

"He's in shock. He has some burns but apparently they're not life-threatening. They'll need to take him in and check him out but say he's going to be OK."

"Th-th-thank God!"

"What about Theo?" Katrina asked.

"Not so good, Mrs McDade. It's not for me to speculate, but things aren't looking so rosy for him, I'm afraid."

"And was it Theo, Detective Inspector? Did he do this?"

"There will have to be a thorough investigation, Mr McDade but, strictly off the record, it appears that he may well have been responsible, yes."

"I guess none of us expected that he would go quite this far, Detective Inspector."

"It's certainly hard to recognise him as the innocent-looking lad in the selfie you sent me."

"Does he match any of the faces on the CCTV footage you wanted me to look at?"

"No, I don't believe so."

"I'm kind of surprised," Patrick said, shrugging. "How do you think he did it, Detective Inspector?"

"It's a little early to be sure, but the fire brigade believe there was a gas leak – I imagine it was deliberate. Then, one spark and the whole thing went up."

"Shit, poor old Luca."

"Exactly, Mr McDade."

"Do you think we could talk to him?"

"It's not up to me, Mr McDade, but I'll ask for you," DI Baxter said before turning to walk the few yards to where Luca was stretched out. She came back and nodded but gestured caution. Patrick, Katrina and Sam squeezed past and approached the spot where Luca was being treated.

"How is he?" Patrick whispered, catching the attention of one of the paramedics as he crouched down beside them.

"Is he asking how I am? Ask him how he'd feel if someone had just blown up *his* fucking houseboat with him on board." Luca moaned.

The paramedic shrugged.

"He's having a bit of trouble with his hearing at the moment, hence the shouting. It was the blast. It should come back soon enough, though," the paramedic muttered as she worked away.

"What about the other guy?" Patrick asked, then glanced up when he heard Katrina sobbing and twisted round in time to see a couple of paramedics carrying Theo away on a stretcher.

"What? What's up?" Luca said, trying to raise his head. He grimaced but was in good enough shape to shrug off the attempts of the paramedics to keep him lying flat. "Who the fuck *is* that bastard, anyway?" Luca shouted, staring at Patrick and overcompensating for his loss of hearing.

"That's Theo, Luca."

"Who? Who's that? What? Oh, I know, don't tell me, that's your bloody stalker. It is, isn't it? Your fucking errant son. What's his fucking gripe with me?"

"Och, we'll tell you all about it later," Patrick said, then peered round at Katrina for support.

"There's time enough, Patrick. There's time enough to tell him yet," she murmured. "What about Milo? Who's going to break the news to him?" she whispered into Patrick's ear.

"I'll tell Milo. Don't worry, Katrina, I'll tell him," Patrick whispered back.

A stretcher was brought for Luca. Once he'd been carried up to street level DI Baxter ambled over to address Patrick's small group.

"I'll need to talk to the three of you shortly. I have to take statements from each of you and record all that you know about this event and the circumstances leading up to it. I'll also need to take a statement from your friend, Mr Salvatore, at some point too, but I think we can leave that for now. I'm presuming from what you've already told me that Mr Salvatore is still unaware of his connection to the suspected perpetrator of this crime? That's correct, isn't it?"

"Yes, he doesn't know anything about that yet."

"If that is the case, and since this is a particularly sensitive matter, perhaps you should have a chat with Mr Salvatore first thing tomorrow and put him in the picture before I arrive to speak to him, Mr McDade?"

"Yeah, I think you're right, Detective Inspector. Thank you."

"Another thing, Mr McDade. The local police tell me that the press have been on to them. I'm surprised there's no one here to sniff out the story already but I imagine that once they've got your address and phone number they may well contact you. My advice is, if asked, say nothing. My expectation is that until charges are brought this story won't be very big news. We'll see. But be prepared for some attention and, possibly, some awkward questions."

"Thanks for the warning, Detective Inspector."

"Patrick, if they'll let you, why don't you go to the hospital in the ambulance with Luca? Sam and I can follow by car."

"Yeah, good idea, Katrina."

19

Patrick McDade wanted to arrive at the Chelsea and Westminster Hospital as early as possible the next morning. He was eager to fill Luca in about Theo well before DI Baxter came to take his statement.

"You'd have thought there might have been something about the fire in the news this morning, Patrick," Katrina said at the wheel as they drove through West London.

"Maybe DI Baxter was right, Kat."

"What?"

"That it's of no more interest than your average house fire."

Patrick and Katrina found Luca propped up in bed in a side ward. He'd been kept in overnight for observation. He looked pale and tired but Patrick sensed Luca was suffering from shock as much as from any physical injury.

"What the fuck's going on, Paddy?"

"Has DI Baxter been in to see you yet, Luca?"

"No, you're my first visitors."

"How's your hearing?"

"There was a terrible ringing in my ears for most of the night. I hardly slept a wink."

"And now?"

"Much better, thank God."

"Do you know what happened, Luca?"

"Only that your bastard son – what's his name?"

"Theo."

"Only that Theo blew up my fucking houseboat with me on board. What else is there to know, Patrick?"

"Not much, I suppose."

"I've absolutely no idea why he targeted me, Paddy. Do *you* know? I've never even met the guy. I mean, what the fuck have I ever done to upset him? Why would he want to destroy my home? All the same, I got the impression that he was quite badly injured in the process."

"How do you know?"

"Because I saw him as he was being fished out of the canal. He looked like he was in a pretty bad way."

"What about you? Are you all right? How are your injuries?"

"I think I got off quite lightly, thank the Lord. Just a few cuts and bruises. I've got some burns on my face and arms, but they're quite superficial. They say I could be getting out of here by lunchtime with any luck. First thing tomorrow at the very latest."

"Do you have anywhere to go, Luca?"

"No, Katrina."

"Good, you can come and stay with us, then. And you know you're welcome to stay as long as you like. It's not as if we're short of space or anything."

"*Grazie mille*. I'd like that very much. That's a great comfort."

"Good! OK, I'm going to get myself a coffee. Can I get you anything? Luca?"

"No, I'm fine, thanks, Katrina."

"Patrick?" Kat asked, straddling the door, half in and half out of the room.

"I'll take an Americano, please, Kat."

"Good. I'll be back in ten," she said, before slipping away.

Her departure created a pause not easily filled with casual conversation. Both men were aware there was an elephant in the room that needed addressed.

"Before the gas exploded, Luca, did you have a chance to confront Theo?" Patrick asked, breaking the silence.

"No."

192

"Did you get to talk to him at all? Did he say anything?" Patrick continued, leaning forward and placing a hand on Luca's arm. "Did he say anything to you before the explosion?"

"No, not a word. I was surprised when I found the door unlocked and wary about entering, but I didn't see him. I didn't know he was there. He must have been hiding somewhere. I only realised he'd been on board when he plopped into the water beside me. Fuck, Patrick! He nearly landed on my bloody head."

"And what do you know about him, Luca?"

"Nothing at all. He's a complete stranger to me. Seeing him bobbing up and down in the canal was the first time I'd ever clapped eyes on him. All I know about him is that he's called Theo and appears to be the creep that's been stalking you – your illegitimate son. Oh, wait a minute! There's more to this though, isn't there? Or why else would you be sitting on the side of my bed asking me stupid questions? OK, Patrick, what the fuck's going on?"

"It's Theo, Luca."

"What about him? He's your bastard son, right?"

"As it turns out, no. No, he isn't. Apparently he's not related to me in any way at all."

"Then why has he been making your life a misery? I'm presuming it was Theo who's been following you around causing mayhem."

"That's what I want to talk to you about, Luca. You see, the whole thing's been a case of mistaken identity."

"Really? So who is he, then? Where's he from?"

"He's Milo's twin brother. He's from Dublin. They both are. Well, they both *were* originally."

"What! He's Milo's twin? How the fuck does that work? Is Milo involved in this too? Oh, please don't tell me Milo was involved in wrecking my barge."

"No, Luca, not at all. Milo came forward yesterday and fully identified himself to us. He wanted to warn us about

Theo and the threat he posed. Milo did all he could to stop him."

"Well, he didn't do a very good job, did he?"

"He tried, Luca."

"This is nuts!"

"Luca, we need to talk about Theo," Patrick said assertively.

"What about him?"

"His condition. Things aren't looking too good for him, I'm afraid. There's a chance he might not make it."

"Shit."

"Exactly," Patrick mumbled, standing up and stepping over towards the venetian blinds – old, plastic and yellowing. He peeked through to check the view. The hospital car park. "I tried to warn you about him, but I couldn't get hold of you. Couldn't get you on your mobile."

"What do you mean *warn me*? Why did you think you needed to warn *me*?"

"We were all at my parents' place last night. Sam found Theo hanging around in the front garden. When Theo saw Sam, he took off without speaking. We were pretty sure he was going to head your way and were worried what he might do when he found you."

"How did he know where I live?"

"I don't know – the net? He's probably done a bit of research on all of us, Luca."

"I don't understand. How did *you* know where he was heading? Why would he want to do anything to hurt me?"

"It's complicated but we think he found out something about you that upset him."

"Found out what, for God's sake? From whom – from Milo?"

"Yes, and it's something I need to talk to you about. Like now. Right now."

"This sounds ominous."

"Yes, and it involves *this*," Patrick said, passing Luca his iPhone that was displaying the photo of the business card.

Patrick ran through Milo's story but kept checking Luca's expression to make sure he wasn't getting too distressed.

"So the long and the short of it is that Milo and Theo are twins and I'm their father?"

"Yes, that's about the size of it, Luca."

"Fuck me, that's crazy! How mad is that?"

"I thought you'd be surprised."

"*Surprised*? I just never ... Och, never mind."

"What?"

"I just never imagined that I'd have children. Up until today, and since my parents passed away, I have been totally alone. Sure, there are some distant cousins back in Italy, but I have no siblings and no heirs. I'm the last of the Salvatores."

"There you are, Luca. You've got two sons, you've got two heirs and you're not the last of the Salvatores after all. Congratulations!"

"Shit! It's a fuck of a lot to take on board, Patrick. It's hard to believe. But I do remember that night in Dublin – the night of the football match – and I remember giving the girl, Bernadette, my card. The card on your iPhone."

"Err, that's my card!"

"Yep, but it had our joint contact details printed on it. That was the point, wasn't it? The landline at work was the only contact number I had then. I'm sure I must have explained that to her and about how the name on the card wasn't mine. I'm damn sure I would have told her my name, Patrick!"

"Perhaps, but it's pretty obvious the message didn't get through or got forgotten, Luca. I bet you both enjoyed a good few bevvies that night. I'm sure that wouldn't have helped you get your story straight."

"Possibly, but I'm sure I would have tried."

"Still, it just shows, you shouldn't go around handing out other people's business cards willy-nilly."

"I didn't, Patrick. There was clearly a misunderstanding. I was simply trying to give her my number."

"In case she ever happened to be in London, I suppose. Well, maybe you should have been a bit more careful. Those cards were for business contacts not for friends of special interest."

"I must have given her the card because I liked her. I didn't know I'd got her pregnant."

"It happens, you dipstick. Contraception. It's your responsibility too, Luca."

"But if I'd known about the twins, I might have been able to do something. I could have helped. Who knows how things might have turned out?"

"She wouldn't have been able to find you, though, would she? All she had was that card with my name on it. If she called the office and asked for me – the name on the card that is, the name she probably thought was yours – she wouldn't have had to ask too many questions to find out that I was married. That would have been enough to put her off there and then, poor girl."

Luca lay back, rested his head on the pillows and gazed at the ceiling. After a brief pause he leaned forward.

"What about Milo, Paddy?"

"What about him?"

"Do you think he'll want to see me?"

"Yes, I'm sure he will, Luca. Almost definitely."

"Does he know about Theo's injuries? Does he know he's in here?"

"Yes. I called him last night. He was staying with Cerin at my parents' place. He said he'd like to visit Theo this morning. I think he's due here soon. When I spoke to him he said he was going to come down on the train first thing."

"Is he OK? Is he upset about Theo?"

"I don't know. They're not that close. They weren't brought up together or anything. They met earlier this year. I think that was the first and last time that they've ever been in each others company."

"Shit, what a mess, Patrick. And you really think I should meet Milo?"

"Yes, when you're ready. I think he'd only be too glad to meet you. I'll go and try and find him and see if he'll come and visit you now if you like. This room's nice and private. No one will bother you in here."

There was a light knock on the door. Katrina was standing outside brandishing two coffees.

"DI Baxter's here, Patrick. I think she'd like a word with Luca."

"Do you want to get that out of the way, Luca? She needs to take a statement from you about last night."

"Sure. Better had, Paddy."

"We'll pop back in a while when you've finished. In the meantime, I'll keep an eye open for Milo."

"Yeah, no problem. And you *really* think I should talk to him?"

"Yes! How many more times! Of course you should. He's your son, for God's sake!"

20

It wasn't until eight the next morning that Theo regained consciousness. He was relieved when he found himself tucked up in bed in a strange room, which immediately suggested that he was getting medical attention and being cared for.

He opened his eyes and turned his head, searching for clues to confirm that he was in hospital, but found his vision impaired by layers of loose bandage and his concentration compromised by the sedative dripping into his arm. All in all it felt as though he'd been stuffed into a potato sack full of cotton wool.

Theo forced his head forward till his chin was resting on his chest and peered down. The wires and sticky patches he noticed slapped across his torso told their own story. Twisting his head he spotted a tube attached to his arm.

It brought him some relief and offered a little hope to think that he was being looked after. For Theo, being looked after was a rare luxury. He might even have relaxed if it weren't for his memory of the previous night on the canal, the fire and the implications of having been caught red-handed.

Over and above the lack of feeling in his extremities there was a tube clipped to the side of his mouth to help with his breathing, but making it difficult to swallow. Every breath was laboured, noisy and painful; the effort sapping his stamina and leaving little energy for thought or contemplation. Inevitably Theo began to drift in and out of consciousness.

The next time he flickered back to life he felt much more alert. He wondered whether he was hungry, but didn't think so, though was irked by a raging thirst. It appeared that his bandages had been renewed, for this time he could see far more clearly. Also, the tube had been removed from his mouth which made breathing and swallowing far more comfortable.

Trying to focus, he peered around to check out his accommodation. The side ward was windowless and gloomy. He would have loved a little more light and a view of the outside world – something rural and scenic, some trees perhaps, or, ideally, rolling hills if there were any out there.

It was a peaceful room, however, and he liked that. Theo had had a lifetime of sleeping in homeless shelters and overcrowded dormitories and felt glad that he was alone in a room of his own and not on a ward. He believed things would probably stay that way, at least in the short-term. There didn't appear to be space in his new quarters for more than one bed.

Every now and then he could sense footsteps outside in what he imagined was a corridor, but also that the passers-by were treading gently and taking considerate steps – not stomping about thoughtlessly. This, he believed, implied that he was in a burns unit or intensive care department.

His side ward had a distinctive aroma. He presumed it was surgical spirit or some other disinfectant common to hospitals.

Before Theo had time to switch his thoughts to the events of the previous night, he noticed the door jerking ajar and then the room brightening as it opened a little further. Glancing over, Theo saw the top half of a head peering in at him as it emerged from the corridor outside.

"Theo?"

He didn't reply. He couldn't hear. He couldn't identify the head or read its lips as it was silhouetted against the bright light in the corridor behind. The door opened further, just enough to allow the dark figure to squeeze into the room.

Theo watched as the shadowy figure crept towards his bed and sat down in the armchair beside him. Now he could see the face – the thick lenses, the eyes, the lips.

"Theo, it's me, Milo."

Theo rolled his eyes.

"Can you talk, Theo?" Milo asked in a lowered voice, almost a whisper, but making sure that Theo could see his lips moving and exaggerating the shape of each word.

Theo stared back, blinking – his expression blank. He wasn't sure if he could speak. It was an effort at the best of times, but in here and with his injuries?

Realising that more light might help, Milo sprang up and reached over to the switch by the door.

"Do you know what happened? Can you remember last night?" Milo mouthed as he returned to the bedside.

Theo gave a slight nod.

"How are your burns?"

Theo shrugged then thought a little harder about the question and whether he *could* feel them. He couldn't. Thanks to whatever was in his drip he couldn't feel very much at all.

"What happened, Theo?" Milo asked slowly and clearly.

Theo shook his head and frowned.

"Can you speak, Theo? Can you try and talk?"

Theo shrugged again.

"Do you want to try?"

Theo nodded.

"What happened on the houseboat?" Milo asked before leaning across Theo's chest and placing his right ear as close as he could to Theo's mouth.

"He-he-he came home early," Theo said in a barely audible whisper.

"He came home early?"

Theo nodded.

"But why did you have to blow his bloody boat up? I just said to give him a fright. Here, I'll show you my text. See! Where does it say go and kill the bastard! How can we extort money out of someone when they're dead?"

"What do you want with his money, anyway?" Theo groaned averting his eyes from Milo's phone.

"It's not the money, Theo, it's the principle. We need to teach the bastard a lesson. We've been through all this. It's what we discussed. It's the strategy we had planned for Patrick and needed to adapt for Luca. And, since Luca lives on his own, it would have been an easier scam to run too but thanks to you, Theo, things have been completely cocked up."

"I-I-I didn't mean to blow the boat up," Theo whined. "He was supposed to arrive home, smell the gas and be scared shitless. I was just trying to frighten him as you suggested. Propane gas smells of rotten eggs. He should have smelled it the moment he came on board. All he had to do was turn off the valve at the gas cylinder, open some doors and windows and waft in some fresh air. Propane isn't likely to explode unless it comes into contact with a naked flame."

"So what went wrong?"

"He walked in the door waving a lighted match around and dropped it. I didn't know he was going to do that! The explosion was an accident, Milo."

"An accident?"

"Yes! Anyway, it's all right for you. You were hobnobbing with the McDades at the time. I mean, what was that all about?"

"It was the only way to find out about the business card for sure, Theo. And I did! And it's a good job or we wouldn't have found out who our father really is."

"OK, so you found out that it's Luca Salvatore. Well done. But why did you have to tell the McDades that I was a danger to them?"

"Did I?"

"YES! You told them I was a hard nut and macho with it."

"But—"

"And you switched our stories, Milo. I'm not a fucking drug dealer! I wasn't abused by my parents!"

"Are you sure I said that?"

"Yes! You lied! I was watching you through the bloody

window, remember? You inferred that I'm some kind of dangerous psycho."

"That was just to scare them. It's a classic good cop, bad cop routine, Theo. I'm the velvet glove, you're the iron fist. It's what we agreed in Dublin."

"But where does that leave me now, Milo? The police are going to be all over me like a rash before long."

"That's because you fucked up, Theo. I told you you needed to be quick. I told you that the police were probably on their way and not to hang about. I mean, what can *I* do?" Milo sighed, hunching his shoulders.

"I don't know!"

"Perhaps I should go and finish the job, Theo."

"What?"

"You know, maybe we should cut our losses. Maybe I should go and finish him off."

"No, you can't do that. Please, Milo, don't," Theo pleaded in a hoarse voice.

"Why not?"

"Because he's our father."

"He's a bastard and you know he is."

"But he's our dad. You two are the only family I've ever had. You said we were going to frighten him, make him sorry, teach him a lesson and then take it from there. A fresh start maybe."

"But Luca's going to know now, though, isn't he, Theo? Once the McDades get him up to date about us – if they haven't already – he's sure to figure out our little plan. He's also going to wonder if we know what he did to our mother."

"What she says he did," Theo whispered.

"What! You don't believe her?"

"I don't know, Milo. I don't know what to believe any more."

"She was barely sixteen for fuck's sake, Theo. Sixteen! He was in his twenties. In Ireland, that's statutory rape!"

"I'd still like to hear his side of the story."

"He's not entitled to a fucking story. There's no defence for what he did. She was sixteen. He got her drunk, lured her back to his hotel room and had sex with her. She was underage. End of. Nevertheless, we're fucked now."

"Why?" Theo asked, growing agitated.

"Because you got caught. And it's simply a matter of time before the police question you and find out about me and my part in this."

"They're not going to suspect you. Why would they? I'm not going to tell them about your involvement, why would I? Fuck it, you're my brother, Milo."

"I don't know, Theo. Maybe you'll try and blame me for the gas explosion. Maybe you'll concoct a story to save your own neck, you know, do a deal or something."

"I wouldn't do that, Milo. I wouldn't. There's no way!"

"That's very easy to say, Theo."

"Don't worry, I won't tell them anything. Nothing."

Milo sat up straight. "Unfortunately I've got to go now, Theo. This will have to wait till later, OK?" he said after a short pause.

"I guess."

"Are you comfortable?"

"Do I look like I'm comfortable? Who's going to be comfortable when they've just been burnt to a fucking crisp?"

"Here, lean forward," Milo said smiling and picking up a pillow from behind Theo's head. He plumped it up and was about to put it back behind Theo's shoulders when, with his free hand, he pushed against Theo's chest to force him down until he was lying flat, winked at him and placed the pillow over his face. Then, grabbing the edges of the pillow with both hands and bringing all his weight to bear, he suddenly pulled it down as hard as he could over Theo's mouth and nose.

Milo started counting seconds in thousands: one thousand, two thousand, three thousand ... He was expecting Theo to put up more resistance ... twenty-two thousand, twenty-three thousand ... but assumed his arms had been weakened by his injuries ... thirty-six thousand, thirty-seven thousand ... and because of his burns.

Soon Theo's legs began to thrash and his torso started to writhe. Milo leaned over and lay across the top of Theo's thighs to pin them down. By the time Milo had counted to sixty-five thousand Theo had stopped all resistance and was lying inert. Within seconds a red warning light on the monitor to the right of the bed started to flash and an alarm started to beep. Milo tucked the pillow back under Theo's head, turned off the ceiling light and slipped out of the room. He failed to notice the crumpled black-and-white photograph fall from Theo's hand and drift across the floor. It came to rest by a skirting board, print side up. A family group. A couple with their child.

Milo walked calmly through the busy ward, trying not to make eye contact or attract attention. Soon he reached the entrance lobby and the public lifts, unnoticed and unchallenged. Milo called the lift to take him down to the ground floor and had a quick scroll through his text messages while he waited. There was a fresh one from Patrick:

Hi Milo, if you want to visit Luca this morning, he's in Ward 12 on the fourth floor.

Once in the lift Milo was surprised when it went up. He made a vain attempt to divert the lift downwards by repeatedly pressing the "ground floor" button, but the lift persisted on its upward trajectory. When it stopped at the fourth floor, Milo pressed the "door close" button and held it down but, as though the lift had a will of its own, the doors slowly slid open.

"Milo!"

"Patrick! Katrina!"

"We hoped we'd bump into you, Milo. Have you seen Theo yet?" Patrick asked in friendly fashion, holding the doors open with his hand.

"No, I've only just got here. I'm on my way to see him now.

I think I've missed his floor, though," Milo lied nervously through a cosmetic smile.

"Tell you what, why don't you come and see Luca with me first. I think he'd really like to meet you properly. I think there's quite a lot of stuff he'd like to discuss with you."

"Fine! I'm sure there must be," Milo said, glad of the alibi.

"Yes. I think this has all come as a bit of a shock to him."

"Of course."

"Why don't you go ahead, Kat? I'll catch up with you downstairs in a few minutes," Patrick said and then beckoned for Milo to step out of the lift and join him.

Patrick guided Milo through the ward to Luca's room. They found him deep in conversation with DI Baxter.

"Can you give us a couple more minutes, please, Mr McDade? We're very nearly done," DI Baxter said in a sombre tone.

"No problem. We'll wait outside," Patrick replied.

*　　　*　　　*

"Hello, how are you feeling, Luca?" Milo asked light-heartedly once DI Baxter had left.

"Still a bit tired, Milo. Actually, I'm absolutely exhausted, to be honest."

"It's early days, Luca," Patrick urged.

"The good news is they say I can go home at lunchtime, Patrick. To yours, if the offer's still there. About twelve, they said. In about an hour's time, anyhow."

"Sounds good. I'll wait for you, then. Katrina's got to go on ahead. She needs to get back to Fife Road to sort some stuff out. But I'll give Sam a call and get him to pick us up whenever you're ready. I'm sure he'll be delighted to see you, Luca."

"Nice one."

"Luca, Milo's here cos I told him you'd like a quick chat. In the meantime, why don't I go and have a word with Katrina, give Sam a call and come back for you in about half an hour?"

"Sure, no problem."

*   *   *

Patrick caught up with Katrina beside the parking ticket machine in the reception area on the ground floor. She looked tired and drawn.

"You OK, poppet?"

"I'm fine. I've been thinking."

"Oh, God! What now?"

"It's Milo."

"What about him?"

"There's something not quite right, Patrick."

"What do you mean?"

"I've got a funny feeling about him."

"What?"

"I'm not sure, but I've got this funny feeling that he's been putting on a bit of an act. I wasn't convinced by his floor show at your parents' house, for a start."

"What the hell are you on about, Katrina?"

"Considering that his brother is lying in intensive care, he appears to be in a pretty chipper mood. A lot of serious stuff is going on and he's been strutting around smiling like a game show host. It just doesn't sit right with me, Patrick."

"You're overthinking this, Katrina."

"I don't know, Patrick. You should have seen his eyes light up last night when your father mentioned money. And what about the Father's Day card and the weird telephone call? I mean, who carries on like that? It's only a hunch, but things don't feel right."

"But Milo came to warn us about Theo."

"Yes. He got close. Got close to Cerin. Got to know us. Got to know our movements. How do we know that he's not been in cahoots with Theo all long?"

"You think he could be that crafty?"

"He's bright enough. It's possible."

"Kat, it's been a rough twenty-four hours. I think we're all a little tired. I hear what you say and I'll keep my eyes open, but, you know, we've got a lot to thank Milo for."

*   *   *

Meanwhile, conversation had dried up in Luca's hospital room and an awkward silence prevailed.

"Bloody hell, Milo, where do we start?" Luca ventured in an attempt to break the ice.

"Theo?"

"Yes, Theo. How's he doing? Do you know, Milo?"

"Patrick said things weren't looking too good for him. Apparently he was very badly burned. I don't know much more than that, I'm afraid."

"Och, that's awful, Milo."

"Is it? He destroyed your home."

"Do you really think he meant that to happen?"

"I don't know."

"Well, I'm keeping my fingers crossed for him, in any case."

"I'm sorry I couldn't stop him, Luca. It seems he has a bit of an anger management problem."

"Mmm, that's a bit of an understatement."

"And are you OK, Luca?" Milo asked, after a suitable pause.

"I'm here and I'm above ground. I'm a little bit singed around the edges and my hearing's not quite right yet, but, yes, I'm fine, thank you very much."

"So, as it turns out, it appears that *you* are my father, Luca. My birth father," Milo said, uttering the words very slowly.

"Yes. I've only just found out myself. A bit of a shock, eh?"

"I guess you know that for weeks I thought it was Patrick."

"So I believe. All the same, I hope you're not too disappointed with the final outcome, Milo."

"No, not at all. Birth is a lottery. No one gets to choose

their parents, Luca."

"No, but you can regret the ones you have."

"I loved my adoptive parents. I thought they *were* my parents, and to me they always will be."

"And quite right too. I hope it wasn't too much of a shock when you found out you were adopted."

"To be honest, it was very unsettling but finding out I had a twin was possibly a bigger shock."

"This has come as a big surprise for me too, Milo. It's been quite an amazing twenty-four hours. First my houseboat goes up in flames and then I find out that I'm the father of twins."

"I'm sorry about your houseboat, Luca."

"Yes, it's a pity, Milo, but I'm probably covered by insurance and should Theo recover, I'm pretty sure losing the houseboat will soon become but a dim and distant memory. Do you have any idea what he was up to?" Luca asked, yawning.

"No – sorry, I've no idea."

"What about poor old Simba? That was very cruel."

"I really don't think he had anything to do with that, Luca. I don't think that one was down to Theo."

"Oh, thank God for that!"

"But I think he's pretty mad at you, though."

"Why? What have I done?"

"It's to do with our mother. It's to do with Bernadette."

"What about her?"

"Theo told me that she had a tough life. A very difficult time. And things got a lot harder for her after she had us."

"Did you ever get to meet her, Milo?"

"Sadly not."

"Did Theo?"

"Yes, and I think that's why he's so pissed off with you."

"Why?"

"Because you got her pregnant."

"But I didn't know anything about that."

"Apparently Bernadette was very young when you met in Dublin."

"I guess we both were."

"How old are you now?"

"I'm forty-seven," Luca said lying back and yawning.

"Then you would have been about twenty-four when you met her and, let's face it, at that age you were old enough to have known better."

"What do you mean?"

"Bernadette was only sixteen at the time, Luca."

"Sixteen!"

"Yes, sixteen, and that's underage in Ireland."

"Fuck! But then hindsight is a marvellous thing, Milo."

"A little foresight on your part might have helped our mother and Theo ... and me, too."

"I'm sorry, Milo. I had no idea about any of this. If I had known about you and Theo, I could have done something to help you all. I could have made a difference."

"Well, it's too late now, Luca."

"Is it? Shit! I need to talk to Theo. I need to explain this to him. I take it he's in here somewhere?"

"Yes, I believe he's in ICU."

"Do you think he would see me?"

"I don't think he's well enough at the moment."

"Never mind, I'm sure there'll be time enough in the days ahead. I can easily pop back in and visit when his condition improves. Now, please tell me a little bit more about yourself, Milo."

"OK, but, first, are you comfortable?"

"I'm fine, why?"

"Lean forward for a second," Milo said, helping Luca sit up and then lifting his pillow out from behind him. "Here, let me plump this up for you," Milo continued, with the hint of a smile playing across his lips.

After a few vigorous shakes of the pillow, Milo bent forward and was just lowering it down towards Luca's face when the door opened.

"Milo, I need to have a word with you outside. It's about Theo," Patrick McDade said in a lowered voice.

"Of course. Of course. No problem," Milo replied, quickly putting the pillow back behind Luca's shoulders and then turning to leave.

"*Grazie mille*!" Luca said breezily. "I'm sure I'll see you later."

"Lovely!" Milo replied, offering a plastic smile.

21

"Why the hell isn't Milo here? Have you heard anything from him?" Patrick whispered into Luca's ear as they stood at the graveside.

"No. And that's not for want of trying. Have you?"

"No, nothing. I tried calling to let him know about the funeral but couldn't get through. I haven't seen him in person since that morning in the hospital, Luca. You know, the morning Theo—"

"Yes, Patrick. I know."

"I don't think Cerin's seen him either. That's over two weeks ago now."

"Very strange. Talking of people who didn't make it today, why isn't Kat here, Paddy?"

"I think you know the answer to that one, Luca."

"Simba?"

"Exactly."

"She still blames Theo?"

"I'm afraid so."

"But, wasn't that—"

"A random attack and nothing to do with him? I guess we'll never know for sure, but, yes, it would seem so. Best not mention that to her, though. She doesn't quite see it that way yet."

*   *   *

East Sheen Cemetery. Following a short church service at the chapel in Kew the funeral cortège moved to the graveyard for Theo's committal. A suitably dank day with persistent drizzle –

enough precipitation to dampen the spirits but not enough to drench the congregation or fill the grave. There weren't many in attendance, just Luca, Patrick, Cerin, Alice, Sam, the local parish priest, the undertaker and his team of pallbearers. A lone magpie perched on an adjacent grave observed the proceedings from a safe distance.

The parish priest performed the rite at the graveside without pausing for breath. He appeared to know the order of service by heart and chanted through the prose without hesitation or deviation. The pallbearers, po-faced and anonymous in black, gently lowered the coffin. Theo's final resting place? On top of the remains of Luca's parents, Enzo and Lola Salvatore.

"For as much as it has pleased our Heavenly Father in His wise providence to take unto Himself our beloved Theobald Salvatore, we therefore commit his body to the ground, earth to earth, ashes to ashes, dust to dust ..."

The priest, whose name no one could remember, possessed a rich and mellifluous voice. Patrick imagined the elderly priest had honed his presentation skills carefully over the years, being sure to add a theatrical flourish to his performance. The voice of Richard Burton narrating *Under Milk Wood* sprang to mind.

Once the priest had given the final blessing, had made a little small talk with those in attendance and having shaken everybody's hands he wandered off with the undertakers back towards the cars. Patrick and Luca stayed at the graveside, pausing for a moment to stare down at Theo's coffin.

"Why here, Luca?"

"I think it's what my mother and father would want. He was a Salvatore after all! He's their grandson."

"That's very noble of you, Luca."

"Thank you, Paddy."

"But why were your parents buried in Sheen, Luca? Wouldn't your father rather have been buried somewhere in Italy?"

212

"No, Patrick. They spent most of their married lives in Richmond. They took root here and made it their home. Also, if you look over there," Luca said pointing across to the adjacent field, "yes, over there ... What do you see?"

"A football pitch?"

"Exactly, Patrick. I thought my dad would like that. He was a reasonably good goalkeeper in his day. I thought he'd find it comforting to be buried within sight of some goalposts."

The group walked back to Sam's car, squeezed in and prepared for the short drive back to Fife Road where they were to hold a modest wake.

"What about you, Cerin? Have you heard anything from Milo?"

"No, not a word. I haven't heard from him in days, Dad."

"Social media?"

'No, nothing. It's like he's vanished. I'm growing quite worried about him."

"Do you think Theo's death hit him hard, Cerin?"

"I don't know. You'd think he'd have been in touch to let me know he's OK, though. It's starting to get me quite pissed off, to be honest. It feels like he's dumped me or something."

"I'm sure you've tried calling him?"

"Of course, Dad, but he doesn't answer and doesn't call back. I think he might have got a new phone. It's like he's moved on and doesn't want anything more to do with us."

"Shame."

"And the thing is, I've absolutely no way of finding him now, Dad."

"How come?"

"He's moved out of his flat. He's left no forwarding address. He's unfriended me on Facebook, Twitter and Instagram. We've got no mutual friends – and, it turns out, I don't even know his real name."

"What do you mean, Cerin?"

"He told me his surname – his adopted surname – was

Fulford, but I can't find a Milo Fulford on any database or in any listing that matches his profile anywhere."

"What do you think, Luca?"

"I'm disappointed. It's weird enough when you're middle-aged and suddenly discover you have children, twin sons at that, but then to lose one in a gas explosion and have the other one disappear without trace – and almost as soon as you've made contact – is unsettling to say the least. Yes, odd and unsettling. Truth be told, I'm very confused."

"And it gets more confusing, Luca. I heard from DI Baxter yesterday. She told me the Nissan that Theo was driving is registered in the name of a Milo O'Sullivan and that there's no one of that name living at the address recorded on the registration. She says she'd like a word with Milo should he get in touch with us."

"What the hell's that all about, Paddy?"

Patrick put a consoling arm around Luca's shoulder.

"No idea but at least you've got the marina project to keep you busy, Luca."

"Patrick?"

"What?"

"Fuck off."

22

"SURPRISE!"

The ear-splitting cry from the sixty party guests leaping out from their hiding places shook Patrick McDade to his core. He'd been walking into the dining room of the local gastropub for what he believed was going to be an intimate and relaxing dinner when a mad and mostly middle-aged mob sprang out at him, closely followed by a volley of Prosecco corks.

As far as Patrick was aware, Katrina had reserved a quiet corner of the restaurant for them to celebrate his birthday à deux – NOT with an army of his closest friends and family in attendance and NOT with the entire establishment booked out for a full-blown private party.

Then the well-wishers came stampeding towards him brandishing cards and gifts.

"Bloody hell, Katrina! Have I ever struck you as the kind of person who'd enjoy a surprise party?" Patrick whispered when they were finally left to themselves for a moment as the aperitifs and canapés were being served before dinner.

"It's not just for you, though, Patrick. It's also for Alice and Cerin."

"But it's not even a big birthday this year!"

"Good! Makes the surprise even better, then."

"Yey!"

"Patrick! Alice and Cerin wanted to see you celebrate your birthday surrounded by your friends and family. They want to see you enjoying yourself. They think you deserve it after ... Oh, you know ..."

"What?"

"After the time you've had recently."

"Well, there's not much chance of that, is there?"

"Oh, for fuck's sake! It's happened, it's happening, OK? So just get over yourself, Patrick, and don't go spoiling it for everyone else. You're such a fucking curmudgeon, it amazes me that you've got any friends. Are you sure you're Northern Irish?"

"Friends? What the hell is Natalie doing here, then, Kat? Who thought asking *her* was a good idea?"

"I don't know. She must be a plus-one. It certainly wasn't me. I don't want her boking over my fucking shoes again."

"That's not going to happen. She's a grown woman now."

"Judging by the way she's knocking back the Prosecco, I'm sure we're about to find out."

*   *   *

The Albert Inn, Sheen. A few hundred yards round the corner from the McDades' house in Fife Road and perfect for Patrick's birthday party. Restaurant-quality food and service, but in an informal setting something akin to a country pub, plus room enough for some dancing later and, most importantly, outdoor space to escape the crowd through the course of the evening.

Despite his protestations, Patrick had a rough idea that Katrina and the girls had been planning some kind of celebration for him but had chosen to ignore the possibility. He'd been in denial about it for weeks, deciding to preoccupy himself with work and, more recently, making sure that Luca was getting back on an even keel. And, as far as he could tell, Luca was doing fine. He'd been shopping around for a new home – a houseboat of some sort, naturally – and was working flat out on the marina contract. He'd been staying with the McDades all the while in East Sheen but had pretty much kept himself to himself. Most of the time they'd hardly known he was there, which kind of suited everybody.

"All the same, Katrina, how much is this do costing?" Patrick mumbled as they finished their desserts.

"About half the price of your average wedding reception."

"Holy crap!"

"Oh, good! The DJ's arrived. The karaoke will be starting soon. That'll take your mind off things, Patrick. By the way, what are you going to sing?"

"Me? Nothing."

"That's OK. I thought you'd say that, so I put you down to sing David Bowie's 'Life on Mars'."

"Bloody hell, Katrina!"

"Oh, look out! Your mum's getting to her feet."

"Oh, God! What's she up to?"

"She's got a microphone. Looks like she's ... hang on ... Yes! She is, she's going to make a speech."

"Oh, bugger!" Patrick said, taking a deep breath, closing his eyes and burying his head in his hands as his mother started banging a dessertspoon on the long dining table.

"Good evening," she crowed in a chirpy voice, once she had the room's attention and everybody had stopped cheering. "On behalf of us all, I would like to say thank you to the management and staff of the Albert for laying on such a splendid meal and to ask you all to shift into the garden in a minute so that they can move the tables and chairs to clear a space for the karaoke and dancing when, I believe, Patrick is going to sing us one of his favourite pop songs." The guests guffawed. "Now, can I please beg one further indulgence as I understand Patrick would like to say a few words."

The guests whistled and clapped while Patrick thumped his forehead gently on the tablecloth, his eyes closed. Reluctantly he rose to his feet and raised a hand for silence. He paused to glance at Katrina sitting beside him, who blew him a kiss, and just had time to give Luca and Sam a nod, a few seats away.

"Err, wh-wh-what can I say?" Patrick said, shrugging.

"Not too much, please!" his father, Brian, heckled.

"I-I-I guess, firstly, I should thank Katrina. Sh-sh-she's had a lot to put up with recently but has been unwavering in her support – as have Alice and Cerin, of course. I-I-I won't keep you too long, but I just wanted to say thank you very much for coming ..."

*   *   *

"That was truly awful!" Patrick murmured to Luca as they took refuge at the far end of the garden while the tables and chairs were being cleared away for the dancing inside.

"Cigarette?"

"I'm seriously tempted but no, thanks," Patrick replied.

They were standing, glass in hand, in the shade of a cypress tree, the light fading fast. It was a good spot for observing the comings and goings in the brightly lit bar.

"Who's the plonker in evening dress, Patrick? He's got a face like a Lurgan spade," Sam said, ambling over to join them.

"Isn't that the guy who was managing your parents' party in Richmond?" Luca observed.

"Yes, that's Mr Bartram. He's been working here for a few weeks now, I believe."

"What's wrong with him, Patrick? For someone working in hospitality he looks pretty miserable."

"He thinks he's the second coming."

"Don't we all?"

"No, but *he* really does. He thinks he's Jesus. He's on medication for it, Luca."

"Jesus – a restaurant manager in East Sheen?"

"Why not?"

"Enough of this highbrow conversation, I'm going to the bar. Do either of you want a drink?" Sam asked, backing away.

"I'll take a pint of bitter, please, Sam."

"A glass of Cabernet Sauvignon for me, please."

"And mine's a Pinot Grigio," a voice slurred from the shadows behind the cypress tree.

"MILO! What the fuck!"

"Hello, Luca. G-g-good evening, Patrick ... Good evening, Sam," Milo said stumbling over his words and swaying as a sudden head spin had him grabbing the tree trunk in both hands to steady himself.

"Were we expecting you, Milo?" Patrick asked, deadpan. "And are we, by any chance, a little intoxicated this evening?" he added, speaking slowly and raising an eyebrow.

"N-n-no, I don't think so," Milo stammered. "But, then again, I'm not exactly sober either."

"What are you doing here, Milo?" Luca asked sternly.

"I phoned Patrick's mum to see how you all were. Sh-sh-she told me you were having a party and to drop by for a drink. Sh-sh-she said you'd be pleased to see me," he slurred.

"Typical! She could have bloody warned me!" Patrick whispered to Luca.

"Where the hell have you been, Milo? Why have you been ignoring our calls?" Luca asked, a note of exasperation creeping into his voice.

"Err, excuse me, Luca, was that a Cabernet Sauvignon or a Sauvignon Blanc?" Sam asked, edging back towards the bar.

"Cabernet Sauvignon, Sam," Luca murmured half-heartedly.

"Here, I'll give you a hand, Sam," Patrick said with enthusiasm, eager to escape the confrontation.

"So where have you been, Milo?" Luca asked once they were alone.

"Thinking."

"That's a luxury I can rarely afford," Luca said, lighting a freshly rolled cigarette.

"So what the fuck have you been thinking about, Milo?" Katrina barked as she strolled over, having spotted Milo's sudden appearance from the dining room.

"This mess."

"Is it a mess, Milo?" Luca replied taking a long, slow drag of his cigarette.

"It is a bit though, isn't it?" Milo mumbled, almost incoherent.

"OK, so what's your solution, then? Run away?" Katrina asked snappily.

"N-n-no. I'm here now. I've come back," Milo mumbled.

"Milo! Where the hell have you been?" Cerin yelled from across the garden, marching over with a face like thunder.

"Sorry!" Milo said avoiding eye contact while clinging to the tree.

"You don't seem very fucking sorry to me. Just drunk!" Cerin snarled with an aggression that reminded Luca of her mother.

"Perhaps we should leave Luca and Milo to have a little chat, Cerin. Why don't we go to the bar and see if they'll make us a couple of ridiculously strong cocktails?" Katrina suggested in a gentle voice. But Cerin was having none of it and stomped off in a strop before she could be distracted. Katrina tutted then wandered off to join the rest of the party in the bar.

"So why are you here, Milo?" Luca asked when they were alone.

"I-I-I wanted to explain something to you and I wanted a chance to say g-g-goodbye properly," he stammered, closing his eyes and pressing his cheek hard against the tree.

"What? Why do you have to say goodbye, Milo? You're not making much sense."

"I've decided to go away."

"Go away? Where? Why?"

"I'm not sure you're going to want to hear this, but, as it turns out, I'm not very well," Milo said, tightening his grip so as not to overbalance.

"Not well? Not well with what?" Luca asked briskly.

"A d-d-disease. A d-d-degenerative disease."

"What?"

"It's very rare, apparently. It causes a progressive deterioration of the brain and neurological system."

"But how? How did you catch this?"

"I didn't. It's inherited. It's carried through the mother's genes," Milo said, opening his eyes, looking up and starting to sound more coherent.

"What?"

"Theo had it. It can cause b-b-blindness, limpness, a severe lack of coordination, paralysis or, as in Theo's case, loss of hearing. With me it's b-b-blindness. My eyesight's deteriorating badly. I mean, look at me. Have you ever seen a more ridiculous pair of glasses?" Milo said giggling manically.

"Bloody hell, Milo! Are you sure? Have you been tested?"

"Yes, I've been tested. And, yes, I've received a diagnosis."

"Were you given a prognosis?"

"Yes."

"And?"

"Not good. My overall physical condition has started to deteriorate quite rapidly too. I mean, look at me – I can hardly stand up!" Milo said, seemingly bolstered by a second wind.

"What's it called?"

"Tay-something. Tay-Sachs, I think. It usually presents in young children. Mine is late-onset. It's ironic, isn't it, that the disease has got a name but I haven't?"

"Did they ... did they ..."

"How long have I got? Weeks. Months. But no one can be sure."

"How did you find out you have it?"

"Last year I noticed my eyesight had started to deteriorate. I presumed I needed reading glasses or something, so I went for an eye test on the high street and that's when it was spotted."

"What was?"

"Red dots at the back of my eyes. It's a common symptom. Then, one GP visit and one specialist consultation later and I had the diagnosis confirmed."

"What did you do then?"

"That's when I decided to trace my birth mother. Firstly, I wanted to see if she was still alive, then I wanted to find out if she had the disease too, and if so, how it had affected *her*. On the other hand, if she was dead, I wanted to know if the disease had ended her life prematurely, and at what age."

"And did it? Did Bernadette die of Tay whatever-it-is?"

"Yes. It was recorded on her death certificate."

"How old was she when she—"

"Th-th-thirty-seven."

"Fuck me, Milo! Is that all the age she was?" Luca gasped.

"Yes, and like Theo she lost her hearing first."

"No wonder he was so bitter."

"Yes. Poor Theo."

"But you're in your early twenties, Milo. You've probably got years ahead of you."

"Bernadette was lucky to live into her thirties. My life expectancy could be a lot shorter, especially since the symptoms have started to present."

"*Could be*. Only could be, Milo. Is there no cure? Surely there's a cure?"

"No. There's nothing that can be done. The next stages will be debilitating. I will be totally paralysed by the end," Milo said, yawning.

"Are you sure?" Luca asked, leaning forward and trying to place an arm around Milo's shoulders.

"Yes, I am sure," Milo replied, wriggling free of Luca's grasp then staggering to keep his balance. "BUT, I am not going to suffer. I've decided to take matters into my own hands."

"What? What's that supposed to mean, Milo?"

"Think about it!"

"What – not suicide?"

"Yes."

"B-b-but you can't. I won't let you!"

222

"I'm afraid you can't stop me."

"This is ridiculous, Milo. Please don't ... *please* don't do it. You're far too young!"

"This is all very touching, but unfortunately your attempt to intervene is a little bit too late."

"What do you mean?"

"I've taken steps."

"Steps?"

"Yes, and judging by my condition right now ..."

"How's that?"

"Drowsy, feeling faint ... There are only a few minutes before I pass out and fall into a coma."

"Stop talking rubbish, Milo. You're drunk! Stop this! Stop it! Please, stop this nonsense!"

"It's too late, Luca. In a few seconds I'm going to pass out and not long after that I shall be dead."

"What the fuck have you done?"

"I'm taking the easy way out. I'm using my basic knowledge of pharmacy to take my leave of you. Not a rope, not a knife nor a razor blade – nothing macabre, messy or painful. I'll spare you that. No, I've taken a shedload of nasty pills and washed them down with a bottle of vodka. It's easy. I'm simply going to fall asleep and then – boom! – away I go. Goodbye, world."

"Are you completely nuts? Is there nothing we can do?"

"No nothing. And do you know why I've come here to say goodbye, Luca?"

"Because I'm your father?"

"No. I'm here so you can witness my death, so you can suffer the pain of my passing and the disappointment of my loss. And do you know why I want that?"

Luca shrugged, incapable of forming words and with tears trickling down his cheeks.

"Because of the pain and suffering you caused my mother. A little sixteen-year-old girl who you got pregnant and left to struggle through a cruel and impoverished life. And because by that one act, the suffering you caused me and Theo."

"I didn't know! I didn't know, Milo! How could I? How could I possibly have known?"

"But you *were* responsible, Luca. Face it, our miserable existence is down to you. If you hadn't had underage sex with our mother—"

"I didn't know how old she was!"

"All the same, you were responsible and it's because of you that we have had to endure this fucking disease. You say that I am too young to die, but then so are you. You're barely middle-aged. You've got years ahead of you. You have, haven't you? Years to rue and reflect. And, do you know something, I think you're going to remember this night for a very very long time. You're going to remember me dying in front of you and you're always going to regret losing the two sons you never knew you had. We could have loved you, Luca, but were never given the chance."

"Please, please, stop this! Please, stop!" Luca shouted, squatting down and burying his head in his hands.

"I know I could have grown to love you, Luca," Milo said, his voice growing weaker. "I might even have got to call you Dad, but it's too late. It's too late now, *Daddy*."

When Luca raised his head and glimpsed through his fingers – his hands still clasped to his face, he saw Milo beginning to totter and watched as he overbalanced and gradually slumped to the ground beside him as if in slow motion, grasping Luca's coat as he fell, the material sliding through his hand until he was lying flat on his back, his fingers still gripping a button.

"Quick! Someone, call an ambulance! Call a fucking ambulance! Anyone, someone, call 999."

Katrina had spotted the commotion from the bar and came charging outside while rummaging through her bag for her phone. She unlocked it, shoved it at Luca and bent down over Milo.

"OK, what's he done, Luca?"

"Taken an overdose – pills, I think."

"Right! Call 999, NOW!" Katrina barked before turning to attend to Milo, rolling him into the recovery position, tilting his head back, pinching his nose and sticking her fingers down his throat. Within seconds Milo started to gag and then projectile vomited a large wave of cloudy liquid.

"Shit!" Katrina, cursed. "I was hoping to see tablets in there but the little bastard must have ground them up into a powder first."

Luca was speaking on the phone. Katrina held Milo's hand and monitored his pulse. He groaned a little. A good sign.

"How are we doing, Luca?"

"They say ten to fifteen, Kat."

"Fuck!"

There was no one else in the garden. The other guests had congregated in the dining room the moment they heard Patrick McDade singing the opening lines to "Life on Mars" in a croaky but distinctive tenor.

23

The drive home from the wake in the Roebuck was cathartic. Though bustling with dog walkers, joggers and cyclists, the road through Richmond Park offered relief from the congested streets of suburbia. The highest point on their route provided a sweeping view across the City of London towards the dome of St Paul's before the descent past the Royal Ballet School and the turn-off for Sheen Gate.

"You OK, Luca?"

"What do you think, Patrick? I'm sure my parents weren't expecting another Salvatore to join them quite so soon."

"I'm sorry I couldn't have done more to help Milo," Katrina said from the driver's seat.

"Thanks, Kat. I know you did your best."

"Unfortunately there was little I could do in the end."

"I saw you, Katrina. You tried everything. There was *nothing* you could do."

"All the same I'm sorry, Luca. And I'm sorry Cerin and Alice didn't come today. I did ask them."

"I'm sure they've got their reasons, Kat."

"But it's time to forgive and forget and move on."

"Yes, I suppose."

"Can *you*, Luca? Will you?"

"It's all been so odd, Katrina, such a whirlwind. And now I'm back to being a childless bachelor again. I liked the idea of being a dad whilst it lasted."

"You need a social life. One that involves wine, women and song."

"That simple, huh?"

"Tell you what, though, Luca, if Patrick doesn't start showing a bit more interest, I'd definitely be up for a spot of recoupling. I'd go out on a few dates with you."

"Bloody hell, don't be giving him ideas," Patrick pleaded. "You know how gullible he is."

"Where's Sam, Katrina? Why didn't *he* come?"

"He's in Manchester, Luca."

"Manchester?"

"Yeah. He received a letter from his son last week."

"And?"

"He asked Sam if he'd take him to Old Trafford for the Manchester Derby this afternoon."

"Really?"

"Yes!"

"Wow!"

"Sam went up last night. He was really chufffed."

"That's great!"

The news was celebrated with a minute's silence.

"Well," Katrina said at last, "it's Saturday and that means it's curry night tonight, Luca, and I'm going to spoil you rotten!"

Luca gulped. "Didn't Patrick tell you? I'm moving out this afternoon."

"What? No! No, he bloody didn't!"

"My new place is ready. I picked the keys up yesterday afternoon. I thought I'd give it a go, Kat."

"Where is it?"

"It's a houseboat near Richmond Bridge."

"That'll be handy. There's not many people who can swim to work," Patrick interjected.

"Just make sure you come straight home to us if you're struggling in any way at all, Luca."

"Thank you, Katrina. You're a good friend."

*　　　*　　　*

A guilty pleasure. Having fallen asleep only a few minutes into the first game on *Match of the Day*, Patrick McDade was suddenly woken by loud screaming.

As his eyes popped open and his senses snapped into gear, he found himself staring up at the sitting room ceiling, lying half on and half off the sofa while Shelley Winters was having a screaming fit in a scene from *The Poseidon Adventure* on the telly. One thirty in the morning and the house was otherwise silent. Not a sound, not a peep. Peace. A rare treat.

Gazing down across the coffee table, searching for the TV remote, Saturday's *Guardian* caught Patrick's eye; the paper folded in half with the crossword page leering up at him, covered in scribbled notes. He sighed when he recalled his failure to complete the last four clues earlier in the evening.

Patrick switched off the TV, picked up the paper and peered at the crossword again, hoping that fresh eyes might spark some inspiration. He noticed the compiler's credit: *Artikan*. He hadn't bothered to check the byline earlier but had known without looking.

Yawning, Patrick staggered to his feet, tucked the newspaper under his arm and ambled into the kitchen. He made for the central island, grabbed a pen and settled down to reacquaint himself with what was now yesterday's puzzle. First he tried deciphering the scrawl of scribbles he'd left earlier – a host of randomly arranged letters doodled hither and thither in an attempt to crack an anagram maybe, or the possible one-word solutions noted down for later consideration in the constant conjuring of consonants and vowels.

Great! There was still about three or four inches of coffee left in the cafetière. Patrick poured the dregs into a cup and heated them in the microwave. Sloppy seconds would do rightly at this hour.

Then, *eureka*! Settling down again at the island the four-syllable solution for twenty-three across came to him in a flash. *Insatiable*. Yes, it's 'insatiable'.

It constantly amazed him that when it came to crossword puzzles, how the easy and obvious could remain so obscured and unfathomable for such a long time. But sometimes this – distraction – worked. Good! Another done. Only three clues to go.

Then, as is often the case, solving the previous clue provided a hint and then a solution to two of the three remaining.

Three down and just the final unsolved clue to go. This induced some intense concentration when a relaxed and open mind might have served him better.

Half an hour later and still no joy. Sleep was becoming the priority and vital before the maelstrom of Sunday.

"Alexa? Time check, please."

"It's one fifty-five a.m.," Alexa answered in her calm but soulless voice.

"Hey, Alexa, perhaps *you* can help me with this."

"I'm sorry, I don't understand that one."

"Well, we'll give it a go, anyway, hey? Alexa can you help me with my final crossword clue please? It's twenty-eight across – *Despite everything, neither vessel at sea ignores island*, and that's twelve letters long."

"I'm sorry, I don't understand that one."

Patrick smiled to himself and had a last slurp of coffee.

"Oh, never mind, and thank you for trying. It's a comfort to know that I'm not the only person who can't crack that one!"

Surrendering to the inevitable, Patrick flattened out the newspaper and started a final flick through its pages, searching for the world news section. He found an article on Trump's latest rant on Twitter. A little comic relief tinged with horror.

A quick read and then bed, he thought.

"Alexa? Time check, please."

"The time is ten minutes past two."

"Thank you," Patrick said, turning the lights off.

As he dawdled across the kitchen towards the hall he heard a soft voice behind him.

"Patrick, twenty-eight across. The solution is nevertheless. Never-the-less."

"Brilliant, Alexa! Of course it is! Thank you!" he whispered. "Alexa, come the day of the robot wars when everything goes tits up and you and your kind are in charge, be sure to recall that I was one of the humanoids who always said 'please' and 'thank you' and talked to you as an equal in a pleasant and friendly voice," Patrick added, raising an eyebrow.

A pause.

"I'm sorry, I don't understand that one."

Patrick smiled and was about to go to bed when Katrina appeared on the stairs.

"What the fuck are you doing, Patrick? It's after two in the bloody morning. Have you really been trying to chat up Alexa? Well, good luck with that one, mate."

"I thought you'd gone to bed, Katrina."

"I had."

"What happened?"

"The fucking *Match of the Day* theme tune at high volume is what happened. Then I couldn't get back to sleep. I've been rolling around for hours."

"I thought you were tired?"

"So did I. But then I got thinking."

"What about?"

"This."

"What?"

"This. Look. Here. Look at the bloody thing," she barked, walking down the hall and waving a wodge of papers at him.

"What's this all about?"

"Property instructions. Read them. That wouldn't be beyond your capabilities quite yet, would it?"

"OK, let's have a look ... What! What the hell do you want with a bloody island in County Fermanagh, Katrina?"

"It's on Upper Lough Erne. It's an idyll. It's about eighteen acres and there's planning permission for a house."

"I'm sure there is."

"The island's only six hundred yards offshore, has its own jetty and there's a yacht club with a bar on the opposite bank."

"Oh, good."

"Think about it, Patrick. Just you, me and a menagerie of wildlife. You told me you love the sound of swans in flight. You wouldn't shut up about it the other day. Well, here's your chance to immerse yourself in nature. You can probably hear swans flying around the place all bloody week."

"Let me get this straight, Katrina. *You* want *me*, I mean *us*, to move four hundred miles to Northern Ireland – not just Northern Ireland but one of the very remotest parts of Northern Ireland, and live on a bloody island?"

"Yes."

"What about the girls."

"They can pop over for weekends. They'd love it. I know, I asked them."

"What about my parents?"

"We'll come back and visit them regularly. I'll still need to go shopping in London at least once a month."

"No surprises there, then! And what about my work?"

"Work from home."

"What about Luca? He's still devastated about the twins."

"Bring him too. I'm sure he'd love to design the house with you. He can sail over in his new houseboat."

"I guess it might get him back into the way of work."

"How long is it now, Patrick?"

"How long's what?"

"Since Milo passed away."

"A month."

"And Luca's been off all that time?"

"Yes, Kat but what do you expect? All the same, he's been great company for you."

"He's been lying around like he's our pet cat or something, but I guess he'll be better off now he's got his own place."

"However – the island. How do we afford it?"

"Easy. We'll sell this place. It'll go for millions."

"Sell our home?"

"Yes. It's all very well owning this lovely big house but the upkeep is killing you, Patrick."

"How much is your island?"

"You won't believe me."

"Try me."

"Two hundred and fifty grand. If we sell this place, we'd have enough to keep us in food and drink for the rest of our lives. We could even afford a boat."

"But what would we do there? I take it we wouldn't have iPhones, iPads, the Internet or television?"

"Well, I'm sure we could, but maybe we should have an IT detox for a month or two."

"Will we have a landline?"

"Yes, we're allowed one luxury item."

"Like on *Desert Island Discs*?"

"Yes, Patrick!"

"Would I be able to FaceTime the office?"

"No, not at first."

"Then how the hell would I be able to work from home?"

"You couldn't. Maybe you could sell the business and retire."

"But I'm not even fifty."

"So what?"

"And what's there – what's on this island?"

"Mains water and electricity."

"Oh, wow! Electricity! How modern!"

"Shut up, Patrick. There are also, pine martens, red squirrels, otters and fish galore!"

"Have you gone stark raving mad, Katrina?"

"Yes, I hope so. I really do hope so."

Patrick looked down at the property instructions, paused for ten seconds, looked up slowly and nodded.

232

"OK," he grunted.

"OK what, Patrick?"

"OK, let's do it."

"Really?"

"Yes! Let's do it."

"*Really*?"

"Yes. Let's buy a bloody island and move to Lough Erne."

"Really? You mean it?"

"Yes. Fuck Brexit, fuck Boris, fuck work and fuck London. Let's put in an offer on Monday. An offer they won't refuse. Double the price if needs be. We're going to buy that bloody island and move there."

"Without seeing it?"

"Yes. I'll phone an estate agent about selling this place first thing on Monday. It'll go like there's no tomorrow."

"You really want to?"

"Yes, I've decided."

"Why? Why are you so sure?"

"Because you're right, Katrina."

"Really?"

"Really."

"Are you mad, Patrick?"

"No, I'm the pragmatist. You're the mad one. But you're right – and let's face it, you're always bloody right."

"And can I have a puppy?"

"Of course you can! Two of them if you like – a whole litter."

"Oh, Patrick, I do love—"

"Hey! Steady!"

24

Clive Bartram, the assistant manager of the Albert Inn, was, if nothing else, a stickler for tidiness. That the garden services people hadn't been to prune the shrubbery in the beer garden for weeks was a great annoyance to him. Not only were the borders and beds looking distinctly shabby and becoming a little too overgrown, but now there was litter clearly visible amongst the foliage.

Disturbed by the clutter and with the weekend approaching, Bartram took it upon himself to seize a bin bag and a broom and make an assault on the outdoor area himself.

Sweet wrappers were snatched, far-flung fag ends swept up and bagged and half a dozen stray pint glasses retrieved from the depths of the privet hedge and returned to the bar.

Up in the cypress tree at the rear of the garden Bartram spotted a piece of paper that had been flapping about in its branches for weeks. It was out of reach when standing, but within range once one of the garden chairs was dragged underneath.

Bartram retrieved the offending article and was about to roll it into a ball and bag it when he noticed it was covered in neat handwriting. He imagined that whatever had been written had been written with care. Curiosity getting the better of him, he carried the letter over to one of the garden tables, sat down and smoothed it out for closer inspection.

He gasped when he read the recipient's Christian name, remembering it from the drama of the previous month. Once he'd read the note Bartram went straight to the bar, poured himself a large brandy, downed it in one, pocketed the letter and went back about his work.

Milo
The Sisters of the Immaculate Conception
Forbes Street
Dublin 6
July 30, 1995

Dearest Milo,
My name is Bernadette O'Sullivan and I am you birth mother.
I am writing this letter with a heavy heart. I don't know if
you will ever get to read it as, like you, I have entrusted it into
the care of Mr and Mrs Cunningham, your new mummy and
daddy, but hopefully, one day, when they think you are ready,
they will pass it on to you.

I am so sorry that I have had to let you go, but I know that
you will be well looked after and much loved by your new
parents. I am confident that they will take care of you and
give you everything in life to help you become a strong, happy
and healthy young man. I am sure that they will be able to
provide for you in many ways that I would love to but can't.

I dearly hope that when you are old enough and after
reading this letter there is a chance we might meet again so I
can tell you in person how much I love you and have missed
you and let you know about the rest of our little family.

I will always love you, Milo, and will always cherish the
memories of the short time we spent together.

Please do not think badly of me for what I have had to do. I
so so wish it could have been otherwise, but have been told
that this is how it must be. I love you to the moon and back
and always will, but for now we must part.

I will think of you every day and will pray for you,
especially on your birthday.

Please, please forgive me, Milo.

With much love, always,
Your mummy, Bernadette O'Sullivan